INSTACRUSH

A ROOKIE REBELS NOVEL

KATE MEADER

Copyright © 2019 by Kate Meader

Cover by Michele Catalano Creative

ISBN: 978-0-9985178-5-8

PROLOGUE

THEO KERSHAW WAS the luckiest guy alive.

With the best hands in hockey and the world at his skates, he had a career anyone would envy. Number three draft two years ago, all the more remarkable because he was a D-man. Defenseman. Thunder thighs—that's what Coach called him. Rock freaking solid in the back third. No one was getting by him.

The LA Quake suited him, even if it felt strange for a Michigan boy to be skating during warm weather. He liked how laidback California was. The team practiced that West coast, earthy-crunchy lifestyle: yoga, meditation, nutrition plans that involved fruits and grains and ingredients Theo had never heard of until a year ago.

Another thing rocking his world? This year, they had a real shot at going all the way. Knocked out of the playoffs during the first round last season, that was about to change. Only five more games to go in the regular season and they were in second place in the conference.

Tonight they were playing Vancouver, the team one spot

ahead of them in the table. You could say they were the team to beat.

Screw that. The Quake was the team to beat and Theo was the D-man to pass.

They were two goals up by the end of the first period, so happy, happy. Theo had defended like he was paid to—which he was. Handsomely.

The second period started, and three minutes in, a killer headache was dragging him down. A migraine, maybe, though he didn't think he'd ever had one. Was it *my*-graine or *mee*-graine?

Distracted, he missed a pass. One second the puck was barreling into his strike zone, the next he'd completely whiffed it. Macker, their goalie managed the block, but what the hell happened there?

The lights glowed brighter, like they were inside his brain, flickering on and off. The contents of his stomach—a very tasty chicken wrap—surged and his mouth watered with that telltale signal: he was going to puke.

Koz, the Vanouver center smashed him against the boards. Standard checking procedure yet Theo lost his balance. He should have been up in half a second, but something was keeping him on his very fine ass. His helmet felt like a crown of pucks.

He tried to push up off the ice, but his head wanted to stay down. Pressure behind his eyelids was pushing, pushing, forcing the ball out. He could already imagine the mess it would make on the shiny white ice, rolling away like a Halloween horror freak show.

"Kershaw, you okay?"

"Yeah," he lied to Gunnar Bond, his captain. "Never better."

Gunnar was looking at him strangely, his blue eyes troubled. Someone pulled Theo's helmet off, which was good because crown of pucks, but bad because he needed that bucket to hold his brain inside his skull.

More people loomed over him: Bond, the ref, looky-loos, all peering at him like he was a circus show weirdo.

"Give him room," Bond said. The ref knelt, and something about what he saw freaked him out. "Medic! We need a medic here."

Suffering Jesus, it's just a headache, people. He tried to tell them he'd be okay in a minute, but the words sounded like garbage from his mouth. Not garbage. Garbled? Garbled garbage. He didn't know, only he never wanted anyone to look at him again like this zebra with the sad-dog eyes.

"Theo, stay with us," Gunnar said, his voice soothing, his eyes really fucking blue. The guy was a great captain, one in a million, and if anyone could stop Theo from going somewhere, it would be Bond.

Besides, where would Theo go? They had a game to win, a series to start, a cup to lift.

The lights were bright, but suddenly not. Suddenly they were dim, dimming, dimmer.

Suddenly they were gone.

1

Two years later

@TheTheoKershaw Are you ready for the holidays? Check out my recs for the hockey lover in your life #TheoDoesChristmas #WrapItUp #HoHoHockey

ELLE BUTLER HAD A MORNING ROUTINE. Coffee, strong, a dab of creamer, half a Splenda. A slice of cinnamon toast (no raisins because *ugh*). Sleeping in until 8 a.m., a luxury after her stint in the military, but necessary given she usually closed out the Empty Net bar, her current place of employment.

Little things, no harm to anyone, and hardly likely to throw the universe's balance out of whack. Elle was big on balance. For four years in the army she'd added entries to the credit side of the ledger. She'd supported her team. Saved the lives of her guys in the field. Served her country with honor.

All so she could atone for a previous lifetime of entries on the debit side.

It was a never-ending task, though. Balance had yet to be restored and on occasion, she slipped, such as this morning.

Fine, most mornings.

Anyone who spied her gazing at her phone, complete with a (usually) shirtless man reporting on *his* morning routine through the magic of Instagram Live video, would be rightly confused. Because Elle Butler was not a hockey fan. She barely knew how the game was played despite working in a sports bar within spitting distance of the Rebels Center, home of the local franchise. Even crashing at the apartment of a player for the team—Levi Hunt, army buddy, former Special Forces, and now the Chicago Rebels latest rookie—hadn't provided any special insight other than that they ate, slept, and banged a lot. Like sharks.

She did not like the sport and she most certainly did not like Theo Kershaw, defenseman for the Rebels. But she liked *looking* at him. He and his "Imma-doing-laundry-shirtless" videos were her guilty pleasure.

And she would die before she admitted it aloud.

This morning was no different. Coffee in hand, toast mid-chew, Elle tapped the icon for Instagram (user name: PuckLover21, the height of sneaky irony) just as Kershaw began to broadcast. He didn't always archive the videos to his regular feed so it was best to catch him live before he headed off to practice.

"Morning, hockey fans! It's another fabulous day in Chicagoland!"

Grrr. He was already irritating her. Why must everything out of his mouth be punctuated with exclamation points? The guy was so extra which was probably why people adored him. As for Elle? She was here for the pretty.

Black, wavy hair that had clearly undergone some sort of finger-rake attack topped his ridiculously handsome head.

His full, sensual lips were perfect for mouthing ludicrous opinions that had invariably bypassed his brain filter. Those cheekbones must have been carved by malevolent angels determined to make every man suffer by comparison, then stumble through the rest of their miserable lives when they realize perfection is unattainable.

But the kicker was the eyes. She'd read somewhere that less than 2% of the world's population had green eyes. Theo's were emerald chips raised to unstinting magnetism by flecks of gold, which was probably even more rare. (Because, Theo.)

Barely ten seconds into the video, and Theo seemed to realize that, as awesome as his cheekbones and hair and eyes were, the effect was magnified ten-fold when he repositioned the camera to take in his broad shoulders and defined pecs. A flurry of emojis flooded the screen. He laughed, knowing exactly how that maneuver would be received.

Elle wasn't laughing. Her mouth had turned as dry as butterless toast. To think she'd met him in person, had served him drinks in her bar, was less than thirty feet away from him *right now*—and she didn't mean the metaphorical distance between his on-screen presence and her hormonal one.

Because Theo Kershaw, defenseman for the Chicago Rebels, teammate to her roommate, known as Superglutes because of his most excellent posterior, was also her neighbor. As in across-the-hall-hey-how-are-ya neighbor.

He was over there now, making this damn video and she was watching the show like a creeper.

Clearly satisfied with the effect his muscles had on his fan base, he brought his camera back in close. "So, we're two days out to Christmas, friends, and I don't have a game until

two days after which means I have time to ... wrap presents!"
He flipped the lens to take in his living room, cluttered with
wrapping paper, scotch tape, and assorted boxes. Something
twanged in Elle's chest. There would be no presents under
her tree this year. Estrangement from one's family tended to
put a damper on the gift exchanges. But she'd made her
decision, choosing her conscience over her blood. Now
wasn't the time for regrets.

Back facing the camera, Theo smiled. Elle swore she
heard the thud of thousands of dropped phones the world
over. "Anyone want to guess what I'm buying for my gran?"

The predictions came in hard and fast, ranging from a
cashmere sweater to scented lotions to inappropriate items
that no guy should be buying for an elderly female relative.

Theo's dark eyebrows (probably professionally shaped)
lowered as he read some of the messages, then raised as he
likely came across the more risqué ones.

"Hold up there, I don't know what kind of relationship
you have with your grandmother, but we're not that kind of
family!" He chuckled, the sound deep and going straight to
her core. She had to give it to him: he knew exactly how to
connect with a million plus people and their genitals.

"Well, I can't tell you what it is because she's probably
watching right now. Hi, Aurora!" He waved. "She's always
been my biggest fan and I can't wait to see her in a couple of
days. But keep those guesses coming and I'll pick a winner
for a signed Rebels jersey. So, let me see, JennyLuvsARebel
is asking ..." His perfect brows knit together while he read
Jenny's question.

"*How do you get your skin to glow like that?* Great question! Well, I've been using Neutrogena Hydro Boost to
cleanse every night and morning. It's really lightweight and
creamy and doesn't leave my skin feeling tight. And it's

incredibly affordable. Thanks for asking, Jenny. I'm going to send you a Neutrogena care package, so get ready for skin that lights up the room! Okay, I'd better get back to it as I have a few more gifts to wrap up. What's that? I should wrap myself up?"

He held the phone camera back to take in his entire torso.

Elle's tongue turned to rubber. #StopDontStop.

"You want me to cover this up? Maybe we should take a vote on it."

A cascade of comments insisting that Theo remain shirt-less flurried like gravity-challenged snowflakes across the screen.

Never!

Don't do it, T.

That bitch is crazeeee!

"Didn't think so," Theo said with a cheeky wink, and then it was over and out, and Elle's world was a little less bright.

Such nonsense! How ridiculous that she would allow a himbo hunk be the highlight of her day, all the more so because she'd met him in person and knew he wasn't worthy of this strange infatuation. He was just another brainless jock who thought he was all that.

Two months ago, she'd shown up on Levi Hunt's doorstep, acting like an unannounced visit to an old army unit-mate was perfectly normal. As if her request to stay in his spare room for a couple of days that had stretched to eight weeks was completely by the book. Hunt had known that she was running from something, but he hadn't pressed. Instead he'd welcomed her with open arms, their connection strong enough for him to treat Elle's situation as need-to-know.

That night, she'd walked in on a Rebels bonding exercise: video games, beers, and pizza with Hunt presiding in that quiet, stoic way of his. Already flustered because she was trying so hard to act like a normal, she'd not been prepared to meet *him*.

"I'm Theo, one of Levi's teammates."

Those green-gold eyes had bathed her with an intensity she would later learn he usually reserved for the ice. Words refused to climb her throat. All she could do was nod in response, feeling like the biggest dummy for being tongue-tied by beauty.

Hunt had made introductions and said something about Theo being a D-man. She didn't know what that was, but it sounded faintly absurd and on the right side of dirty. She angled for the upper hand with a playful retort that came out much sharper than intended.

"D-man? What the hell is that?"

"Stands for defense," Theo had said. *"And other things."* His perfect lips stretched wide into a grin, revealing straight, white teeth and a mouthful of privilege.

She'd met guys like him in her various walks through life—cocky grunts who thought the only female in the unit would automatically put out. Arrogant Wall Street types who assumed their waitress would gladly serve more than fifty-dollar prime rib to earn that 20% tip. Pro athletes were just another genus of the same species.

D stands for defense ... and other things? Sure.

She settled on dismissal. *"Way to sell it, Dick-Man."*

He didn't take offense, which she soon learned was his standard response when poked. It had set the tone between them.

Ever since, she'd gone out of her way to ignore him (in person). Might even have overcompensated by being rude.

Self-preservation was key. Better to enjoy Theo Kershaw from afar, in the privacy of her—or Hunt's—kitchen. He would never know that she got a kick out of the doofus's muscles, sparkling green eyes, or knock-em-dead smile.

He would never know what she truly thought of him at all.

2

THE KNOCK on the door was loud enough to make Elle jump. She closed her laptop on the search she'd been running. Checking up on her family was a full-time job, and she needed to know they weren't up to anything—or at least anything she couldn't scupper before significant damage was done.

Hunt was out of town for the holidays, and the building he lived in, with a lease set up by the Chicago Rebels, was relatively quiet. Most people had already headed to wherever their holiday plans would take them.

It might be him. Theo.

Unlikely, though. Levi had given his teammate-neighbor a key and he liked to pop in and raid their fridge on the regular, which she'd added to the running tab of things Theo Kershaw did to step on her nerves, after looking so fine and placing unreasonable demands on her attention. She paid for those groceries and did he ever return the favor? That would be a negative. But Levi made up the difference, so she remained quiet. Guys like Theo Kershaw assumed people were put on this earth to feed and service them.

The knock came again, louder, more insistent. With a stealthy slide forward, she checked the peephole.

It *was* him.

A glance ceiling-ward held no answers, so she squinted through the hole again. Shiny hair, square jaw, naked … shoulders. It was one thing to view them with the protective distance of Instagram—this was not her preferred method of interaction.

"Come on, Sergeant Cupcake, I'm freezing my ass off out here."

His ass. Meaning *that* ass, the world's eighth wonder.

Hauling in a deep breath, she opened the door, ready to be miffed. Theo Kershaw, hockey god, grocery thief, and possessor of the finest ass she'd ever ogled, stood before her wearing a towel and a frown.

"About time."

He took a step forward.

She took a step back.

This little dance was enough to signal invitation to come in but not quite enough to give him space to do it. "I got locked out. Any idea where—"

"Hold up." Her instincts to defend her turf and the remains of her dignity caused her to place her hands up awkwardly and graze his chest.

Heat. So much heat even with that mere brush of a touch. She recoiled.

He raised an eyebrow. "I'm not radioactive, y'know. If you want to touch, just ask."

Irritation flared. "I don't. I'm merely trying to halt the strange man invading my home." Slightly hyperbolic, but he'd caught her on the back foot.

He clutched his chest. "That hurts, Cupcake. Neighbors can't be strangers. You've lived here for over six weeks now."

Eight, actually, and not for much longer. The question was whether she wanted to stay in Chicago. Right now, it seemed as good a place as any to lay low and escape the grasping hooks of her family, especially as she had a job and a couple of friends in Hunt and his girlfriend, ace sports reporter, Jordan.

Ensuring her eyes remained north of the action, she folded her arms. "Can I help you?" She held up a hand immediately to forestall whatever smart-ass comment was coming next. Better rephrase. "Why are you here?"

"I locked myself out."

"Let me guess. One of your honeys left her underwear and you had to chase her down?" She'd never actually seen any women visiting his apartment, but belligerence was her default in Kershaw's presence and the wheels had been set in motion.

"That would be no. My intercom buzzer doesn't work and I had to run down to let the delivery guy in because there's no way I'm allowing someone to steal my package."

That almost made her laugh because "my package" was just perfect.

"And this is my problem how?"

"Hunt has my spare key."

"Why didn't you say so?"

"I—" He ran a hand through his damp hair and she was oddly jealous of that hand. What was wrong with her? "You know what?" he went on. "I tried to say so, but you were too busy feeling me up to let me get a word in."

"That was an accident," she grated, feeling a pang of guilt because he had a point.

"Tell it to the judge. So you're not going home for the holidays?"

She jerked at the sudden subject change, or maybe it was the mention of home. Not wanting to sound like a sad sack, she responded with a white lie. "Sure. Tomorrow." It wasn't completely inaccurate. Levi's apartment felt like home anyway.

Though she knew Theo was heading home with his wrapped gifts for grandma, he didn't know she knew, so she asked the obligatory, "You?"

"Yep. Saugatuck."

"Where's that?"

"Michigan. Of course, that's dependent on me getting into my apartment because I sure as hell can't drive home in a towel. Just think of the looks I'd get!" He grinned, which made her smile. That was kind of funny.

Not enjoying the sudden burst of camaraderie, she sought hormone-suppressing focus. Warm fuzzies, especially in relation to a body like Theo's, made her nervous.

"Where's the spare key?" She walked by him as she asked, careful to avoid any accidental towel-snags. This was all a little too makings-of-a-porn-movie clichéd.

"No idea."

She whipped around. "But I don't know where it is."

"Then you'll have to text Hunt and ask him."

Order dispensed, he walked by her into the kitchen where he opened the fridge and started rummaging around. "Got any of that—there you are, my beauty!" Out came *her* Gouda cheese, *her* fresh deli turkey slices, and *her* wheat bread.

Anger bubbled beneath the surface at his presumption. "I guess I'll text Hunt, then."

"Thanks, Cupcake." With his back to her, he gave an ass twitch. She was being thanked by his ass!

Damn, it was fine, though. This guy could represent backsides for his country.

Text. Hunt. Now.

She shot off a message. Thirty seconds of watching Theo make a sandwich—okay, watching his fine towel-shod glutes, which she gladly took as her due for the "borrowed" sandwich fixins—and Hunt had not replied.

"Maybe he's not near his phone."

"Probably giving it good to his lady." He turned, the sandwich already in his mouth. After a decent chew, he eyed her over the crust. "Maybe he'll take his time. He's the kind of guy who probably thinks it's bad manners to get off without giving his woman three orgasms first."

"Unlike you, I suppose, who wouldn't want to spend so much time away from the fridge."

"I do like to eat," he said, passing over her snark. He was definitely one of those "water off a duck's back" types.

She looked at her phone. Nothing from Hunt.

How long was she supposed to stand here, gazing at Theo Kershaw's naked chest when all that separated her from a peek-a-boo at the goods was that loosely-knotted towel? Anxious for something to occupy her itchy hands and overactive imagination, she walked to the nearest drawer and yanked it open.

"Maybe he put the key here." Take-out menus, duct tape, assorted screws. They could have themselves quite the party ...

"Maybe it's in his bedroom," Theo offered.

She didn't relish the idea of going into Hunt's private space. He'd been really good about giving her room and she repaid the favor by staying out of his way, even working double-shifts at the bar so she could pad her oh-shit fund.

No incoming messages arrived to save her.

Theo remained unusually quiet while finishing his sandwich along with a glass of OJ he'd helped himself to.

"That was my juice, by the way."

"I'll pay you back." He eyed the open drawer. "No luck with the key?"

"No. And Hunt's not texting back." She threw a glance toward the main door to the apartment.

"Think I could borrow some sweats from Hunt?"

"No."

"No?"

"You're in here eating our food and drinking my OJ and generally making yourself at home. But wearing Hunt's clothes is probably not part of the neighbor contract."

Was it possible she wanted him to remain in that towel? No. She was just protective of Hunt's turf. That was all. She looked away, not wanting to be caught staring at his half-nakedness, imagining all the things she couldn't have because a guy this hot wouldn't deign to lower himself to her level. Stay in her dreams, please.

"You okay? You're acting kind of weird." He stared at her for a long, penetrating second. There was something almost knowing about that gaze, which was strange with a guy who seemed to have no reflective capabilities whatsoever. That towel, though. She swore it was slung lower on his hips than before. Never had her brain and hormones been so ready to duke it out.

Slip that knot, sexy towel.

Don't even think about it, terrycloth terrorist!

The hormones were winning.

"I'm fine." She checked her phone again. Nada.

"You sure, Elle-oh-Elle?"

"Yes!"

He moved toward her, slowly, a swagger to his hips, and she held her breath, uncertain what she would do if he touched her. *Ohgodohgodohgod.*

He walked right past her. *Phew*, right?

Much too close for comfort and enough to have her sex antenna go zing. Clean, fresh man. No better scent. He headed to the door and a small—very small—voice in her head cried out in protest. *Don't leave.*

He left.

And returned.

With a large box that was taped up so well that it would require a chainsaw to get through it. Tons of stickers blanketed it—Christmas trees, pink hearts, Pokemon, My Little Pony, and every emoji known to man.

"Someone went nuts at the craft store," she commented.

Theo placed it on Hunt's coffee table. "From my gran."

She liked how his voice softened at the mention. "And this is the package you needed so badly you locked yourself out." In a towel. *Let's not forget the specifics.*

"This is it."

They both stared at the package.

"The best brownies you'll ever eat," he added.

"I've eaten my fair share of brownies so that's quite the claim."

He took a seat on the sofa. "So you want to try my ... sweet treats?"

Okay, time they had this out. "What's your game?"

He blinked. "My game?"

"You always seem to be so ... on. Is this how you talk to every woman of your acquaintance? 'Cause it must be exhausting for you." She didn't believe for a second that he was actually interested in her. The Theo Kershaws of this world would never go there but his flirtatious nature stretched her nerves taut.

"I'm just a chatty person. I've always been but especially since—" Something flickered across his expression. "It's called being friendly, Cupcake. You ought to try it sometime."

She wished her thoughts about Theo Kershaw would stay in the realm of friendly. "Maybe tone it down."

"It?" He leaned back, one strong, muscled arm over the top of the sofa, which showed to perfection his beautiful pecs, toned abs, and a strangely attractive tuft of underarm hair. "Are we talking about my unrelenting charisma and incalculable sex appeal? You realize I'm in my prime, sitting in a towel on your sofa, offering you homemade brownies, and you expect me to tone all that down?"

Maybe it was too much of an ask. "I'll find you a sweater."

3

THEO STARED at Elle's departing back, liking that her exit gave him leave to do that uninhibited. Full-figured, with more curves than a stash of hockey blades, she was taller than most women he usually encountered, maybe a couple of inches short of six feet. Her chestnut hair, pinned in a messy knot atop her head, gave the impression of someone at ease with herself and the world around her.

But it was merely a cover. Those blue-gray eyes of hers carried the weight of that world, while the stubborn set to her jaw signaled a lifetime of disagreements with whatever man or woman might be willing to match her tart tongue. Elle Butler was a serious person with a smart mouth. She had a sense of humor, all right, just not when it came to him.

He liked her, though she clearly didn't return the sentiment. What kind of person didn't enjoy a friendly neighbor? Most people got upset if someone didn't like them, but Theo had plenty of people who considered him awesome. When one didn't jump on board the Theo train, it excited his interest. It was more fun trying to puzzle out his neighbor.

He wandered back into the kitchen to look for scissors. If

he couldn't be dressed, at least he could be sated. Brownie-sated.

He'd like to be sexually sated though.

Despite his claims to be in his prime, Theo wasn't feeling quite the king of all he surveyed lately. He'd only felt "normal" for the last six months after eighteen months of being locked in the body of someone else. Learning to hold a knife and fork again, move a mouse (hell on his porn viewing), even getting dressed, had all taken a toll on his time and mental fortitude. Thankfully his speech hadn't been affected by the aneurysm rupture and subsequent surgery, but his mind had. It ran a million miles a minute, only resting when he slept—and he couldn't sleep for longer than a few hours at a time. He'd always been hyper but since his brain exploded, he was hyper squared. And strangely lacking in confidence when it came to women.

He had no shortage of offers. But he didn't feel ready to dip his toes back into the sexual shark-infested waters yet. Except ... he might make an exception for Elle which was pretty screwed up because she would certainly not be making an exception for him.

In the kitchen, he opened a drawer of flatware and found scissors. Then he headed out to the package and attacked it.

Thank God for Aurora. Or Saint Aurora, because his grandmother had nursed him back to health in Saugatuck. He couldn't imagine anyone else stepping up, though there was someone more obvious who could have. *Dear old Dad.* Theo wasn't given to self-pitying sarcasm, even in his head, so he was annoyed as hell when that unlikely voice popped in for a visit. He stabbed the package with a bit more force than necessary.

"Hey, watch the brownies!"

Elle stood at the entrance to living room, her brow in its default setting: furrowed.

"Yeah, I know. Must protect the sweet treats." He schooled his expression, drawing on years of ignoring whatever might bother him. He cut through the tape sealing the box.

Before he could get further, a soft ball of cotton fabric landed on top of the box.

He held it up. "What's this?"

"It should cover up all that."

All that. So his near nakedness did bother her, and he was fairly sure it wasn't because she was a prude. *Still got it, Kershaw.*

He put down the scissors and held up what she'd given him: a tee with a picture of the captain from Star Trek. Bald, British, and badass. Beneath his cue ball head, crinkly blues, and smirky-hot grin (he assumed that was what @Sir-PatStew was going for) was the slogan: *Tea, Earl Grey, hot.*

Weird for a catchphrase, but those Trekkies were even more rabid than hockey fans.

He checked the tag. Large. But for a lady?

"This is big on you?"

"Sure." She grinned, a little evilly.

He shouldn't like that because he was probably the butt of a joke, but he did all the same. Better to view it as a weakness on her part: she wanted to see him in a muscle shirt that highlighted his superior physique. Joke was on her! Theo was never afraid of looking stupid or gorgeous. People expected him to display epic doofus qualities and he found it tended to get him further in life.

He put the shirt on. As he suspected, it was tight and had more of a crop-top look to it, meaning his abs were getting plenty of air. Perfect.

"Any pants?"

"You'll have to stick with the towel until we hear from Hunt."

"Knew you dug it."

Slight head shake. *Sah-weet.*

"Ready for a brownie?"

"I'm ready to test your claims to having the best brownie ever created."

He extracted the lipstick-blotted note Aurora had written, knowing the contents without needing to unfold it (*I'm so proud of you, Theo,* and other rah-rah encouragements. The woman was a fucking treasure) and put it to one side, then took out a giant Tupperware box. Placing the lid under Elle's snooty nose, he popped the corner so she got all that sugary, chocolate goodness first.

Theo Kershaw, giver in the extreme.

"It does smell good," she said with just the right amount of skepticism.

He unsealed the lid and offered the box to her, filled with an assortment of half double-chocolate, half cream-cheese swirl, as well as classic chocolate. "Have one of my gran's brownies, Elle-oh-Elle."

She smiled, bit her lip, and wow, that was something special. His pulse skipped a few beats, then thundered hard when it found its rhythm again. Plucking out one of the classics, she examined it and took a tentative bite.

"Oh," she said around her chewing.

"Oh?"

"That's ..."

"That's ...?"

"Absolutely amazing!" She took another bite, bigger this time. Shaking her head, she turned back to him, her eyes wide and lust-stoked ... for the brownie. A boy could dream. "Your grandmother made these? She ought to sell them."

"She gives them away at the gallery."

"The gallery?"

"Yeah, the art gallery she owns back home in Saugatuck."

Elle looked taken aback. "Your grandmother owns an art gallery?"

He folded his arms across the Star Trek captain's bald head, stretched to thread-snapping limits by his pecs. "Yep. She's a pretty cool lady who marches to the beat of her own bongo. You'd like her." *She'd like you.*

"And Saugatuck? That's where you're going for the holiday?"

"Yeah." He bit into a brownie. "These treats are actually for the team. I was supposed to drop them off at the player lounge before everyone flew out but Aurora—that's my gran—sent them late. So where are you headed tomorrow?"

She frowned, paused for a moment, then proceeded to lie her ass off. "New York. Flying out in the morning. Super early."

Huh, what was that about? Was she lying about the location, the flight time, or the fact that she was going at all?

"Who's at home, waiting for Sergeant Cupcake?"

"Mom, Dad, sister. And you? Just your art-loving, brownie-baking grandma?"

Whiplash on the subject change there, making it clear she didn't want to talk about her folks. Fair enough. He could talk enough for both of them.

"Yeah, but she's got a ton of friends who are like aunts, I guess. Theo's Tarts."

Another brow furrow. "Theo's what?"

"They're my grandmother's friends, kind of like her posse."

"Your grandmother has a posse? Called Theo's Tarts?"

He laughed. "I didn't give them that name! Once a month, they come up to the city to watch a game. They wear jackets with my face on them and generally embarrass everyone within a twenty-row radius. These women are raucous. But hey, they're my biggest fans."

Who couldn't love a troupe of ladies of a certain age swearing like sailors, putting the fear of Gretzky into grown men, and telling the officials how to do their jobs? "Anyway, they'll be at my gran's for Christmas dinner and they'll probably have a highlight reel of my best moments since the season began. It's an event whenever I go home."

She looked a touch wistful—and for the briefest moment, sad. "Saugatuck's favorite son."

"Less than a thousand people so it wouldn't be hard."

She smiled at him again, the rarity of it so unusual that his breath caught once more. Her phone buzzed. "That'll be Hunt." She looked at it, frowned, then turned the phone over. "Not him."

He could say he was disappointed but that'd be a big old whopper. Sitting in a too-tight Jean Luc Picard tee and a towel, eating Aurora's brownies, and chatting with Elle Butler was actually a very pleasant way to spend an hour.

"So, if Hunt doesn't call, I may have to stay here."

"Oh, he'll call. And if he doesn't, then we'll get a hold of the landlord." Was that trepidation he heard in her voice? He knew she wasn't afraid of him harming her, and she sure as hell wouldn't be acting like this because she hated listening to him, which left one possible conclusion: she was worried she couldn't keep her hands off him.

That sounded about right. That sounded about perfect.

"So what should we do?" he asked to test his theory.

She gave him the once-over, her eyes lingering on his chest, then with a lick of her lips, she stood quickly. "I was kind of in the middle of something when you knocked."

"Middle of something?"

"Yes. I should get back to it."

She backed up a couple of steps. Her gaze skittered over his thighs, outlined nicely through the not-fluffy-enough towel. His adductors looked *that* good.

"I'm just ..." She thumbed over her shoulder.

"Going to get back to it?" He put his hands behind his head, which showed his triceps to perfection.

"Yes." She swallowed, and he got the impression she was taking inventory of his sexiest parts.

"Best get to *it*, then. I'll catch up with my stories." A big *Days of Our Lives* fan, he often watched the episodes here because Hunt had a bigger TV. He picked up the remote. "I'll be out here if you need me."

"I won't."

"Or if you need a brownie."

Her eyebrows slammed together. "I'll just take one. In case."

"In case you have problems working up an appetite. For it."

She rolled her eyes.

"It's masturbating, isn't it?" he asked.

"Idiot," she muttered, before heading off in a huff.

Smiling to himself, he took another bite of brownie and settled in.

4

ELLE TRIED to focus on the Financial Theory class she was taking for free online through Yale's Open University. Going to school was one of her goals since discharging from the army but she didn't want to pay tuition until she had an idea of where her interests might lie. So far she'd enjoyed Financial Theory more than Ancient Greek literature and Early Modern England more than Dante in Translation, but the four factors of production couldn't compete with the knowledge that Theo was in the living room wearing that ridiculous Jean Luc Picard tee and a towel.

She'd thought it would be amusing to put him in that shirt. Knock him off that pedestal her hormones had placed him on. But it molded to his chest like latex, highlighting every muscle better than if he'd been naked.

As for that knowing look of his when she took the brownie, his sly comment about masturbating? As if he *knew* he was her guilty pleasure every morning. That she checked in along with thousands of other drooling men and women just to watch Theo Kershaw talking about protein shakes or the special pants he needed to cover his glutes or whichever moisturizer he was being paid to recommend this month. And his skin did glow! #NoFilter

She squirmed on her bed, trying to get relief or work up some friction or—no! She would not be getting herself off while a half-naked Theo Kershaw watched his soaps in the other room.

Research would be her weapon. Forewarned was forearmed.

She'd already checked out his Wikipedia page a few weeks ago around the time she started watching his videos, so she knew the basics. He was twenty five, a year younger than her. Born in Chicago, raised in Saugatuck. Played college hockey in Vermont. Number three draft pick four years ago to LA.

Then disaster struck one night on the ice, a ruptured brain aneurysm that left him unconscious in the ICU for a few days and close to death. It took him over eighteen months to recover, after which he was signed by the Rebels.

Hunt had mentioned Theo's health scare before and every online article about him referenced it, but she hadn't dug much deeper. A quick check of survival rates for aneurysms revealed terrifying statistics. Sixty percent usually bled out, seventy percent of the survivors had permanent neurological deficits. Her heart contracted. That must have been hell to overcome.

He seemed pretty quick off the mark, never lagging in response to her jibes. As for whether he was a good player, pro hockey was a business like any other, no room for senti- ment. He'd clearly made a recovery in all the areas that mattered.

Maybe there were other issues that could be credited to his injury. The lack of forethought when it came to speech. The motor mouth. The food thievery.

Someone ought to research that.

She tried to imagine how such a health setback might affect her: she'd be grateful for surviving, for that second chance. She knew all about do-overs. It was why she was here, trying to balance her ledger.

Theo had almost died a couple of years ago. Wow. And she was in here being snarky and rude and horny. It wouldn't hurt to be nicer to him. He was actually quite funny, even when he was being as irksome as a handsome gnat.

Was that her conscience or her neglected vagina talking?

Her phone buzzed with a call from—thank God—Hunt.

"Where the hell have you been?"

"Scrabble."

"Seriously?"

He sighed, but she knew his moods. He wasn't really all that put out. "You know how some families are into skiing or touch football or pickup games?"

Not really, but she went with it. "Uh huh."

"Jordan's parents are scrabble people, but it's a phones-off scenario. Hushed tones in keeping with the gravity of the situation."

"How about telling me if you're having a good time meeting your new girlfriend's family?" Men. Never knew when to get to the good stuff.

"They're really nice. I was a bit worried that they'd expect something else, but so far they've been great."

Levi Hunt had been best friends with Jordan's husband, who died in Afghanistan five years ago. Hooking up with your friend's woman was apparently some bro code no-no but they'd soldiered on and found their happily-ever-after.

"Well, quit jabbering about yourself, Hunt. Your

neighbor is locked out and we need his spare key or you'll come home to find half the sofa chewed off."

He chuckled, which was beyond weird. The man had always been so serious back at Fort Campbell, where Elle had worked in Special Forces support. Falling in love had lightened him up.

"I have his spare key."

"Which is ...?"

"On my keychain. Here in DC."

She groaned. "What good is it there? What if you lost it?"

"I won't because I have my keys with me at all times. I've never lost them. Ever."

Unsurprising. Hunt probably had an internal GPS that knew if he'd strayed more than fifty feet from any target.

"But he's here. Eating." In a towel, emitting sexiness to beat the band, not that she should mention that. As much as Hunt liked Theo, he didn't like when he flirted with her. Her roommate was strangely protective which she kind of enjoyed, never having had a big brother.

Only parents. Incredibly difficult, grasping parents.

"Call the super. He's on the first floor."

"There's a super on site?" If that were true, why hadn't Theo thought of it?

"Yeah. Number's on the fridge."

"The one that will be empty if I don't get him the hell out."

She felt the air change all the way from DC as Hunt put two and two together and came up pissed. "Has he tried anything with you?"

"No," she answered far too quickly. Because he hadn't but ... she wouldn't mind if he did? As if a guy like Theo Kershaw would ever think of her that way. His flirting was all a grand joke. "No," she said again as much to herself as to Hunt. "He's just talking all the time."

Hunt laughed again. Falling in love evidently caused some sort of head trauma to hard-ass former Green Berets. "A lot of words in that brain of his."

"And he seems determined to speak every single one. That aneurysm business sounded really serious."

"Yeah, it was. Most people wouldn't make it back to regular life, never mind their peak in pro hockey. The kid's something else." Hunt's admiration was obvious and meant something as he was notoriously stingy with his compliments. "I'd like to say there were no side effects but this is Kershaw we're talking about. You flying home tomorrow?"

"Yes, early. Into JFK." She stopped there. No more embellishing in case she was caught out in a lie. "But it'll be a short trip. I'll be home before you, probably."

"We should talk about that when I get back."

"You chucking me out?"

"Not exactly but I'll probably move in with Jordan soon and as the apartment is leased by the Rebels org—"

"I need to figure out a plan. Don't worry, I've been saving and looking for my own place."

"Good to hear, but there's no hurry. You won't be homeless, Butler—I'll make sure of it. All right, have a nice holiday and let me know if you need anything."

She smiled, grateful to have him in her corner, yet determined that he should never feel responsible for her. She could take care of herself. "Say hi to Jordan for me."

"Will do." He clicked off.

"No luck then?"

Theo stood in the doorway to her bedroom, thick forearms folded over his Picarded pecs.

"We need to call the super." At his blank look, she said,

"Landlord." She walked by him into the kitchen and found the number for "Ivor the super." She'd never noticed it before.

"You probably should call, seeing as how you're an official tenant and all. In fact, why didn't you already?" She handed over her phone.

"And miss out on these fun times with my snarky neighbor? No chance." Theo left a message. "Might be hard to get a hold of him. It's his day with Daisy."

"Daisy?"

"His blow-up doll."

She shook her head. "Excuse me?"

"I walked in on him once. We don't speak of it, but there are special days for him and Daisy. That's all you need to know. So you're moving out?"

How long had he been standing at the bedroom door listening? "Have to eventually. This was always a short-term arrangement." Tina, her boss at the bar had offered an apartment above the Empty Net. It would be more expensive than rent-free but she needed to get situated and the commute couldn't be beat.

Her phone buzzed in his hand and he looked down. "Who's Dee?"

She snatched back the phone.

"Says she needs to talk to you. Called you Eloise."

Her mother called her Eloise—even by text—when she was mad at her, which she had been for ... oh, going on five years now. But it was Elle's latest stunt that had the family creating a dark-haired doll in army fatigues that served nicely as a pincushion.

"Just someone I know."

He snorted. "Obviously a ploy."

"A ploy?"

"This act of yours. To make you seem more interesting that you really are. A woman of mystery who shows up out of the blue and won't reveal anything about her dark, secret past."

She offered her most blasé shrug. "You want the boring details? I was honorably discharged from the army six months ago. I used to work with Hunt in Special Forces support as a comms specialist—"

"A come specialist?"

Her sigh implied the eye roll she couldn't be bothered giving. "Now I'm figuring out next steps while I tend bar at the Empty Net."

"What kind of next steps?"

"Free online classes. Trying to decide what I like before I spend my tuition assistance on it."

"That's cool. You don't like hockey." Kershaw wasn't one for dwelling on a subject, that was for sure.

"Not a big sports person."

"I got that. What do you like? What does Sergeant Cupcake want to be?"

Free. Not tied down. No responsibilities.

Absolved.

"Not to be called Sergeant Cupcake, for a start. I was a corporal."

"Even better! I love a nice alliterative phrase. And I only give nicknames to people I like."

She resisted the urge to enjoy the hell out of Theo liking her. In that space while she tried not to take pleasure, he remained silent. This was strange on him—and strangely arousing, particularly because of how he was looking at her.

He moved closer. Too close. Not close enough. Maybe he had skincare recommendations to make.

The corners of his mouth kicked up in a blinding grin.

Please God, don't. And then he did something that slayed her: he rubbed his thumb over her jaw. Gently, like he was worried about frightening the wounded animal.

"Maybe we should start over. Hi, Elle. I'm Theo."

No, you're trouble. Was he going to kiss her? That wasn't what she needed. Her body thrummed with want but not for a kiss. Not for this tenderness.

He stood close now, peering down on her like an immortal descended from the heavens to play around with plain old Elle. For a moment, she let herself dream. She'd been a good girl for a while now, working on her ledger. Didn't she deserve a little fun?

She touched her hand to Jean Luc Picard's dome, stretched taut across Theo Kershaw's pecs. Just one touch for now because she didn't want to be greedy.

You're so selfish, Eloise. You never think of anyone but yourself.

So she was selfish. Why break the habits of a lifetime? Why not indulge in the feast on offer? Her hand brushed one pec, then pressed against it to test its solidity. His pure, unyielding maleness.

His eyelids flickered, enough to seed a doubt in her chest. He didn't want her. Not really. She was merely convenient.

She drew back. "I suppose I'm some sort of challenge for you."

"Oh, you're a challenge all right. But not in the way you think."

Rejecting that dime store psychoanalysis, she shored up those defenses that had briefly slipped with the unsteady beat of her heart.

"Doesn't matter anyway because you don't do it for me,

Superglutes." She injected 100ccs of sarcasm into the nickname coined by Hunt.

"No?" Said in that lazy I-don't-believe-you-for-a-second way of his. "I'm kind of popular."

"Yes, I've seen those billboards for your underwear."

"Fender bender when you did, right?"

"Oh, I have epic self-control. But seeing them made me realize that you're a bit too pretty. I kind of like 'em rougher." She placed a finger under his chin and tilted it for inspection. "You ever get into a fight? And I don't mean those phony ballets you perform on the ice for your fan base."

"I'm more a lover than a fighter."

She scoffed, reluctantly withdrawing her touch. "Thought as much. Wouldn't want to risk getting that perfect nose broken."

He didn't take offense. She wondered what in the world would ever bother *The* Theo Kershaw.

"So we've established I'm not manly enough for you. Any other comments?"

"Oh, I'd never be one to criticize."

He waved a hand. "Help me out, Elle-oh-Elle. Give me some pointers on how to win a real woman such as yourself."

She thought about it for a moment, her blood fizzing with the fun of sparring with him. "You'd need to be a completely different person. But don't fret, your current vapid personality is probably cleaning up so don't change a thing, 'kay?"

He didn't look put out, probably because her jab carried no heat. They both knew she wouldn't be talking to him like this if she really believed he was dumb and vain.

"Yeah, good thing I'm doing okay. It's just you're here and

I'm here ..." The implication being that only proximity would force him to lower his standards.

She patted his chest and suppressed a groan at how hard it felt under her fingertips. "I know you can't help yourself. You've got a penis that seeks out the nearest vagina like a diving rod. It's really not your fault."

"True. I can't be held accountable for my incorrigible flirting."

He grinned and she grinned back, and that fizz in her veins bubbled bright. He'd figured out her game, matched her quip for quip. They understood each other and now they were ... friends?

How odd.

And surprisingly sweet.

Theo Kershaw was smarter than he looked. Confusion must have registered on her face because he seemed to be closer, more present. A rush of awareness overtook her, not just of him, but of *them* and the sparking connection being formed in this moment, more powerful than mere sexual attraction.

"Theo, I—" The cock in her hand buzzed. No, the phone. *The phone.* "Super," she murmured.

"Yeah, it will be," he rasped right back.

Shaking her head to break free of her lust-fogged daze, she slipped out of the pocket she'd become trapped in against the kitchen island and held up the phone. "The super. Your landlord."

He took it, spoke a few words she barely heard, and hung up. "He's going to come up and let me in."

"Daisy can spare him?"

"She's very understanding." He crossed his arms and flashed those pearly whites. "So, where were we?"

"Nowhere."

He clutched his chest, typical over-the-top Theo. "You're going to give in one day. And I'm going to laugh my head off when you do."

Fortunately, her sanity had made a late but necessary entry into the proceedings. "Never going to happen, Kershaw. It's bad enough you waltz in unannounced, steal our food, and generally act like this is a frat house, you're not going to get me thrown in as a perk."

"What's that saying about protesting too much?"

A loud knock sounded. "There's your ride. Have a nice holiday."

5

@TheTheoKershaw Fun on Christmas Eve!
#SecretSanta #TheoDoesChristmas #WhatsInYourSack

THEO ADJUSTED his fur-trimmed red velvet hat, picked up his sack of goodies, and pressed record on his phone.

"Hey guys! Just a short video to say hi to everyone on this beautiful Christmas Eve and to wish you all a happy, happy holiday. I'll be heading home in a few minutes but first up, I wanted to play Santa and drop off a gift for my neighbor—oh, you like the hat?" A flurry of hearts floated up from the comments section and soon his video was dive-bombed with fire emojis, likes, and comments about his Santa hat.

"Yeah, I know I should have worn a beard, but that itches. This is just for you, the best fans in the whole world."

He put Hunt's spare key in the door while still holding the camera up. "Sorry if it gets a little bumpy. Now you guys know that Levi Hunt, superhero, former Green Beret, Rebels center, and totally awesome dude is my neighbor. He'll be back in town before me and I didn't give him a gift before I left because if I give one gift, I'll have to get something for all of them. Basically, Petrov is a nightmare to shop for. But I had this awesome idea for Hunt. You'll think it's really boring but I'm always raiding his fridge and eating his food, so my gift to him is to stock his larder. Okay, that came out wrong. The guy is taken, so I'm not looking to stock his larder in that way. If that even *is* a way."

Yesterday, Sergeant—no, Corporal—Cupcake had accused Theo of stealing. The nerve. He'd always thought they had a *mi casa es su casa* thing going on, but now that he gave it a more weighty consideration, Hunt didn't step across the hall all that often. Meaning, never. As for Elle, her usually lush mouth got that pinched look yesterday when he'd finished off her precious OJ. Was this really what the world had come to? Claiming ownership of the communal food like they were back in the college dorm?

Theo was here to show her that he always repaid his debts. Still filming and treading as light as a cat burglar-slash-hot-Father Christmas, he headed into the kitchen with his sack and opened the fridge. For the benefit of the video, he added a cheery "Ho, ho—"

"What the hell are you doing here?"

"Shit!" He dropped the sack—on his foot—and turned to find his cranky neighbor at the entrance to the kitchen. Shock soon gave way to *hello there* because damn, she was wearing lace-trimmed shorts and a sexy black camisole with thin little straps.

"You're not supposed to be here," he muttered to her chest because that was a nice rack right there. He'd guessed as much but to be confronted with the rounded, supple evidence was most assuring.

"That's it!" She pointed at him. "I want that key back now."

I've eaten since the season started. My fans like videos of my adventures but this turned out to be more of an adventure than I expected."

Her brow puckered. "Thought you were heading to Michigan."

"Later this afternoon." He should be leaving right after the Santa-bandit escapade but he had plenty of time. Just a three-hour drive belting out his tunes after sneaking a peppermint mocha from Starbucks, which was hell on his regimen. But he'd happily delay as Elle looked like she could do with a friend. "Let me take care of this pantry stocking business like the good little Santa I am and then I'll make French toast."

"Kershaw, you don't have to—"

"Yes, I do. I've stolen your food and been a nuisance for months now. The least I can do is make you a pre-holiday breakfast. You won't regret it, I promise." He smiled, and she smiled back, and something caught in his chest that panged. Smiles shouldn't hurt, should they?

While he put away the groceries, she left to cover up, a sad, but necessary-for-his-dick turn of events. When she returned, she wore a baggy hoodie with the Cookie Monster saying "Why You Delete Cookies?" and flannel plaid PJs that he was pretty sure his dick could work with.

He checked cupboards, looking for the extra nutmeg, cinnamon, and vanilla he would need to whisk up the French toast batter the way his gran had taught him. He'd only ever made this for her, actually. Even when he indulged in some fun Theo time—eons ago, it seemed—he didn't usually offer his lady friends anything in the morning. Kind of rude, now that he thought of it, but French toast production was exactly that—a production—and implied a certain consideration. Anyone getting a bite of his toast was one lucky lady.

Elle sat at the kitchen island, checking her phone, then finally looked up. "Anything I can do?"

"Now she asks!" He beat the batter and shot her his hammiest wink. "Talk to me while I work. Tell me why you joined the army."

"Why does anyone do anything?"

"Not an answer."

She sighed. "I wanted to do something useful. Growing up, I didn't have a lot of opportunities for that. I was looking for some way to be shaped, I suppose."

To be shaped. Kind of an odd way to put it, as if her influences up until that point might *mis*shape her. It made him wonder about her family.

It made him wonder about a lot of things.

THE FRENCH TOAST WAS AMAZING. One more check in Kershaw's perfection column, which was getting longer than a CVS receipt—and just as annoying.

Elle eyed him over her coffee mug. "So, you've had these cooking skills in your back pocket and you've chosen instead to raid Hunt's fridge for sandwich and salad fixings on a daily basis?"

He tapped his stomach, covered with a reindeer sweater that unfortunately wasn't snug enough to be interesting. "Got to watch my girlish figure. I can't be eating like this during the season."

"Isn't it still during the season?"

"I can take a break to indulge a little." His eyelids were

"That was just a Merry Christmas, thanks for breakfast, safe travels kiss."

He licked his lips, tasting her and the syrup, and she imagined that tongue tasting other things. It had been far too long.

His hands still rested on her ass.

Yes, much too long.

"I don't have to leave just yet," he whispered, though it was only her to hear him. It made the words seem naughtier.

"I don't need you to stay." *Except for the good hard body you could provide because it's been that long since I've had a good hard body—beside, over, inside me.*

"But ..." He cocked his head, those molten shamrocks eyes assessing. "Would you like me to?"

He wanted her to beg? She'd already kissed him. Wasn't that enough?

Apparently she'd given him cause to doubt, even with the kiss. Even with the fond thoughts she tried to telepathically inject into his brain. Couldn't he figure it out that yes, she'd like him to stay without actually having to say, yes, she'd like him to stay.

Men. Hopeless.

"Tell me your Christmas wish, Ellie."

Ellie. Did she like that? She might.

Her Christmas wish? To forget about her problems. To be unreasonably distracted. Theo could do that for her. Theo could be the perfect gift.

"To see you in nothing but that hat."

His eyes burst into green-gold flames. "Think I can arrange that. But first ..."

Their lips met once more in a haze of wet-mouthed heat and lust, a live current rippling and reforming the space between them. Within seconds, control had slipped—for both of them—as the kiss turned deeper, frenzied, needful. She needed naked Theo now, quickly followed by erect Theo, and inside-her Theo.

She pulled at the hem of his reindeer sweater. "Could you ...?"

"Oh, yeah, right." He peeled it off, and *hello, pectorals, how ya been*? My God, this man had a body that should not be possible without Photoshop.

He grabbed his hat where it had been tangled in his sweater and put it back on. "Important," he muttered.

"Very."

Standing back, he unlaced his boots and peeled them off, throwing them casually to the side. Should she help?

No. Just watch, girl. Savor and enjoy.

He must have read her mind because he smirked, or maybe that was just his default expression when performing a holiday striptease in a desperate woman's kitchen.

Finally, he got to the good stuff: the snap on his jeans, the scrape of the zipper, the unmistakable bulge fighting to escape once given room to work.

"You sure about this?" he teased.

"Just do it before I change my mind, Kershaw."

He chuckled, a sound that said no one would be changing their mind here. The die had been cast. The dick was on stage.

The jeans went the way of the sweater, i.e. the floor. Best place for them. Never looked right on the man.

There he stood in a Santa hat and snug boxer briefs with ... were those dinosaurs?

She blinked, covered her mouth, and giggled. "Nice underwear."

"Gift from my gran. Now, you."

That wasn't how this was going to work. She pushed off from the counter, where she'd had to lean to catch her breath and save herself from melted-knee syndrome, and moved in close. Her hand strayed to his chest, brushed across one copper-pennied nipple.

"I'm not an exhibitionist like you."

He shrugged. "I'm not ashamed. You got it, you flaunt it."

Easy for him to say. She was no prude, but she wasn't able to compete with the level she saw before her. Nothing sculpted or honed about her body. She'd kept fit in the military but hadn't been maintaining her regimen as diligently since leaving. Stripping in the unflattering light of Levi Hunt's kitchen was not on the menu.

He seemed to sense her confusion. He placed a hand on her hip, the other at the nape of her neck.

"You okay?"

"I'm not sure."

"We don't have to do this."

It wasn't that she didn't want to. It would be wonderful, she was sure of it. A clearing of the pipes. A beautiful male body used as the gods intended. But that was it: she would be using him—and she'd been making a concerted effort not to do that to people. She came from a long line of takers, and while she had no doubt this would be a mutual exchange of pleasure and bodily fluids, she still felt weird about it.

"You'd be okay with me changing my mind?"

"This is your show, Ellie." But even as he said it, his cock twitched. She felt its sad poke against her stomach. Not a happy penis.

She looked down at it. Covered by the head of a cartoon T-rex, it was still impressive.

"Sorry," she whispered.

Theo laughed, the sound slightly pained. "Yeah, you should definitely apologize to my dick. The big guy's never gonna forgive us for getting him all worked up." He kissed her softly, which was much more than she deserved for being such a tease. "Not a big deal. You want me out of your hair?" He tangled a finger in one of her errant curls.

"Don't you have to head home?"

"Not for a while yet. But if you want to be alone, I can make that happen." He waggled both eyebrows. "Or I could make Christmas lunch."

"We just had breakfast."

He waved it off. "Merely the appetizer."

"You mean you'd actually cook for me after I led you to the brink—"

"Hardly the brink."

"And made your dick cranky."

With his hands still cradling her hips, he held her back a few inches and peered down at his groin. "You cranky, bud?"

"Oh, God." That was Elle, not Theo's penis, speaking.

He continued conversing with his chatty dick. "A little? Don't worry, we'll have some alone time later. A few happy, holiday tugs and you won't even remember the mean lady who looked a hung-like-a-gift horse in the mouth." All smiles, he met her astonished gaze once more. "We're good."

Were they? Was she crazy to turn down an offer like this? Her ovaries certainly thought so.

She stepped back, struck by the notion that leaving his arms was a mistake. That she might like to stay wrapped in them for a while longer and that she'd missed out on not just great sex, but self-care with a wonderful guy.

He's not for you, Eloise.

Theo made no moves to redress, just started rinsing off dishes. "So, what were your plans today?"

"Cereal for breakfast, lunch, and dinner. Binge watch Hallmark Christmas movies. Paint my toes."

"I can paint toes."

That would make a good video for his social, and she kind of liked the idea of helping him with that. "If you're hanging around thinking I'll change my mind ..."

"I'm not, though we both know if I stay like this, dazzling in my dino-briefs, your resistance will eventually falter."

"You think I'll break down?"

"I'm going to make you lunch, and then I'll have you eating out of my hand. Chicken parm sound good?"

It sounded amazing. It was nice to have someone taking care of her—she wasn't used to that. She didn't want to *get* used to that, but surely a few hours at the holidays wouldn't hurt. A few hours to forget that she was more alone this season than at any other time in her life.

She wouldn't fall for his charms. She'd enjoy them from a distance, safe in the knowledge that they were just two neighbors being neighborly while one of them cooked lunch in his underwear. Sure, completely normal. So what if she wanted more. We don't always get what we wish.

"Hey, Elle." He waved in front of her face. "Where'd you go?"

She managed a smile. "Chicken parm would be great. Just tell me what to do."

6

WHILE THEO WAS DETERMINED to see this underwear-only challenge through, he did don an apron to flash-fry the chicken cutlets because oil spatter on a naked chest was no joke. But he saw no reason why he should hide his great ass on the day before the baby Jesus was born.

Elle sneaked plenty of looks, too. After she'd helped him find the ingredients—flour and breadcrumbs, he'd brought the rest—she settled with a glass of wine at the kitchen island.

"If your fans could see you now. Want me to film a few seconds?"

"No," he said quickly, then when she looked at him strangely, he explained. "After this morning, people will start wondering about you. Add in the mystery woman I'm cooking for while dressed in these bad boys, and there'll be questions. Unless you want to be hounded, you probably should stay on the down low."

She'd gone nuts about that video this morning and made him delete it. He got it. Not everyone enjoyed the limelight.

"You're right. I didn't think—I thought I could give your rabid fans something to make up for the deleted video."

Theo grabbed a jar of Paul Newman's marinara sauce. Into his head popped an image of Cool Hand Luke himself puttering about in a kitchen, working on sauce recipes, Scott Joplin playing *The Sting* theme on a piano in the corner. Yeah, that probably happened.

"You were kind of crazy about being on camera. You don't seem the shy type. Or is it so horrifying to be connected to me?" No doubt she thought he was just another dumb jock.

That's why you like her, Kershaw. Because she's made it clear you're not special.

But you are special, baby boy, his brain chimed in, in the voice of his gran. Good old Aurora, his greatest cheerleader.

"I don't like to filmed, that's all. It's not personal."

"A lot of people would jump at the chance to be seen with me, y'know."

Her expression was pitying. "Poor Superglutes, aren't you getting enough attention from your millions of Instagram followers? Is it lonely being adored by all your fans?"

"Very! All they see is this amazing body and gorgeous hair and beautiful cheekbones. Sure, I'm hilarious and great in bed, but do they appreciate it? Do *you* appreciate it?"

She was rolling in her lips, trying not to laugh.

"I know. You're impossible to break. But wait until you've tried my chicken parm, then you'll be begging for—"

"More chicken parm?"

"Yes!"

She laughed, and it was nice to be responsible for that, even if she was laughing at him rather than with him.

"I'll set the table." She looked in the drawers and found placemats, then set out flatware and wine glasses. She even lit a small candle which smelled like cinnamon and pine cones. Within minutes, he was serving up bowls of angel hair pasta topped with a perfectly crusted golden chicken parm cutlet, sauce, and melted mozz.

"An extra hour on the treadmill tomorrow," he said, patting his naked abs.

She was pouring wine and missed the glass.

He grinned.

"Can it," she grated.

"They're just abs, Elle-oh-Elle, and you claim to be so above it all."

She pushed a glass his way. "No one likes a braggart, Kershaw."

"What'll we drink to?" He held up his wine glass. A half hour of crunches unless he could get some exercise in a more pleasurable way.

"A full fridge I didn't pay for," she said. "Finally."

"Good food and good company," he finished, clinking her glass.

She held his stare as if they'd both made the most significant toast ever. He wasn't sure why but breaking bread with her meant something.

"Tell me about your home town," she asked after she'd had a glass of wine.

"It's right on Lake Michigan and has about a thousand inhabitants in winter and ten times that in the summer. At the turn of the last century, it was home to an artists' colony trying to get some inspiration outside of Chicago. It's really beautiful. The water's different, the sky's kind of alien. It was a good place to grow up, for the most part."

"All your family's still there?"

"Just my gran." The image of another family, just a few miles away in Chicago, tried to take hold. His bio-dad was probably putting up the tree, making a last-minute eggnog run to Target, hiding wrapped presents for his boys under the bed. Since Theo's hospitalization, Nick usually checked in every few months with a bland *hi-how-are-ya* text. He had to know Theo was based in Chicago now, but still no invite to Casa Isner.

Theo refocused on Elle. "Where did you grow up?"

"Oh, all over. We moved around a lot." She cast a quick glance over the empty plates, clearly looking to change the subject. "We did good work here."

"We did," he said solemnly. So she didn't want to talk about her family and he wasn't dying to spill about his except for Aurora, who he really needed to call. "How about you head out to the sofa and get it warm for me?"

Skeptical silver-blue eyes met his.

"While I take care of dessert and the dishes."

"You're gonna make someone a lovely wife, Kershaw."

She headed out and he rinsed off the dishes and loaded them in the dishwasher. Then he made the call he should have made a couple of hours ago.

"Hey!" he said to his grandmother, with a double injection of holiday cheer so she wouldn't think something was wrong.

"THEO, BABY BOY! Are you almost here?"

"Not quite." He lowered his voice. "Something came up."

"Your penis, I hope. I've been worried about you."

"Aurora!" He shout-whispered into the phone. "And at the holidays, too."

"Well, I *have* been concerned. I'm hoping someone else is involved and it's not just you and your right hand."

He hadn't been with anyone since before the surgery— almost two years—and while his grandmother didn't know that for sure, she had a pretty good idea. The woman kept track of his social and social media life like a bloodhound. Apparently inserting his penis into someone was the ultimate sign he'd recovered.

"This isn't about a woman."

"You're whispering," she whispered loudly. "Is she in the bed beside you?"

"No, she is not!" Though not for lack of trying.

"So, it *is* a woman. I saw your video this morning before you took it down. Everyone's commenting on your previous post asking who she is and what's going on."

The perils of being a social media superstar. "My neighbor was on her own so I stopped in to make breakfast and it turned into lunch. That's all."

"I hoped there'd be more to it."

So did he. Despite that explosive kiss, he got the impression Elle didn't think much of him beyond his excellent physique, pretty face, and killer smile. Or maybe he got that impression because that's *exactly* what she'd told him.

"There isn't anything going on. I'll leave here in about an hour and see you by dinner time."

"All right, drive safe. I miss you, baby boy."

"ARE you seriously not going to put your clothes back on?"

"Why, is it too much for you, Elle-oh-Elle?"

Curling up in the corner of the sofa with a blanket was Elle's best defense against Theo, who was still walking around in his underwear. She should have insisted he put his jeans back on, minimum, but his cocky swagger had made her bristle and accept the challenge he presented.

And challenge it was. His thick thighs made her mouth water (not drool, thank you, just liquid that remained *inside* her mouth which she considered progress from her morning Insta check-ins). They were hairy, too, which she'd never thought was a turn on. But with Theo, everything was arousing. Leg hair, calf muscles, even his toes. The man had very attractive foot digits.

Thankfully, he was sitting at the other end of the sofa, the cushions, uh, cushioning his lovely globes. Did she miss them as they pranced and preened around her kitchen while he cooked? Sort of. But this was for the best.

"Do you need your sweater?" she asked, torn between hope and lust.

"Nah, I'm fine." He reached for his water glass and took a sip; the movement highlighted his lats, which were as sexy as the rest of him.

Sighing, she turned on the TV and queued up Christmas Jingle Jangle: Ambitious City Girl Gives Up Job of Her Dreams to Bake Cookies in Small Town and Lock Down Inn Owner/Christmas Tree Farmer/Local Vet (not it's real title).

Within ten minutes, Theo was fidgeting.

Within twenty he was sprawled on two thirds of the sofa, one outsized foot planted on the middle cushion, a position that stretched his dino-briefs taut against his impressive package. There was no mistaking the outline, the length, the sheer girth of what he was working with.

"Quit it," she muttered.

"Pardon?" Polite, as if they were in a Jane Austen production.

"You know."

"I'm sure I don't."

Taking the blanket with her as she stood, she placed it over his lower half. "There, much better."

"You are the envy of women the world over and this is how you treat your opportunity? Tut tut."

"Is there an elderly maiden aunt hidden beneath those gaudy muscles?"

He smiled wistfully. "Just something my gran says."

"You guys sound close."

"She raised me and did an amazing job."

"Such modesty."

"I was complimenting my grandmother."

She wondered about his parents but asking would open up the floor for questions about the Butler clan of miscreants. *Next.*

On the TV, Blond Chick was dressing a tree with spray-painted popcorn on a string.

"I've never understood that," Elle said. "Why go to all that trouble when you could just buy a garland or something?"

"Didn't you make holiday decorations when you were a kid?"

She shrugged. "No. I bought them like a normal person. I'm guessing this is something you and your sainted granny did."

A shadow crossed his brow, a flash of remembered pain. "Yeah, we did. She's pretty creative." He didn't elaborate, and she got the impression that it killed him to hold back. The guy was chatty to a fault.

"She must have been worried sick about you when you had your ruptured aneurysm."

He leveled a curious gaze at her. "She was. I wouldn't have made it back without her."

"Hunt thinks you're some sort of wunderkind because you're back to your peak. Maybe even better than before."

"I do feel like that sometimes. New and improved."

She didn't know what he was like before, but he couldn't be exactly the same now. "Maybe it rewired your brain differently."

"Maybe, but then the rink has always felt like the safest place in the world. Within my control."

Elle had felt something like that in the army. It's what she'd sought—a measure of control over the chaos.

"If only I could bring some of that to the rest of my life," Theo added.

"Looks like you're doing okay with your Instagram videos."

Oh. Shit.

"You watch my videos?" No need to verify that smirk was fully activated; its cockiness drenched the room.

"I may have seen one or two on my travels."

He moved in closer, bringing all that heat. "Are you a ... *fan*? I'm over there filming my morning routine and you're over here ... *watching*?"

He made it sound so creepy. She was no creepier than any of his adoring fans. Not that she was like them. Not at all.

"Like I said, just happened on one or two while scrolling my feed and drinking my coffee. And you always seem your usual cocksure, arrogant, king-of-the-world self."

His humor faded. "It's what the fans want to see. Funny, sexy, no filter Theo."

"Aw, so sad. When all those fangirls send their hearts and tell you how good your abs look, don't you feel like a god?" Especially since he'd survived such a harrowing experience. Some people might come out feeling blessed, even invincible.

He shrugged those broad shoulders. "All my confidence

is reserved for the ice. Off it ... well, let's just say I haven't returned to peak conditioning there."

Was he saying—? "You mean the D in D-man has performance issues?"

"Not performance issues! There's nothing wrong with my equipment. I've just lost some of my mojo, that's all." He folded his arms.

"This is your play, Kershaw?"

He looked confused. "Play?"

"Making me breakfast and lunch didn't work, hanging out in your underwear didn't cut it, and that barely passable kiss—"

"Hey!"

"Didn't get you in my boy shorts. So you're going with the pity angle. You expect me to believe that *The* Theo Kershaw might be going through a sex drought because he's lost a little confidence?"

He stared hard, burning a hole in her head, then broke into a sexy grin. "Figured it was worth a shot."

She pushed playfully at his arm and had to fight not to linger with her horny knuckles. "You probably should get going. Home to your gran."

"I suppose so. I'll just grab my clothes."

When he returned, his jeans were on, half-snapped, his sweater in his hand. Disappointment should not have been her primary emotion. Theo had been nice enough to hang with her for most of the day, he'd made her breakfast and lunch, and hadn't annoyed her nearly as much as she'd expected during her Hallmark movie binge—all fifty-four minutes of it.

She walked with him to the door. "Thanks for sticking around—that was really nice of you."

"I'm a nice guy," he said, the words muffled by the

sweater he was pulling over his head. It sent static through his usually perfect hair and made him look boyish. She preferred when he was muscled and objectifiable. This Theo was a little too human for her liking.

He seemed to hover until she took a step toward the door, then he followed her lead. Now it was her turn to linger. She'd become quite used to catching up-close-and-shirtless Theo in her periphery that it was almost strange to see him covered up.

They both stood, expectant.

"Well, that was—"

"Happy hol—"

Talking over each other prompted nervous laughs, and then he leaned in to capture her joy with his lips on hers. Perhaps he'd meant it to be quick. Perhaps he'd meant it to be friendly. But her body had the jump on her brain. She responded hungrily, drawing his moan, a deep, heartfelt sound that vibrated through her body. Pent up frustration found its release with her hands going straight to his ass.

She'd never have forgiven herself for not taking advantage.

He felt good. Firm and tight and meaty.

He separated from her, his lips wet, his eyes wild. "I should ... what should I do?"

For too long, she'd resisted anything or anyone that might throw her plans for balance out of whack. Indulging in a treat like Theo might be bad for her—but like all useless calories, she could spend time burning them off later. Right now, she needed this. She needed him.

"You should get going?" His gaze dimmed, and she added with a grin, "Into my bedroom."

7

EYES STOKED WITH LUST, he smiled—not smugly but like he knew her secrets. She had to be clear about the rules.

"Just this once, Kershaw. There'll be no future drop-ins or booty calls or quickies against the juke box down at the bar after closing."

"Thought about that, have you?"

"Oh shut up." She kissed him because it was plain her vocal cords were the problem here.

"Thank Christ," he muttered. "I want you so bad, Ellie."

Ellie. She let the way he said her name wash through her veins, enjoying the sparkle. And then she was two feet off the ground with Theo Kershaw's big, hockey stick-holding hands molded to her ass and his big hockey-skate wearing feet walking her back the way they'd come.

"Your bedroom?" he panted against her lips.

"Near the bathroom." She didn't want him to trip so she refrained from kissing him, just watched as he watched her on his path to her bedroom.

She was going to have sex with Theo Kershaw. Was this a terrible idea? Probably. Did she care? Not anymore.

Happy holidays to her!

He placed her down on the (unmade) bed, and she winced at her slobbishness. "Sorry for the mess, I wasn't expecting—"

"To be getting down and dirty with your grocery-wielding, lunch-cooking, next-door neighbor?"

"Well, no." Nice of him not to mention hockey-playing or underwear-hawking or Instagram-influencing.

He pulled off his sweater. "Put like that, it sounds like a porn plot."

"If it was, we would have done it in the kitchen or on the sofa or even at the door. Instead of vanilla in the bedroom."

He smirked. "Vanilla? There will be nothing vanilla about what's happening here."

She didn't care if was vanilla, chocolate, or rocky road. She just wanted to be fucked thoroughly for Christmas.

Soon he was down to his dino-briefs and she was faced with all that man.

"Up," he said in a tone that sounded like ... an order? From nice guy Theo Kershaw? Not expecting that.

She stood and let him undress her. First her hoodie, which made her consider for the first time what she wore beneath. A plain black bra wasn't exactly thrilling for him but she figured they were beyond this. Anything would suffice after the sexual tension she'd barely survived this afternoon.

Before he went further, those green eyes perused her body with a hunger she didn't expect. She'd known he was turned on—guys turned hard at the slightest thing—but she hadn't foreseen this level of intensity from Theo.

It surprised her so much she felt self-conscious. She pushed at her PJ bottoms to distract him.

He stopped her hand. "Hold on, let me savor this."

Savor? Wasn't this supposed to be a quick roll, happy holidays, then be on their way?

"Oh, okay."

He grazed the tops of her breasts with his knuckles, gently teasing, and her entire body goosefleshed. "Beautiful."

She swallowed, uncomfortable with the complement. She wasn't the beautiful one. He was perfection and she was convenient, though that was unfair to both of them. She knew he wanted her, but she wasn't sure there was more to it than geography.

He captured her breast in his big hand and squeezed, causing her to shiver with pleasure.

"You feel really good, Ellie."

"Grrr ..." This was the sound that emerged from her mouth. His hand on her breast had rendered her a savage.

He chuckled and captured her lips in a kiss. So good, like wine and cinnamon, a festive party in her mouth. She pulled his body over hers, loving the weight of him, the solidity of all that muscle, a comforting blanket with sexy intentions.

He fed kisses down her throat to the V of her bra and sucked through the fabric. Then he continued blazing a path down her rib cage, stopping to dip his tongue in her belly button before tugging at her PJs.

"I'm—oh, shit."

He looked up, his eyes smoky with lust. "What?"

"It's a little disheveled down there. I wasn't prepared for this."

"Don't care. Any guy who says he does is a fucking liar."

Within five seconds her PJs were off. Within twenty, she was halfway to heaven as Theo demonstrated one more spoke in his wheel of perfection.

She couldn't help her hip swivel, her begging with her body for him to taste and suck and lick. She clamped her mouth shut, letting her hips do the talking. Better that than cry out his name, give voice to this fantasy coming to life. Trapped in her throat, that one word struggled to break free. *Tee ... Tee ... Tee-Oh!*

His fingers got in on the act, slipping, sliding, while his tongue lapped and licked. The flood of pleasure caught her by surprise and she screamed out ...

... something that was not his name.

Surely not.

Theo was still below deck, his cheek resting against her inner thigh. His shoulders shook with ... laughter.

"Did you just call out T-Rex when you came?" Before she could answer, he collapsed in hysterics.

She'd been trying so hard not to say his name that she said the first thing that occurred to her. Blame the dino-briefs.

"What? You've never had a girl invoke her favorite dinosaur when she gets there?"

He crawled up her body and kissed her thoroughly. "No, that's a first. You're a first, Ellie. A complete original."

Because he was being such a good sport, she figured she owed him an explanation. "I didn't want to say your name because your head's already big enough."

"I have no problem being compared to the king of the Cretaceous period."

"But he had such tiny ... hands."

He laughed. "Pretty sure no correlations can be made in that area. I'm plenty big enough to satisfy you, Ellie."

"Oh yeah? Let's see." She cupped his cock through the dino-briefs, the proof in the prick. His thickness expanded in her hand, so she stroked hard and let all that leashed power thrill through her.

He closed his eyes in ecstasy, then opened them lazily. "Condoms? I have some but they're back in my apartment."

She leaned over to her nightstand, pulled open the drawer, and withdrew a three-pack.

"Army issue?"

"I bought them at the base, so yeah."

"Thanks, Uncle Sam." *Bye bye, dino-briefs. Hello, rubber friend.* And then he kissed her again, so sweetly. "You ready?"

"Yes."

He pushed inside her, slowly, testing her ability to take him.

"Christ, you feel so good," he murmured against her mouth.

She wanted to scream, *No, you do!* She'd loved his tongue on her, bringing her to orgasm (T-rex! Would she ever live it down?) but this fullness felt so much deeper. Connected.

He withdrew an inch or two, then moved inside her again. Further, fuller. His hand trailed down her arm until it found and interlocked with her fingers. There was a sweetness about that gesture that unlocked something in her chest.

It was too much. Too real.

"That's it, Dino-Boy. Just like that."

He chuckled, thrust again, squeezed her hand tighter. "Whatever you need, Ellie." His eyes remained focused on hers, telling her he wasn't buying her efforts at distance. He knew her game and he could play it better than her.

So she stopped playing and started feeling. Let herself enjoy Theo's singular attention. With each stroke and molten look, he touched a private and usually inaccessible spot inside her. Joking Elle would say it was her cervix, but that version wasn't here. In her place was a woman moved by how good it felt to have another person inside you, a man who looked at you like you were the center of his universe, if only for a little while.

The time for jesting was over. Racing toward a peak was her only goal, and Theo knew what she needed. Gave it to her so good. He thumbed her clit and drove her over the edge, and this time she whispered his name into his shoulder, a soft sound that was all she could manage in the wake of such relief.

But Theo's sounds weren't soft or gentle—he was loud and lusty and possessed of a pretty filthy vocabulary that his brownie-baking grandma would most definitely not approve of.

ELLE AWOKE in the middle of the night, or maybe it was the middle of the morning. Time seemed to have no hold here in the warm, blanket-shrouded dark.

A large hand was positioned between her legs.

Oh.

She adjusted her thighs. The hand twitched, then stroked with a light, lazy motion. *Ohhhh.*

A whimper escaped her. Encouraged, the hand clamped tighter, cupping, drawing her body back into the cradle of his.

Theo.

This was crazy, but then her life right now was crazy. Unconnected, loose-limbed, no traction.

"You have to go," she murmured, in direct conflict to her basest needs.

He buried a groan in her hair. "Too comfortable. Too turned on." Then he pulled a groan from her—easily—with that sensuous tease of the sensitive flesh between her thighs.

"You have to start your trip," she said at the same time she opened her legs to give him better access. "Be home before grandma gets up." She didn't want him to leave, but he'd already stayed long past his initial promise of breakfast and lunch. Dinner was cereal and popcorn, dessert was sex on the sofa while Hallmark movies played in the background (sacrilege, and so deliciously naughty).

But she couldn't have him here with her on Christmas Day. He had a family he needed to see and she had a family she needed to hide.

His fingers continued their maddening torture, and after a few more strokes he had her on her back and his mouth stamped over hers. "Holiday delivery. Right here." Two fingers now, a luxurious stretch. A few more minutes wouldn't hurt, even though she knew every passing second dragged her deeper into the lure of him.

More rubbing and stroking and *there, so good, yes, yes, yes* and she could feel that perfect coil of pressure tightening.

"More," she urged.

His big palm spread her wide. "I'll take care of you, Ellie. I'll take care of you so good."

His voice was thick with lust and she could feel him, huge, urgent, against her thigh. She needed to be filled. She needed something she couldn't articulate properly. Him, but more.

"Please. Oh, please."

The crinkle of the condom wrapper registered in her ears, and he gave her what she needed. She fell asleep wrapped in Instagram-worthy arms.

When she woke again, he was sitting on the bed, leaning

over her. She could make out bright eyes, white teeth. Could hear his fertile brain ticking over.

"You know, Ellie, you could—"

"Let's just leave it at this, Kershaw. Lovely night, morning delight, and no strings."

"I was going to ask—"

She touched her fingertips to his lips. "I know what you were going to ask." *Come home with me. You'd be welcome in Saugatuck. I'd feel bad leaving you here alone.* "But like I said yesterday, this is a one-off."

"Several orgasms delivered is more like a five-off. But I'm not counting or anything."

One last ego stroke wouldn't hurt. It had been a perfect day and night after all.

"You rocked my world, Superglutes. Now go home to your granny."

8

Six weeks later

THEO GRABBED a Henley from his locker then switched it up for one of his team jerseys. He shut the door and put his foot on the bench to Velcro his sneakers.

A seated Levi Hunt looked up and delivered the Special Forces squint. "Wearing your own jersey off the ice is a bit much even for you, Kershaw."

"Funny. Not leaving just yet. I need to do a meet 'n' greet with some kids who won a contest on my Instagram."

"Is that what we're calling them now?"

Theo grinned. "You just wish you had fans."

"Regular, mind-blowing sex is preferable." At Theo's pained expression, he patted his arm. "Sorry, sore spot?"

"Blue spot, as in balled."

"You mean to tell me a good-looking guy like you with a zillion fans on Facebook—"

"Instagram, dude. Facebook is for my grandmother and her posse."

Hunt waved that off. "So what's up? Or not ... up?"

"Just going through a dry patch." Since he'd unwrapped a sexy package on Christmas Eve and proceeded to wrap himself in the body of his hot, gorgeous neighbor.

Tonight Theo was going to see her for the first time in several weeks. He wouldn't go so far as to say that he'd been avoiding the Empty Net bar. Rather, he'd been *selective* about his coming and goings. He had good reasons, mostly to do with Elle.

Fine, all to do with Elle.

Why subject the poor woman to the potentially hurtful sight of a hockey god in his prime being pounced on by his considerable fandom? Since that fabulous night, she'd moved out of Hunt's place and into her own apartment above the Empty Net where she worked. Theo flaunting his assets in front of a former fling seemed less than classy, even if the former fling had made it clear she was not interested in him beyond that one night.

Someone else—Theo didn't have a name for this exceptionally irritating someone—might have come up with an alternative theory on his absence.

Avoidance cut both ways.

Theo didn't want to inflict his fans on Elle, and likewise, he wasn't in the mood to watch her flirting with the male clientele. Sure, she was just being friendly, doing her job, working it for a better tip. He *knew* that, but it was tougher than he'd expected to be a fly on the wall. He hadn't had a crush like this since Janie Michelson in the sixth grade. (And that had ended terribly with Janie sending a Valentine's card to Kevin Corrigan because his family owned stables. Hard to compete with horses.)

However, today was their goalie, Erik Jorgensen's birthday, and he'd asked to celebrate this joyous occasion at the Empty Net. *We could head to a club downtown, Fish. Meet a couple of hot girls.* But the Swede had his heart set on the local drinking establishment, and the birthday boy would get his wish.

Later. First some fun with his fans.

Shondra, the team's publicist, appeared with a gaggle of wide-eyed youngsters, mostly boys in the ten to fourteen-year range, though a couple of girls were there, too.

Theo loved meeting junior fans. Some of today's guests had brought parents with them for a backstage tour. It was like Willy Wonka—and Theo had the keys to the chocolate factory.

"Hey, guys! Great to see you. Welcome to the Rebels locker room."

The kids blinked, looking around in awe, pointing at the names of their favorites above each cubby.

"Any hockey players here?"

They all raised their hands, even the girls, which was awesome.

"Cool! We can start the tour here. First up is this marble statue beside me depicting a cross between grumpy guy who really needs a cupcake and too-old-and-barely-hacking-it hockey player who wishes he'd left five minutes ago. Anyone want to guess who this is?"

"Levi Hunt!" Several of the kids shouted as if this was a valid question, and Levi was actually an immobile statue who was part of the tour. Animatronic legends in the Hockey Hall of Fame? Theo filed it away.

"Hey, there." Misery guts Hunt's attempt to persuade the group he was actually a real, live man. "You guys enjoy the practice?"

The kids asked about the drills and plays they'd just seen. One of the dads queried Hunt about his military service, which was always guaranteed to kill a few minutes.

People were pretty obsessed with that shit. While Hunt yammered on about ripping up trees and chopping fire-wood with his bare Special Forces hands (Theo assumed this is what he talked about, he usually tuned out), Theo spotted a kid arriving late to the locker room. Something familiar about him pinged his chest. A woman's hand landed on the kid's shoulder, pushing him forward and guiding him in place.

Theo recognized her. Shit.

Jenny Isner, wife to Nick Isner, Chicago alderman, and more important—to Theo anyway—his biological father.

He'd seen pictures of them online, all American smiles and family values, and while Nick knew Theo existed, he'd made it clear that his oldest son wasn't welcome to join Team Isner.

Theo had made peace with that years ago. He had people who loved him and he wasn't going to beg for more. Occasionally he checked out the guy's Facebook page looking for mentions of Nick's other sons. Wondering if they were happy and safe.

His eyes latched onto the kid, the spitting image of Nick. Mid-brown hair, freckles splashed on his nose, green eyes the same as Theo.

Did Nick even know they were here? Probably not, because there was no way he'd condone this visit. Theo smiled at the kid, certain it came off as weird because it felt like he'd never smiled before in his damn life.

The kid—his half-brother—returned a funhouse mirror version of Theo's smile, then looked shyly at his mom.

"Right, Kershaw?"

He turned to Hunt who must have been trying to get his attention for a while. "Uh, what's that?"

"Just telling them that Boston's defense could give us trouble."

Theo tried laughing off his discomfort. His kid brother was here—and he had no idea who Theo truly was. "That's *your* problem, Hunt. I've got *my* zone covered. Okay! You guys want to see the equipment room?"

A chorus of shouts went up, and in a daze, Theo led the kids to the next stop. They donned shin guards and elbow pads while Shondra snapped pics for Theo's and the team's social.

"Hey, try on these shoulder pads," he said to his brother, who looked like the younger one. "What's your name?"

"Jason," he said while pulling the pad frame over his head. The pads swamped his small body.

"You play hockey, Jason?"

"Yeah. I want to be a defenseman but my coach thinks I'm too short."

"It seems dangerous out there," his mom said.

"Not if you're padded right." Theo patted the sternum plate. "And maybe develop a few muscles. How old are you?"

"Almost twelve."

"I was about your size when I was twelve but then I had a growth spurt."

Jason nodded wisely, then eyed his mom. "See?"

The lady Isner remained unmoved. Her nose twitched, probably at the equipment funk which Theo was well used to. A mom of tweens should be used to it, too, but maybe that's not how it went in their household.

"You'll want to make sure you're eating a sh—a whole lot of fruits and vegetables. You set good habits now and the muscles will follow." He smiled at Nick's wife, who smiled back, liking anything that encouraged her kid to chow down on greens.

"Listen to Mr. ..." She looked lost.

"It's Theo. Theo Kershaw." *One. Two. Nothing.* No apparent recognition at the mention of his name, so still the dirty secret. Nice.

"You always have those protein shakes in the morning," Jason said to Theo. "But Mom said I'm too young for that."

"She's right. That's a special diet planned by the team here. But you can get a lot of the same benefits if you listen to your mom and eat everything she tells you. She knows best."

Obviously bored with the food talk, Jason fingered the straps of the padding. "Could I see your hockey stick?"

"Thought you'd never ask!"

~

MEETING his brother had been a surreal experience. Walking into the Empty Net bar for Erik's birthday drinks, Theo pondered what might happen next. Would Jason mention the visit to his dad? Surely Nick's wife would say something to her husband?

Seven years ago Theo had visited Nick at his law offices in Chicago, and was told "now wasn't a good time." Theo had thought it the perfect time. He was headed to Vermont on his hockey scholarship. He didn't need money or even regular meet-ups with his biological father, who had knocked up Theo's sixteen-year-old mom in high school when he was seventeen. But his mother had recently passed and Theo didn't want to waste any time on *if only*.

His father's rejection of his oldest son hadn't really surprised him; he'd had eighteen years to reach out, after all. Theo was an optimist to his core and to not try wasn't in his nature. With his enthusiasm and ego bruised, he left those law offices and never looked back—except for the odd sneaky look at Facebook.

But seeing his half-brother today plucked at something raw inside him, something that could only be appeased by seeing Elle. He needed her snark, her set-downs, and her hard-won smiles.

Theo approached the bar to place an order. No sign of the woman on his mind, so maybe it was her night off. His shoulders sank in disappointment.

Tina, the woman who owned the Empty Net, spotted him. "What'll it be, Theo?"

"Hey, Tina," he said. "Two IPAs, a pint of Guinness, and a Brandy Alexander for the birthday boy, please." Erik had some shady taste in cocktails.

"The birthday boy?"

His heart kicked hard at the sight of Elle, newly arrived from the other side of the bar. Her hair was tied back, her face shiny with the heat, which reminded him of her glossy and sweaty underneath his body. She'd made those quiet, desperate moans when he touched her and ... now he had the makings of a damn fine erection.

That was the other reason for cutting down on his bar visits. Balls of blue were no fun.

"Jorgenson. It's his birthday." He lowered his voice and leaned in. "How've you been?"

"Fine." She dragged it out, then mirrored his lean, coming close enough that he could smell sweet mint on her breath. "How've *you* been?"

"Like you care. You never call. You never write." He added a cheeky grin to let her know it was all a joke, even though inside he was a touch frosted that they'd been reduced to this level of awkwardness.

"I see you on TV." She pointed at one of the many screens, currently tuned to last night's game, which they'd won. He'd played awesome. "Looks like things are coming together. Or so Hunt says."

Still talking to Hunt, then. He had no reason to be jealous of his teammate, who had known Elle back in the military and was recently engaged and very happy—or as happy as the sour bastard was capable—with Jordan Cooke, sports reporter extraordinaire.

"Yeah, season's turning around. We might even qualify for the playoffs, which I know you don't care about."

"If it makes people spend more money in here, I am your biggest fan, Kershaw."

"Hi, Theo!" An unfamiliar voice cut in, and he had to look down to meet the big brown eyes of a blond pixie type. She wore a Rebels T-shirt, had more teeth than should be possible in one mouth, and smelled nice.

"Hi, there."

"You probably don't remember me, but I'm Kylie and I work at the Riverbrook Animal Shelter? We chatted at that charity brunch in December? You said you wanted to help with our spaying and neutering program?"

Right. Theo actually remembered this woman from that charity thing. She was pretty rabid about de-balling puppies, so he actually believed this wasn't a sneaky way of getting his digits. He never handed them out unless absolutely necessary.

"Sorry, with the holidays, it fell off my radar, but just tell me what you need and I'll be all over it."

"You're so sweet. Money would help? But also a mention

on your Instagram would be fantastic. Maybe I could get your number?"

He checked his pockets and pulled out a business card. "My publicist. She can get you what you need."

Her gaze narrowed on the card. "Wonderful! Thanks so much." She leaned up on her tiptoes and kissed him on the cheek, then skipped off to a table near the juke box—the one he wouldn't be pushing Elle against anytime soon per her post-fling rules. He considered making a joke about that, but sometime during his chat with Kylie, Elle had vanished.

Well, that sucked.

Tina loaded all the drinks on the bar. "Start a tab, Theo?"

"You bet. Got to keep the birthday boy happy." At least one of them would be tonight.

9

WHERE THE HELL ARE YOU?

Elle had texted Jordan hours ago—okay, five minutes—
and she still hadn't come up to the apartment. She checked
her phone and found a new message: *On my way!*

Maybe it was a mistake to do this on her break but
seeing Theo downstairs had pushed her to a decision. What
she really needed right now was Jordan's sunny can-do optimism. She needed someone who would tell her it was going
to be fine.

"Hello?"

"I'm in here," Elle called back.

Jordan's steady tread got louder until the redhead
appeared at the entrance to Elle's bathroom. "You okay? You
sounded—whoa!" Her gaze fell on the bomb in the room.

The pee-stick-shaped bomb.

"Is that what I think it is?"

"Well, it's not a new kind of pimple popper. God knows I
wish it was." She examined her face in the mirror. Was her
skin starting to break out from the stress? No surprise there.
"I did it about three minutes ago, so it should be ready."

Nothing on the readout, yet. No news is good news, right?

Jordan put her arm around her, which she just about managed despite being a good six inches shorter than Elle. "No matter what happens, we're going to get through this. Levi and I will be—"

"No to the nopity no. You cannot tell Hunt. You know how he gets."

Jordan tilted her head, a splash of freckles on her nose glowing in the bad light of the bathroom. "No, I don't. Do tell."

Elle responded as if Jordan hadn't said that with a slightly sarcastic twist to it. "He'll be weird and patriarchal and will probably want to beat up someone." A certain someone.

"*Riiiight.* I hear you, but he also recognizes that you're an autonomous person who's free to sleep with whomever you want and own all the consequences of that."

After a beat, they both burst out laughing.

Jordan grimaced. "Theo?"

"Is it so obvious?"

"Not really, but he's always seemed interested in you. He doesn't come in here much anymore so I figured something might have happened and it was awkward."

So she wasn't the only one who'd noticed his absence. Boy, was she annoyed at how pleased she was to see him tonight after so long without. She'd made it clear that she wouldn't be clingy, that it was a one-time deal, and that he should have nothing to worry about ... except for the possible surprise pregnancy! So much for no strings.

The man could barely look at her, and now this. "Theo is the last person I want holding my hand in this situation."

"I know he's sort of absurd, but he's also kind of sweet."

That was the problem. He was far too sweet for her.

She frowned at Jordan. *You all are. If only you had the slightest idea of where I'm from and the havoc I wreak everywhere I go.* Exhibit A: Got knocked up by America's Favorite Ass.

"He's not terrible, but—" An ominous here's-your-future beep cut her off. "I can't look at it. Could you do it for—"

"It's positive." Jordan had already picked it up and was now waving it like it was a Polaroid and shaking it could make it clearer, or change the result.

Elle snatched it back and promptly started to do the same thing. "Maybe it's wrong."

"99.2% accurate says the box."

"Well, I could be the .8%. Which is why I also bought three others and peed on them at the same time." She pulled back the shower curtain and gestured to the three differently-branded test sticks now lying in the bathtub like a blind-date TV show where the results were (a) catastrophe, (b) loss of freedom and (c) you're screwed.

Those baby bombs portrayed two straight lines (fuck), a plus sign (double fuck), and a smiley face (huh?) respectively. She grabbed the smiley-face one because that was some presumptive shit right there. If it meant what she thought it did, they were assuming this was her most heartfelt wish and joy was all around. Baby poop, vomit, and shackles for her never-ever-after.

She checked the box. Smiley face meant "congrats, Mama to be."

"This sucks."

"It doesn't have to." Jordan gathered up all the tests and looked at each one carefully. "You're pregnant but you don't have to be. We can figure this out."

Elle sat on the toilet seat, her head in her hands.

"He'll think it's a scam. That I'm after his money."

"Why would he think that? Why would you think he would think that?"

Hold up, Eloise. Your bad girl cynicism is showing. That's not going to fly with Susie Sunshine here.

She peeked out from behind her fingers. "He's rich and single. Have you seen how women are always throwing themselves at him?" *Spaying and neutering program my ass.*

"That's par for the course for all the pros. They're not all looking to scam him. Okay, some of them might be, but you? No way. Kershaw won't think that."

The sound of movement outside the door caught their attention.

"Hey, Jordan, where are—oh, hey."

Damn. Hunt.

His eyes flew wide at the sight of Jordan holding a bouquet of disaster-sticks in her hand. "What the—"

"Hell." Jordan slammed the door in his face.

"What did you do that for?" Elle hissed.

"I panicked!" She dropped the tests in the sink, then made a "yikes" gesture with her mouth. "Be right out!"

Elle grabbed the tests and put them in the trash. Jordan was waving her hands and miming something.

"What?" Elle snapped.

"I don't know."

"You're useless. Why is he even here?"

"I told him to come upstairs when he was ready to leave and I must have left the door open. I'm sorry."

Elle yanked open the door. "Hunt! Can't a couple of gal pals pee alone?"

Hunt stood on the threshold, soldier-still, arms crossed, every ounce of his military training reactivated. "What's going on here?"

"Nothing," Elle said because muteness had struck Jordan, who was washing her hands and ignoring her fiancé. "Think I've got a zit, right under my skin, so Jordan was trying to figure out what I could do to keep it at bay. You know, girl stuff."

"Girl stuff. From the two least girly people I know."

"Hey!" Jordan finally came to life, pushing him back from the bathroom door with wet hands. "We can be girly, so quit with the judgments just because she's ex-army and I'm a sports-loving chick."

Not budging, Hunt just stared at Jordan. His ice-chip gaze softened. "Are you—baby, just tell me, are you pregnant?"

"Me?" Jordan flashed a sidelong glance at Elle, assuring everyone present that Meryl's acting crown was not in imminent danger. Clearly not wanting to drop Elle in it, she pushed ineffectually at Hunt's chest again. "Let's chat when we get home."

"It's me, Hunt," Elle said, resigned to the ugly truth. "I'm pregnant."

A curt nod was his response. Then another. His jaw bunched. A muscle ticked. The squint got squintier. The whole rainbow of constipated hard-ass reaction happened before their eyes.

"Kershaw did this to you?"

Was this thing between her and Kershaw really so obvious? "No one *did* it to me. Sure, if we're talking specifics, it takes two, but I'm not a pliant victim waiting for a willing penis to fall inside me. I'm as responsible as the, uh, penis ..." She left it there, hoping that was enough to satisfy him. Like a willing penis.

He turned heel and walked away. Elle and Jordan

exchanged quick glances, then Elle asked the million-dollar question.

"Is Theo still down there?"

Jordan took off with Elle in hot pursuit.

~

THEO DIDN'T SEE it coming.

One second, he was laughing his head off at Erik and Cade's argument over whether doing weights "every other day" meant there were actually eight days in a week, but that the calendar was wrong. This made no sense, but Theo was happy to listen to the two knuckleheads tie themselves into knots.

Until he landed on the floor with a force that made him think he was getting checked by an elephant in last night's game.

His palm went instinctively to his jaw because it hurt, along with his ass and his ego. He looked up.

Levi Hunt stood over him, fist cocked, blue eyes blazing. "You just had to fucking go there, Kershaw."

"Hey!" Theo rubbed his jaw and shook his head, trying to absorb some knowledge he didn't have about this situation into his tired brain.

"Levi, don't!"

That sounded like Elle, who in Theo's entire recollection, had never once called Hunt by his first name. Her face was twisted in discomfort … for Theo?

Still not getting it.

"Want to tell me what your problem is, Hunt?"

"Levi, honey, let's figure this out." Calmer, softer, from Jordan. She placed her hand on his arm, and he relaxed by a hair, just enough that Theo felt he could stand and not walk into Hunt's fist.

The former Green Beret—extremely relevant to this situation, Theo thought—was shaking his head, disgust rolling off him that would give anyone pause. Theo felt disappointed in himself—and he didn't even know what he'd done!

"Theo, could you join us over here for a minute?" Jordan's expression was pleading. Behind her, Elle stood fidgeting, looking distinctly unlike herself. Not that he knew her all that well, but he liked to think he knew that much.

Then he got it: Hunt had somehow found out about Christmas Eve and was here to tear him limb from limb.

"So I can be pulverized to a pulp by Rambo here?"

"No one is going to hit anyone," Jordan said with a grim determination. "Again."

Levi sneered. "Don't bet on it."

The guys were looking on, not interfering—*thankseversomuch!*—evidently having decided this was better left to the two of them to work it out. Sure, Levi Hunt was a reasonable fella so Theo *must* have had it coming. Plenty of people at the bar were rubbernecking, cameras out and pointed, and this had the makings of a PR nightmare. From a public opinion standpoint, Theo had already lost the room.

Who cares what the public thinks? You need to stay in the moment, Kershaw.

He stood and took a step toward Levi who was not backing the fuck down. Jordan stepped in between them and placed her hand on Levi's chest. "In the back. Now."

Theo wasn't so sure about that. Going in back took him outside the realm of the group. Not that he was afraid of Hunt, but he had a feeling that once people heard the reason why Hunt was going with fists first as his strategy, Theo would look less like the asshole here.

A glance Elle's way decided it for him. Still fidgeting, still nervous, still not her usual self. Surely, she wasn't that upset that Hunt had found out about their holiday hijinks. Moving past Jordan and Hunt, he put his hand on Elle's arm. This was between them.

"Are you okay, Ellie?"

She bit her lip, in a way that would normally have had him aching with lust but right now had him concerned. "I'm fine, really. Hunt's making a big deal of it, but I'm okay. Jordan's right. We need to talk."

She turned and walked away, and he followed, thinking he didn't mind. That he might follow her anywhere which was a weird notion to have this second. His brain was a circus in there, and the clowns were getting ready to enter the ring on unicycles, and … *Calm down, Kershaw.*

She led the way to the corridor where the restrooms were located, then past them to a door marked "Staff Only." Hunt's ominous step echoed behind him. What was going on that the guy felt the need to be *this* involved?

Theo turned before they entered. "Is this really any of your business?"

Hunt's face, usually so impassive, split in fury. "*She's* my business."

"Hunt, it's okay," Elle said, her voice more in control again, that nervous quiver no more. "Theo and I need to discuss this alone." She took his hand, led him into the office and shut the door in Hunt's face. Hand on her brow, she closed her eyes and took a moment.

Theo wasn't good with silences especially when someone looked as stricken as Elle did right now. "I know you said you were okay but I'm getting really worried. What's—"

"I'm pregnant."

Two words, so soft, yet heavy as cement. His world stopped, his heart with it, and all he could do was stare at her.

"Theo, did you hear me?"

"Hunt knows this before me?"

Her eyes widened. Okay, maybe that shouldn't have been his first reaction, but what the living hell?

"It was accidental, both the pregnancy and the reveal. I just took the test upstairs with Jordan and he walked in. That's when he put two and two together and came down here to lay you out. I'm sorry about that. Truly."

About that. About Levi punching him. Not that she had anything else to be sorry for but shit, how had this happened?

You know how it happened.

Before he could get into the nitty gritty, she spoke. "Condoms have a 2-4% failure rate and I'm not using anything else. I swear this was an accident. I know you're rich and famous but I didn't do this on purpose to trap you. I promise!"

Her voice rose with each word spoken until it reached a fever pitch at the end. That she would have tried to trap him never occurred to him. If that was her game, she was a scammer without par. Anyone looking to snag a rich pro athlete would have hedged their bets. Fucked him a few more times. Would have been nicer to him.

He placed a hand on her shoulder, a finger under her chin. "Elle, I would never think that."

Her eyes flashed. "Well, you should! You should be

suspicious of every woman in your orbit. You're the perfect mark: rich, hot, famous, and gullible as all hell."

"Gullible? How so?"

"You fell for this, didn't you?" She waved a dismissive hand over her body. "Only a super nice innocent like you would think I'm worth bothering with."

This was a side of Elle Theo hadn't expected to see. She's never struck him as the self-loathing type and he didn't like it. "So, I'm guessing those preggo hormones are already kicking in because excuse me for saying, you sound like a crazy person right now. I thought you were worth bothering with because you're a hot, sexy woman who says it like it is and played hard to get and that's pretty much my catnip. Yeah, I'm super nice but innocent? Not in the slightest. I have very dirty thoughts about you on a regular basis and I don't regret a single thing about what happened here."

She gusted out a breath, clearly seeking calm. "I'm pregnant, Theo. I'm carrying your angel spawn. And I am not in any way prepared to be a mom. My life is a mess, I'm barely getting by, and now I have to be responsible for another living being? This is a disaster."

"Have a seat, Ellie."

"Theo—"

"Now."

She blinked at the force of his order, but immediately sat. The only other thing to sit on was one of those step stools. A little snug with his many-muscled ass, but it would have to do. He moved in close so their knees touched and he could hold both her hands. "We're both responsible. Surprise pregnancies are always going to be scary. I know because I once was one. Now, technically I don't remember how that felt—"

"Well, technically it didn't happen to you."

He continued, undeterred by pesky logic. "But I do remember what it felt like later because my sperm donor didn't stick around." Nick Isner had headed off to Harvard, leaving his family to pay off the girl he'd knocked up. Even when he had a chance to do the right thing, he'd failed. That would not be happening here.

"You're not alone. I'm with you every step of the way, on board with whatever decision you make."

"Even if I don't keep it? Or maybe that's what you want? It would make things easier all around."

He wasn't sure about that. A part of him would always wonder, what if. But he didn't want to pressure her into one decision or the other.

"We have time. Maybe a few weeks? No decision has to be made immediately but I'm down with whatever you want. I'll be as involved as you want me to be on whichever path you choose. We're lucky that we don't have to consider the economics here. Money's sorted, so we can put that aside as a—what do you call it?"

"Confounding factor?"

He smiled. "Right, confounding factor. It's gone. I know you're worried about how to earn a living and how a baby might figure into that. You want to go back to school and a kid would definitely make that tougher. But not impossible. If you decide to keep it, then I'll support you financially and emotionally. You're my baby mama."

"Theo—"

"Or if you want to terminate, I'll support you through that as well," he cut in, realizing that the term "baby mama" was loaded to the max. "You have to do what's best for you."

Her expression was one of shock, like she'd never been offered that before. This was her body and her decision, though it did have him thinking about his own mom—

sixteen, terrified, knocked up by the high school fucking quarterback. Luckily she'd had Aurora to support her through it, but if she hadn't? If she'd been on her own like Elle seemed to be, what then? The Rebels wouldn't have the best defense in the NHL, that's what.

But he couldn't let that influence what happened here. Elle was her own person.

"I—I need to think about it," she said. "I don't want you to feel obligated."

"Too late for that." But he smiled so she wouldn't think he felt trapped. Pregnant. He'd done that. A swell of pride was building in him now that the initial shock had worn off. "What I mean is that whichever way it goes, I'm on the hook for taking care of you, and if necessary, a kid until he turns eighteen. By then, he should have figured out what he wants or be really good at something like his dad and—"

"Oh, God, you've already raised him and thrown him out of the house."

He chuckled, feeling foolishly giddy. He was just kidding about what would happen when the kid turned eighteen. He would love and care for and support that child forever— if it came to that.

He squeezed her hands, then realized he'd been holding them the whole time. He liked being this close to her for non-sexy reasons. Sexy ones, too. Just in general.

And if she decided to keep the baby, would he like that then? His gran would know what to do.

"What?" she asked. "You look like something horrible occurred to you."

"Not horrible. Just thinking about my grandmother and how she's going to react."

"You might not have to tell her."

True. "Thing is, I tell her most everything. And then she tells the girls who put it on Facebook. They have a group."

"That Tarts thing? Maybe don't tell anyone yet. Levi and Jordan will stay quiet and you can tell the guys that he was upset about you sleeping with me."

Would they believe that? Probably. "Okay, I'll keep it to myself."

"I mean it, Theo. No one can know." Her eyes implored his cooperation. "Once it gets out, that changes how we go forward. I'll feel pressured because everyone will think I'm a cold-hearted bitch if I don't go through with the pregnancy."

He curled a hand around the nape of her neck and pulled her close, his lips brushing like a whisper across her forehead. "I won't breathe a word until you're ready. It's the two of us in this." *The two of us.* That sounded nice and cozy and couple-y. He was such a sap.

And this sap might soon be a daddy.

10

ELLE HAD NEVER BEEN SO popular, not even during the fifth grade when she brought in chocolate cupcakes with kitten whiskers icing. (The popularity lasted all of ten minutes as the cupcakes had been overdosed with salt by her mother who lacked in all things maternal.)

This morning, everyone wanted to talk to her. All Elle wanted was to gently hug the toilet bowl and tell it all her secrets.

First, from Jordan: *How are you? We need to make a doctor's appointment so you can get all your options. I've done some research ...* followed by a list of OBs.

Next came Levi, practical to the core: *Let me know if you need anything. Groceries, chocolate, cyanide for Kershaw, etc.*

With fabulous timing, even her sister chimed in: *You can't hide forever.*

Huh. Watch me. If anything assured her that she should *not* go through with this, it was a reminder that her wolf pack of a family existed.

The one person she'd have liked to hear from was strangely incommunicado. She wanted everyone to leave

her alone, but she wouldn't mind a dumb text from Kershaw
—he'd asked for her number last night after all.

Her phone rang and she sighed at the name on the
screen. She'd been avoiding calls from her sister for months
as she tried to build her new life—and look how fabulously
that had worked out. But right now, Elle needed to hear
from someone who knew her—the real her—even if she
couldn't actually tell her sister the specifics.

She clicked accept. "Hey."

"Hey?" Amelia said. "That's all you've got after four
months of cowardice?"

Amy was definitely the most dramatic twin. Being five
minutes older, she'd sucked all the oxygen out of the room
when she exited Mom's uterus.

"You know I did the right thing," Elle said. "He was in
love with you!"

"Uh, yeah, that was the point and how the family makes
a living, sis. Love, marriage, empty the joint accounts, and
move on to the next sucker. We were doing pretty well while
you were on your high and mighty God Bless America tour
in the army."

Elle closed her eyes. Her sister didn't know any better.
All her life, she'd been raised to believe a dollar scored was
better than a dollar earned. Honest work was for suckers,
and one was born every minute.

"I needed to do something for me."

"Sure, but no one said you should interfere in long-
running strategies the minute you discharge. Dad's still
pissed at you."

Elle's heart squeezed. She loved her family but she didn't
love how they earned a crust. In olden times, people called
it grifting. These days, plain old con artist would do—
though her father insisted he was a con *artiste*. *That 'e'*

denotes our skill, Eloise. As if they were descendants of old acrobatic performers and theirs was a dying art.

She'd enlisted because she couldn't take being part of the scamming anymore. It was time to give back, be useful, perform a duty that might somehow mitigate all the crap from before. She'd done things she was ashamed of, and yes, some of the marks deserved it. Too horny, too greedy, too willing to look for a shortcut. Half of them were criminals themselves so she could almost justify some of the cons.

But when she was invited to her sister's wedding four months ago and saw how devoted the groom was, how naïve, and in the not so distant future, how poor, she had to act. Telling him enough to scare him off was a betrayal of her family. She knew that. She hated that.

"So, are you going to tell me where you are?"

Elle grimaced. "I'm just taking a break from all the drama."

"Like you did in the army? Running away from who we are. Who *you* are."

"That's not how I want to live my life, Ames." She wanted something of her own. For a brief moment of insanity, she'd indulged in that want with the hottest guy on the planet and now she was being punished for it. "So how are things?"

"The usual. Dad's running a few bump-and-pay-up, just penny-ante stuff." Schemes where someone braked quickly and forced a fender-bender. They worked best when the mark wanted to handle it outside their insurance company. "I'm crawling the business section, checking my stocks."

Stocks were what Amy called her speculative investments —guys she took a closer look at to see if they were worth pursuing. A marriage con was a long game, though usually they tried not to let it go that far. It was easier to get paid off, usually through blackmail or extortion, than deal with the paperwork of a divorce.

Melancholy gripped her, bone-deep sorrow for how they'd been raised. "Ames, do you ever think there has to be something else? Another path you could take?"

"Like you did?" Her voice softened, not laced with her usual mockery. "I'm not like you, Elle-Belle. Mom always said you didn't have the stomach for the biz, but she was wrong. You're tougher than all of us. It's almost harder to make that choice, to go against what you know and strike out on your own. I could never do that. I'm only good ... at this."

Elle's heart sank. "That's not true. You could do anything, be anything. No one's locked into one fate."

"Perhaps." Her sister sighed. "Perhaps I'll come visit— wherever you are."

Elle stiffened, on alert once more. She wanted to encourage her sister to use her talents for good but placing her in Theo's orbit right now would be a temptation her grifter brain would be unable to resist.

"Maybe in a while. I do miss you," Elle said. "I know you're angry with me—that you all are—but I do miss you." She just couldn't be near them now, but mostly she couldn't let them within a ten-mile radius of Theo. If they found out what she'd done and the mistake she'd made, they'd be all over him, ready to squeeze the man dry.

If he knew what she was, he'd think the obvious: gold digger.

Before they'd conceived a life, she wouldn't have cared about that, but now? The sooner she removed the problem, the sooner she could get on with her plans.

"I know you're mad. I just thought I'd answer your call so you don't worry."

"Well, I *was* worried. As if I don't have enough on my plate."

Elle snapped to attention. Amy sounded ... off. "What's going on?"

"Nothing you can help with unless you've got a spare twenty grand lying around."

"Let me check the seat cushions."

"Ha ha." Said without any trace of amusement. "Miss you, too, Elle-Belle." Her sister clicked off.

Elle blew out a weary breath and pressed her fingers to her eyes to stave off tears. Hormonal, that's what she was.

Her intercom buzzer sounded. Probably Jordan or Levi trying to be good friends. Better friends would ignore her until this was all over.

What did she want? She rubbed a hand over her stomach. On the outside, nothing had changed, more like her traditional food baby than an actual baby. But whatever was in there wanted to make itself known. She retched, but nothing came out. She'd already unloaded half an English muffin and a cup of green tea. She didn't even like green tea but coffee probably wasn't good for the sprog.

The buzzer went again. They'd call Tina to get access if she didn't answer.

She answered. "Yeah?"

"It's Theo."

Oh. Her heart fluttered, or maybe it was further down. She wanted to think it was *much* further down but it was more the stomach/baby vessel area that liked the sound of that. This kid was already sucking up to Daddy.

She pressed the button to let him in and opened the door.

He bounded up the stairs like a herd of rhinoceri, and just the sight of him with a big grin made her teary. Rather than give in to that, she steeled her spine and snapped, "It's too early for a decision, Kershaw."

"I know that!" He held up a plastic Walgreen's bag. "We didn't get a chance to talk about how you're feeling physically. In case you have morning sickness, I brought over supplies."

"You did?" Surprised, she stood back to let him in.

"Yep." He looked around, keen eyes assessing her hovel and no doubt finding it wanting as the future home of Baby Kershaw. "So this is your place?"

"Sure is." She'd not done much to brighten it up, preferring to spend most of her time in the bar so she could save enough for when she needed to move on. She'd been building her oh-shit fund for such an eventuality.

Theo turned to her, his expression open and non-judgmental. "How are you feeling?"

Like I've betrayed the people of my heart. Like I've made a mess of everything. Like I really need a hug and your arms look perfect.

Knowing that relying on Theo for comfort was what got her into this pickle in the first place, she wrapped her arms around her body. Self-love was her best option. "A little queasy. I just threw up though, so I'll probably be okay for a while."

He looked like he wanted to … hug her, perhaps? The inclination evidently passed. "I did some research on morning sickness and bought this stuff." He emptied the bag of purchases onto the coffee table: pre-natal vitamins, mints, lemon-scented lotion, ginger, candy, and a tiny plush toy.

A purple dinosaur.

She picked it up. "This is supposed to be good for morning sickness?"

"Oh, that." He took it from her hand and positioned it on the table it so it faced her mid-roar, then took a seat on her sofa, a careworn piece she'd found in an alley two blocks over. "I saw it in the drug store and—well, you might remember, I like dinosaurs."

"How could I forget those dino-briefs?"

"And how could I forget your mating call?" He cupped his mouth and yelled, "Teee-Rexxxxx!"

Her palms flew to her burning cheeks. "I can't believe that came out of my mouth."

"That mouth was quite the surprise all right."

Heat swirled between them, delicious and dangerous. She would say it was a problem except the disaster had already occurred.

Dragging her gaze away from his, she blinked at the rest of his offerings. "Sour patch candy?"

"Yeah, sour tasting things can help. Ginger will settle the stomach. Mints, for obvious reasons. If those don't work, I've also booked a session with an acupuncturist. And I have the team's nutritionist on call so we can discuss a plan. Some of the research says that smoothies are a good way to keep hydrated and full, but not too full. There's also an exercise regimen—"

"Theo." Elle held up her hand. "An acupuncturist? A nutritionist? You told someone else on the team about this?"

"Not yet. I just told her that I might need some tweaking to my nutrition plan. I swear, this is undercover until we—you—make a decision."

He took the sour patch candy package and ripped it open with those big, beautiful, magic-producing hands. But then again, those hands had also gotten them into trouble so she really should be mad at them. Those awful, baby-making, orgasms-in-their-fingertips hands ...

He offered her candy. "Come on, Elle, have a seat. Let's chew and chat."

She sat a couple of feet away from him. Chewing the candy, she told herself she felt better, but it wasn't the candy. It was Theo, taking charge when she felt like she was spiraling.

She never would have expected it. He'd make a great dad one day, just not in seven months. Because she couldn't do it to him. Involve him in all her mess.

But neither could she say it yet. He was here, as excited as a puppy with his morning sickness solutions and his acupuncturist appointments and his heart-stopping smile.

"What did you want to talk about?"

He scrunched up his mouth, looked at the ceiling, and let out a long humming noise, which made her laugh. What else could they possibly talk about? There was only one, crazy, life-changing thing.

"My grandmother wants to meet you."

"Your grandmother?"

"I told her about you. Not about the baby, but just that I'd met this cool girl who was kind of interesting with her military background and smart mouth and fierce eyes hiding all these secrets."

Shock at his description of her warred with annoyance at his jumping the gun. "But I can't! What if I go the way that results in no-baby? How do I look her in the eye then?"

"I didn't say you *had* to meet her. Just that I made you sound interesting enough for her to *want* to meet you. She's kind of interesting herself—an artist, a creative type. Not like me, but more like you. You'd get along well and no matter what we—you—decide, you'll still both be interesting people who would find each other equally interesting."

No pressure, then. "I'm not creative." What gave him that idea?

"Pretty creative in the sack. That move with your finger—"

"Theo. Could you stay on track?"

He shrugged and popped a piece of candy in his mouth. "We should see a doctor. Get you checked out. I know you're sure but ..."

"Worried I might be trying to pull one over on you? You should be suspicious."

"I'm not worried. Unless you've been with someone else around the same time."

"No one else." At his smug look, she added, "Not that I haven't had offers. That bar downstairs is brimming with offers."

"Sure you have. But you've not gone there because you're worried no one will match up to what I brought."

"Your ego."

He grinned. "Just kidding. But not really. Also, why are you so sure I'll think this is a scam? You said that yesterday. A very cynical take, Sergeant Cupcake."

"It's Corporal Cupcake. Don't you have tons of gold diggers trying to jump on board the Kershaw Caboose for a ride up the altar?"

"That's just the nature of the fame and celebrity beast. Sure, I have to be careful but I don't think you're like that. Hell, you don't even like me except for how good I can do you."

Because he didn't even look offended by this self-own, she decided to be offended on his behalf.

"You're not just a pretty face, Kershaw." She gestured at

the stash he'd bought. "This is a nice thing you've done. A kind thing." Too kind. He was being such a sweetheart and someone was going to tear him to shreds one day.

She had to make sure it wouldn't be her.

His phone buzzed and he dragged it out of his pocket, his brow crumpling as he denied the call. "I'm late for morning skate." He jumped up. "You working later?"

"Yeah, I'll be in the bar."

He looked thoughtful then seemed to change his mind about whatever he was going to say. "Let's talk then. And if none of these make you feel better, we'll think of the next solution. You're not alone, Ellie."

She nodded because if she spoke, she'd be unable to do so without sobbing.

11

OUTSIDE THE EMPTY NET BAR, Theo checked the text message he'd received while sitting on Elle's sofa and gave it a long, hard stare.

This is Nick Isner. Got a second?

Bio-Dad was reaching out. Deliberately.

Theo was under no illusions that this was the dawn of a brave new world where Nick actually wanted his oldest son in his life. No, he could already see how this would go. Evidently terrified that his carefully-planned world might be crumbling around him, Daddy-O was conducting damage control after yesterday's locker room visit from his wife and kid.

Theo wasn't going to make it easy on him with a stilted text conversation. If Nick wanted him gone—again—he'd have to say it to him using his fucking words. He dialed the number.

"Hello, this is Nick Isner."

"It's Theo."

His father cleared his throat. "Thanks for getting back to

me. I want you to know that I had no part in planning that visit by my son yesterday."

"Figured as much."

Silence.

"Unless ... did you know he entered that contest?"

This was where his mind had gone? "Right, it was a trap to get your kid into my orbit so he'd see what a great guy I am and somehow, I dunno, *feel* our brotherly connection."

"I'm sorry, but it's quite a coincidence."

Theo wanted to smash the phone into tiny fragments. "Believe it or not, I actually pay people to manage my social media busywork like picking winners for contests. I had no fucking idea your son was a fan or had won that visit or even what his Instagram handle is. And by the way the recommended minimum age for Insta is thirteen so maybe you should keep a better eye on your kid's social media use so he can't enter contests to meet his long-lost secret brother!"

Jesus, *Days of Our Lives* couldn't have scripted it better.

"I shouldn't have said that." Nick sounded embarrassed. "Or thought that. It was just weird."

"Is that all you wanted to say?"

A long beat passed before he said, "Things seem to be going well for you. Your season's turning around."

What the hell. "You want to talk ... hockey?"

Nick cleared his throat. "Maybe we could get together and chat. About everything."

"Are you kidding? What was it you said last time? *'I'm just not sure what's to be gained by raking all this up again after all these years.'* Those were your exact words." That Theo remembered it verbatim—not fucking embarrassing at all.

"Theo, listen—"

"No, you listen. Aurora did a great job. Whatever money

your family sent did the trick. I turned out just fine and you had zero to do with it."

That would have been the perfect time to hang up, but Theo waited, hoping Nick would say the magic words—words Theo couldn't even imagine existing—to make this better.

"Look, Theo, I'm not a bad person. I've never told my wife, my boys. I'd need some time to figure that out."

My boys.

"You've got a lot to lose. I understand." Nothing to gain, it seemed. A son who'd overcome tragedy and life-threatening injury. A son who was a success in his chosen profession and loved by millions. All these reasons and Theo still wasn't good enough for Nick Isner.

Oh, and by the way, you're going to be a grandpappy!

"Jason's a big fan," Nick said. "He was thrilled to meet you and your teammates."

"Yeah, he seems like a good kid. Listen, I've got to go."

"Oh, okay." Christ, did this asshole actually sound disappointed? More likely, he wanted to control how the conversation ended. Like all politicians, he was clearly a sociopath. "Good luck in your next game."

"Yeah, thanks."

Ten minutes later, he walked into the locker room ahead of morning skate, expecting that everyone would take one look and know what a bad boy he'd been. He'd left the bar by the side entrance last night, so the crew were still in the dark about why Levi had brought the Hunt Hammer down on Theo's beautiful face.

"Superglutes," Ford called out, grabbing everyone's attention, "sounds like you got some 'splaining to do!"

"A gentleman doesn't kiss and tell."

"But you're not a gentleman," Cade said. "At least if that dark look on Hunt's face right now is anything to go by."

Hunt stood at the door, thick arms crossed, his flinty eyes trained on Theo. "A word in your ear, Kershaw."

"Need protection?" Erik offered.

Theo turned to Levi. "Do I?"

"Not this time. Out here." Theo followed Levi into the corridor and found him outside a door to one of the exam rooms.

Get him alone. Cut him into tiny pieces. Stash him in the hot tub.

That'd be Theo's preferred strategy if he were in Hunt's skates. He walked inside and waited for Levi to shut them in and begin the dismemberment. Just more shit to add to his shitty day, except ... seeing Elle was nice. He wished he'd given her a hug, though. She'd looked like she needed one, only he just wasn't sure of the rules yet.

Hunt squinted, folded his arms, sniffed, unfolded his arms, and finally, grunted.

"How's Elle? I assume you went over to see her this morning."

And if he hadn't? Thank the ghost of Gordie Howe that he'd gone there first thing. It had never occurred to him not to drop by. She was scared and she needed to know he had her back.

"She's okay. I dropped off some stuff to help with the morning sickness. And I'm going to talk to Sadie about drawing up a nutrition plan."

Hunt did a double take. "You're planning to tell her what to eat?"

"Just recommendations. With a certain diet she might not feel so ill."

"She won't want to hear orders. It's one thing when

you're getting paid to in the army, but a guy telling her what to do ..." Levi shook his head in disbelief, and Theo took grave offense at the notion that Hunt had the inside track on Elle. Maybe he did, but he needn't be such a know-it-all about it.

"About last night," Hunt continued.

"Apology accepted."

"I have no intention of apologizing, asshole. I was about to say that I don't like this situation one bit so I'll be keeping my eye on you. If you pressure her into a decision, a little boxing in a bar will be the least of your worries."

After that call with Nick "Dad of the Year" Isner, Theo was a match strike away from a powder keg explosion.

"I have no intention of pressuring her. She's a grown woman who can make her own decisions. We've talked like adults, she knows that I'll support her no matter which direction she goes in, so I'd appreciate if you got off my case and quit being such a fucking dick!"

Hunt's expression barely changed, though that tick in his jaw fluttered like a tiny bug beneath his skin.

"Got an opinion either way on whether you want to be a daddy or not?"

Theo crossed his arms. "As if I'd tell you."

That, of all things, made Hunt smile.

"What's so funny?"

"I was hard on you and you haven't crumbled. It sounds like you're trying to do the right thing, so if you need my advice or assistance, I'm here for you, kid." Hunt offered his hand.

Theo stared at it, then grasped it because he could do with all the friends he could get.

A quick nod from Hunt, and he turned to leave. That was it? So much for the friendly ear.

"I'm fucking terrified, man."

"I know." Hunt pivoted and waited for the typical Theo verbal vomit.

"If we were in a relationship and we'd planned it—"

"But you're not and you didn't."

"Thanks, Captain Obvious."

Levi's hard blue eyes softened. "What's your gut here?"

"I want this baby. I don't want to force Elle to keep it but if I had a choice in the matter, I'd want to keep it."

"Maybe tell her that."

"And put pressure on her? No. I'm just telling you my first instinct here. Hell, she might decide bye-bye-baby and I'll collapse in relief. But right now, at this moment in time, I feel like I'm being given this opportunity to do something momentous. Is that the word?"

"It's *a* word." Hunt smiled again, which was fucking creepy because Hunt never smiled. Falling in love had *a lot* to answer for. "A baby is a huge life change for everyone involved. It sounds like this might be not such a bad outcome for you except for the not being in an actual relationship with the mother part."

"Yeah. That. She's not interested in me at all, which kind of makes me think she's going to go the other direction. She doesn't want to get tied down or make connections." He thought on it for a second. "Do you know anything about her people?"

Hunt squinted. "Her family's from New York, which is part of the reason why we get along, me being from Jersey. There's a sister but I don't think they're all that close. She went there for the holidays."

"Not exactly."

"Meaning?"

Theo wouldn't normally be a tattle tale but this was

important. If Elle didn't have a good support network, they might need to help her create one here. "She said she was going but she didn't leave. She stayed at your old place. Got the impression she didn't want anyone feeling sorry for her."

This put Hunt on edge again. "And you were there to play Santa and deliver your dick in a box?"

Theo met his gaze levelly. "Not going to apologize for that. She's a grown woman and you need to cut out the scary-dad-with-shotgun shit."

That earned him another stare down, then finally: "Okay. You're right."

Theo took out his phone and pressed record. "Say that again."

Hunt leaned over the phone and spoke into it, enunciating each word. "Fuck you, Superglutes." But he was smiling as he said it.

ELLE HAD NEVER BEEN to a live hockey game. Watching while pregnant was probably not the best way to pop her cherry but Jordan had invited her to sit in the press box, so she could at least get in and get out without Theo knowing.

As to why she wanted to hide this information from him, she wasn't sure. She told herself it was because she was on a fact-finding mission. If she kept the baby and the daddy was playing this dumb game and getting pounded every night, then Elle needed to know what that felt like. What her child would feel if its father was in danger of being hurt.

Strange, perhaps, but she'd already started to think long-term about how this might actually work.

Theo shouldn't have come by with his stupid sour patch

candy but something had melted inside her when he produced it. Along with his research. And that cute dinosaur. He cared about this kid already.

The press box was something else and she liked that the view was from far away. She couldn't make out Theo's handsome face or clear green eyes or even his strong jaw. His ass, though—you could see that puppy from space.

"Want something to eat?"

Jordan gestured at the table of treats behind her, most of which Elle would be all over if she wasn't feeling like an alien was zapping her life force.

"Not right now, thanks." She really should eat something because she'd only chomped on a few crackers earlier. "Give me the sixty-second version of what I'm watching. I assume goals are important."

Jordan's face brightened, obviously in her element. "Goals are indeed important, my young padawan. Everything else comes second, goals are the thing."

Jordan went on to explain who the players were, their positions, why some kind of bodily or stick contact was okay and some wasn't. She half-listened while Theo did a decent impression of a human wall.

"So, is Kershaw considered ... good at this?" She assumed he was because no one paid big bucks for mediocrity. Still, she'd like a professional opinion.

Jordan nodded. "He and Burnett are one of the most solid defensive lines in the league. Before Kershaw came on board, Burnett was holding down the fort—just—but since Theo was acquired, they've really gelled. I think they're going to get to the playoffs and it'll be because of that defense."

"The playoffs are the big kahuna, right?"

"Well, half the teams qualify but there are three rounds

of best-of-seven over a couple of months. Making the final round of that is the thing, but the Rebels have been off their game for the last few years. Getting to the playoffs would be a good step for them. Putting in a decent showing would be awesome, but I think Harper and Dante will be happy if they can make good use of this new blood and build on it for next year."

Elle had done her research this morning. Harper Chase was CEO and the eldest Chase sister, one of the team's co-owners along with her two half-sisters. Apparently a female-run team was a big deal. They'd inherited from their father, a famous hockey-playing dickhead in his heyday, and managed to defy all expectations, winning the Cup in their first year out. As if the lady bosses weren't enough to piss everyone off, they'd hired a gay guy—Dante Moretti—as general manager.

Elle liked the idea of Theo and Hunt working for such a progressive leadership, though she'd heard that players had little to no control over where they were traded. What if Theo was sent to another team? Was she expected to move so he could be close to his kid? Would he let her build a life separately from his?

"It's a wonder he can focus with what's going on in his personal life," she muttered.

"Once they're out there, they're really good at shutting off everything else. It's remarkable how tunnel-visioned they become." Jordan smiled and leaned in close so the other reporters wouldn't get a scoop. "Whatever decision you make, you don't have to worry about it making his game dip."

"I just—I just don't want it to have *any* impact on our lives but that's impossible, isn't it?" She lowered her voice to a whisper. "This is another human being we're talking about. A helpless bundle of fucking joy that's going to keep me up all night and turn my body into a wasteland."

"Babies. Life, body, and vag-destroyers."

"They are! Especially when you don't plan for it. I'm not ready to settle down."

Jordan squeezed her arm. "You don't want the husband, the kids, the picket fence?"

Coming from her family? God, no. She'd just be creating a meal ticket they could use for their nefarious purposes.

"I haven't had great role models."

"Parents divorced?"

If only. The world would be safer. "No. Just not the kind of people I'd want my kid to be around."

Jordan looked sympathetic but didn't press. Bad reporter, better friend. "Doesn't mean you can't want good things for yourself. A good guy. A good life. Why not with Theo? Is he too nice? Too goofy? Too good in bed?"

"All of the above. And not my type—for a long-term thing." Not that anyone was, but she tended to gravitate toward men with a similar worldview to her own: realistic, sharp, cynical. "He's so fresh-faced and pure."

"You were impregnated by a Ken doll, I suppose?"

"What does that mean?"

Jordan tilted her head. "I'm assuming that lustful animal urges were in play prior to conception. No one is that fresh-faced and pure. Stop making Theo out to be some sort of saint."

"Why? Because Hunt, aka Father Theresa, has a lock on the do-gooder market?" Hunt was known for his good works and holy ways, spending much of his spare time volunteering at a homeless shelter. These hockey players were something else. "What I mean is that Theo's the kind of guy who would bruise easily. He's not tough enough.

People will walk all over him and I'd hate to see him hurt."

Her friend shook her head. "You're being far too kind to him and far too hard on yourself. So maybe you're not compatible outside the bedroom—did this happen in a bedroom?"

"It might have been the shower or the sofa or over the kitchen island," she said morosely because now the great sex was tainted with the horror of conception. "Who's to say which condom failed its job?"

Jordan grinned, then turned serious. "But that doesn't mean you can't find common ground."

Not wanting to argue with her—Jordan was really too sweet to contradict—Elle refocused on the game. She didn't understand everything that was going on, but the basics were obvious: put the puck into the opposing team's net as often as possible.

The visiting team, Detroit, was having a hard time getting anything by Theo. As soon as the puck came within five feet of him, he smothered it and blasted it out of his zone. There was something oddly comforting about that protectiveness. Theo with his thunderous thighs and bubble butt wasn't letting these assaults on his defenses go unanswered.

Best not to read into that. She had no doubt that Theo would do the best he could as a dad: he'd provide money and security and a better role model than she'd known herself.

He had just blocked another shot to the raucous cheers of the crowd when the Jumbotron zeroed in on one section. Three women in hot pink jackets had their backs to the rink. Was that—*no!*

"Is that Kershaw's face on those jackets?"

Jordan laughed. "Yep, Theo's fan club. Led by his grandmother."

His grandmother was in the building?

"Theo's Tarts," Elle murmured in recognition. "I had no idea."

The women were shaking their booties, the camera close enough to read a bejeweled "Thirsty for Theo" emblazoned beneath his pretty face. "That is wild."

"I'm going to have to invite them on the podcast," Jordan said. "We're all about celebrating the crazy in hockey."

And this was the world Elle was considering bringing a child into?

Two minutes later, the period had ended and the other reporters were milling around the food table and cracking open beers. All except one: a bearded lumberjack type, who sat at the end of the viewing bar doing a thousand-yard-stare out onto the empty ice rink. In profile, he looked like he was carved from granite, his dark blond hair thick and lustrous on both his head and his jaw. He didn't have a computer like everyone else, just a small notebook.

Elle was about to ask Jordan about him, when her friend stood and stretched. "I've got to make a phone call. You okay here for a few?"

"I'll manage."

"Help yourself to the spread."

Once the wildebeest had made room at the trough, Elle stepped forward to check her options: a fair bit of healthy stuff like salads and grains, which made her shudder. The sushi looked good, but she'd read somewhere that raw fish was a big no-no in her condition.

She sighed. Decision-ing while pregnant was hard.

"Have the cookie," a deep voice said behind her.

She turned, sensing it would be the statue who had sparked her curiosity before and glad to get a better look at him. Tall with hard-packed muscle, he held himself tautly, fighting the confines of his suit jacket, which had the effect of making him look like a prisoner forced to wear a suit for court. Long-healed scars weathered the right side of his face near his ear and that nose had to have been broken multiple times.

His dark brown eyes met hers, and she felt strangely soothed.

"I want to take advantage of the free food," she said. "A cookie seems to be letting them off easy."

"Wouldn't want to do that, the bastards."

She laughed, pleased he'd run with her joke. "I'm in your way," she said, moving aside.

"Just headed to the fridge. Need something?"

She shook her head, feeling sad about that. All these sacrifices when she'd vowed not to be shackled to anyone or anything. This was supposed to be her time!

The nice stranger returned with a bottle of beer and handed off a water to her. "Best to stay hydrated. Staring at free food is thirsty work."

The bottle had barely touched her fingertips when the room swirled around her. The next thing she knew she was seated near the window. Her dizziness started to ease once she was settled.

"Sorry, I didn't eat much today," she said to the stranger who stood over her, his face echoing his obvious concern. She'd felt nauseous earlier, and then nervous about what she could eat that wouldn't make her more nervous or damage the peanut. How could she already care about this blob inside her—and how could she be so dumb to be already putting it at risk by starving herself?

She was clearly not qualified to take care of herself, never mind a child.

"You should drink some of this." He unscrewed the water bottle and placed it in front of her.

"I'm not usually this pathetic."

"Who said anything about pathetic?"

"I'm a fainting sack of weakness, but I'm usually quite sturdy. Well, look at me."

He gave her body a cursory look, purely to be polite. There was no carnal interest in it. "We all have bad days, but you need to be careful. It's not just about you now."

"Not sure what you mean," she said defensively.

"Fair enough." He looked away toward the ice, giving her the time to think over what he'd said and her reaction to it.

She took a sip of the water, a few deep breaths, and a furtive gander at his profile.

"What are you, some sort of fetus whisperer? Or do I already look like a haunted mom-to-be?"

"You do look a little peaky. I recognize the signs ..." He reversed course. "You've been holding a hand over your stomach since you sat down. Figured you were feeling protective of something."

She was. Of her lost dreams now that this kid was demanding her time and attention.

"I'm trying to decide what to do. It's going to change my life and I'm not sure I'm ..." Her voice petered out, unable to finish the thought.

"What?"

"Good enough," she whispered. Embarrassed at her admission, she looked away.

"Are you on your own?" When she refocused on him, he shook his head. "Not trying to ascertain your single status, just wondering if you have a support system."

As this guy was likely a reporter, chatting about the famous father of her child was probably not the savviest of moves.

"I'm not completely alone. The other party would be involved but his job makes the full-time dad thing difficult. Plus, we're not actually together. It wasn't planned."

"Sounds complicated."

"It is."

He gazed out over the ice again. "Anything I can get for you? Anyone I can call?"

She shook her head. "Thanks for saving me from falling flat on my ass."

"No problem. I'll leave you to your thoughts."

"Oh, okay." It had been kind of nice having him there while she puzzled through it but she couldn't beg a complete stranger to stick around. And then he was gone, the air a little chillier for his absence.

A few minutes later, Jordan appeared just as the players were coming back on the ice. "What are you doing sitting down here?"

"Just getting a different perspective."

12

THEO WASN'T QUITE sure what was happening. He rubbed his eyes again to check on the mirage before him: Elle Butler, his baby mama (and yes, he knew that was just asking for trouble to even *think* it) was in the locker room. She looked a little pale. Had something happened?

He lowered his voice. "Are you okay?"

"Quit yer clucking, Kershaw, I'm fine. Jordan invited me into the press box so I thought I'd finish off the evening with a look-see behind the curtain. And I don't mean your towel."

Something in his chest lurched. She sounded like the funny, sharp-tongued Elle of old. "Are you saying you actually watched a game? But you hate hockey."

Her brow pleated, like she'd been caught out. "I don't *hate* it. I just don't know anything about it, and I figured I should check it out while I have such great connections."

He stepped in closer. "How are you feeling?"

"Better," she murmured with a quick glance around to make sure no one was in earshot. "The sour stuff actually helped. The ginger, too. Thanks for that."

"Good to hear it. I've been thinking of you all day."

She made a face. "I don't want to distract you while you're out there. What you're doing is important."

"Is it?" Right this minute, it didn't feel so important, except as a means to pay the bills and make sure Elle and his baby had the best possible life. He wanted to give them that, both of them.

"Of course it's important. Jordan told me you guys have a shot at the playoffs."

"Your luscious lips to God's sexy ears."

She shook her head. "You're so weird."

"I get that a lot."

That made her smile, which made him smile, and now they were two smiling fools.

She gave a shifty look around. "So, we probably should talk."

"Definitely. Thing is, my —"

"WHERE'S MY BOY?"

Yep, there she was. He'd known she was here but how in the hell did she get access to the locker room? Aurora came flying at him, arms ready to bear hug him even though she was a third his size.

"Gran! What are you doing back here?"

"Darling, how many times have I told you that I don't need you reminding the world that I'm old enough to be your grandmother?"

He looked over her shoulder to find a smiling Harper Chase, also known as the Rebel Queen.

"She texted," Harper said.

He mouthed "sorry." Once he was acquired by the Rebels, his grandmother had insisted on constant contact with the powers that be, as in Coach, Harper, and Dante, all in the name of monitoring his health since his surgery. She texted his bosses weekly to make sure he wasn't doing anything he shouldn't: exercise, diet, or fun-wise.

She meant well but damn, she could be exhausting. He held her back to take a better look at her. Smart grey bob, sharp blue eyes, hooker red lipstick, the scent of lemons that rolled back the years. She was also wearing that incredibly embarrassing jacket with his face on it, just like the Pink Ladies in *Grease*.

Aurora wasn't quite like other grandmothers. In elementary school, he'd been mortified every time she waltzed in with her Audrey Hepburn glasses and glamorpuss lips. Older than the other moms—he'd still thought she was his mom then—she'd reveled in defying convention, and after a while, Theo had gotten used to it. He soon figured out that he had enough personality not to have to worry about whether his friends thought she was weird and he was happy to put the beatdown on anyone who said a word against her.

Having moved to Saugatuck from Chicago when Theo was three, no one knew that Aurora was his grandmother and that Candy, the woman he'd thought was his older sister, was his mom. When he found his birth certificate while looking for information about his father, it had crushed him that she'd lied.

That they'd both lied.

Forgiving Aurora came easier—or more quickly—than Candy. His grandmother was doing her best in a bad situation, but his mother? That betrayal had stung deep. He'd never gotten over it, and by the time he was ready to forgive her, it was too late. Candy was gone.

Shaking off those ghosts, he asked, "Where's the posse?"

"Wandering around, flirting with security. Harper wouldn't let them all in, worried about overwhelming the team. They can be a bit embarrassing." Said with no irony whatsoever.

He caught the eye of a grinning Elle.

"Nice jacket," she said to Aurora. "We could see it in all its glory from the press box."

"You think so?" Aurora gave a twirl. "Limited edition, though I could probably get one for a true fan." She took a closer look. "Theodore, aren't you going to introduce me?"

"Aurora, this is Elle. She's a ... new to hockey and someone was giving her a tour."

"Elle? You mean, Elle, YOUR CHRISTMAS FLING?"

Oh, Aurora, you treacherous big mouth.

His gran grabbed Elle and pulled her into a hug. "Why, she is GORGEOUS, but a little pale. Are you feeling okay, dear? It looks like you should sit down."

"I'm fine," Elle squeaked, shocked at being put on the spot. Elle glared at Theo, and all he could do was shrug back.

"I might have mentioned my regret about leaving you alone. I'd already called Aurora at Christmas to make sure it was okay to bring you but you didn't want to come and she could tell I was disappointed. She likes to draw her own conclusions."

Elle opened her mouth. Closed it again. So, he'd revealed too much there, but what the hell. Let her know he meant business. That if she wanted to keep this baby, he wouldn't be half-assing it. He'd be superglutinous-to-the-maxing it.

"I'm THRILLED you two kids are giving it a shot!"

"Now, Aurora ..." Theo warned.

"We're just friends," Elle said quickly, her eyes pleading with him to be cool.

"Yeah, we're just friends. Stop being so pushy."

"I'm not! I just want you to find a NICE GIRL to settle down with."

Theo tried a tentative grin at Elle—*wanna be that nice girl?*—and she let him off the hook. "It was great to meet you, Mrs. Kershaw."

"It's Aurora, darling, and let me know if you want a jacket. We could make you an honorary member of the crew." To Theo, she winked and said, "I'll see you outside, baby boy."

"Sure thing, grandmother."

"Oh, he's mad at me." She nudged Elle conspiratorially. "Calls me 'grandmother' when he's annoyed." With a classic cheek-pinch to seal the deal, she was gone.

He turned back to Elle who was cracking up. "Does she have any idea what "thirsty" means?"

"She saw it on Twitter and thought it was perfect because she's all about the alliteration. And she'll make you a jacket whether you want it or not."

"I'll wear it with pride, *baby boy*."

So she was kidding but he still liked the sound of that.

"It's kind of cool that you're here, y'know," he said quietly, feeling hope blooming in his chest.

She shrugged it off. "So I still don't know much about hockey but I could tell that you seem to know what you're doing out there."

He did know. But he also sensed that he'd passed some test with Elle. As for the subject, he couldn't quite say.

13

@TheTheoKershaw Are your quads too epic or glutes too thicc? Check out this line of dress pants specifically made for hockey butt. #Superglutes #BootyHug #NotASeamsBuster

NON-GAME NIGHTS at the Empty Net were often as busy as game nights, mostly because the players hung out there and the fans knew what they wanted.

To get up close and personal with their favorites.

Theo was one of those favorites. Looking at his Instagram page and his one million plus followers was a revelation to Elle. So many photos of biceps and abs and so much squeeing and hearts and fire emojis in response. It had been both a relief and a disappointment not to see much of him in the weeks since they'd connected horizontally.

But since the big reveal, he was here every night the team wasn't playing or traveling. Worse, she was actually looking forward to seeing him. How ridiculous was that?

She was just finishing slicing up limes behind the bar when a message came in from Dee: *We need to talk, Eloise.*

Even by text, her mother managed to sound imperious.

Not wanting to answer the summons immediately, she spent a few minutes loading the imports fridge with Newcastle Brown Ale. Done, she turned to Tina.

"Mind if I take five before the madness begins?" By eight it would be wall-to-wall and breaks would be impossible.

Tina nodded, and Elle headed back to the office to call her mother back.

"Eloise, have you heard from your sister?"

No hello, no preamble. *Me? Oh, I'm just fine, Mom.*

"A couple of days ago. Why? Is something wrong?"

"She's not answering my calls. Maybe she has something on the hook and she's trying to go it alone." Dee and George never appreciated being cut out of a con. "I heard you made up, though. Did you give her your holier-than-thou fire-and-brimstone act?"

"Not an act, Mom. I really am holier than thou."

"How I raised such different girls I will never know."

Elle had heard a version of this every day of her waking life. Amelia was the more talented one: slim, beautiful, fatally charming. Where Amy's attributes were an obvious boon to the family business, Elle's were useless.

A conscience tended to get in the way of criminal activity.

Elle eyed the Rebels calendar hanging on the wall of the back office, annotated with reminders about beer distributor deliveries and the team's game schedule. Absently, she flipped through the calendar but it was Theo-free, made before he was acquired. That Vadim Petrov was pretty fine, though.

"How's Dad?"

"His heart is weak. Weakened more since our latest job dried up."

Her own heart squeezed. She knew it was pure manipulation on the part of her mother, but like all family, she had the capacity to push buttons that no one else knew the shape of.

"You could just claim disability. Or get a job."

She practically heard her mother's head shake. "Yes, that's what we'll do. Eloise, I don't want to fight. So we've always seen things differently, but there's no reason why we can't be friends."

Friends? She'd wanted a mother, not a grifter mentor.

"I don't wish you any harm, Mom. I just don't want you to hurt anyone."

"Yes, well, we all have to make a living. There's predator and prey. You'll do well to remember that."

What did that make her? She didn't want to be either.

"Give my love to Dad," she said finally because there didn't seem to be anything left.

"You'll always be one of us. I know you'd rather not be, but you're part of the fabric of this family. Don't shut us out."

"As long as I turn a blind eye?"

"That moral compass of yours is such a drag, my love. If you hear from your sister, let me know." She hung up.

Elle felt ill, and it wasn't entirely because of her condition. How could she even think of introducing a baby into a world where his grandparents would be grasping at every opportunity a connection like Theo would provide? She couldn't twist Theo up in her fucktangle of a life.

Hard to believe that four nights ago she'd sat in this swivel chair after telling Theo the news that would entwine them forever. His reaction had floored her. She'd expected he'd try to steer her in whichever direction suited him, but so far, he'd been nothing but respectful. Unlike her, he'd been raised right.

Last night, meeting Theo's grandmother and seeing the

oodles of love they had for each other had inspired in her such a yearning. When she came home, she'd cried for an hour. She wanted someone to love her that much, without strings, without expectation.

Maybe ... it was selfish but this baby would love her unconditionally.

She wouldn't need Theo or anyone else because the baby would be the center of her world. No man or avaricious family members could fill that gap for her. She would be the anchor for her child and the child would be the anchor for her.

A strange calm descended over her, and not even the buzz in the bar which signaled a crazy night ahead, could throw her off stride. She needed to be clear about her needs to Theo. No doubt he'd want to throw money at the problem. Fine, she'd take a few dollars for the baby but when all was said and done, this was her responsibility. Her opportunity to find purpose.

Feeling like the threads of her previously-slippery control were reweaving and giving her strength, she headed out to the bar, grabbing another crate of beer as she went.

"Put that down now!"

Shocked at the harsh tone, she looked up into the furious moss-green eyes of a Rebels D-man. Tina had stopped a Guinness mid-pour. A couple of bar patrons watched curiously.

"Excuse me?" Elle asked.

"I mean it," he gritted out. "Don't make me come around there."

Anxious to divert the increasing attention to them, Elle put the crate down. "Happy?"

Theo was not happy, if his dramatic hand-wave to

include Tina was any indication. "Those crates are too heavy."

Elle's boss screwed up her mouth, trying to get a read on the situation. "Are they?"

"No!"

"Yes!"

Tina looked amused. "How about I leave you kids to decide for yourselves?" She headed off to the other end of the bar to deal with someone less trying who wasn't losing her money.

Elle growled. "What do you think you're doing?"

"You've got to be careful," he hissed. "Lifting crates of beer is not being careful."

"Not an invalid, Kershaw. Can still do all the things and I'd rather you didn't shout to the entire bar your concerns about my condition. Clear case of none-ya as in none of your—"

"Yeah, yeah, I get it. Though I don't agree."

"Objection noted. Now what can I get you?"

He rattled off his order—he often paid the entire tab for the team on any given night because he was the Merriam-Webster definition of "sucker." While she worked, he took a seat at the bar, his watchful eye giving her tingles. When she looked up, he flashed a cheeky grin and her stomach wriggled predictably.

"Stop it," she muttered.

"Stop what?"

"You know."

He grinned. He knew.

"Aurora was impressed with you."

The compliment felt nicer than it should have. "She seems like a cool lady."

"She's the best. No better woman to have on your side."

She placed two bottles of IPA, two pints of Bud, and a cider on the bar. "Start a tab?"

"Sure."

Tina stopped on a pass by. "Nice video this morning, Theo. You wearing those hockey butt pants tonight?"

"Oh, you liked those?" Chuckling, he stood and twirled, showcasing his lovely denim-clad ass. "Jeans tonight. Those pants are for game days, though people sure did seem to enjoy the fashion show. One of my most popular posts!"

Her boss nudged her. "You catch Theo's Insta video this morning?"

You mean the one where he did lunges with his amazing butt front and center to advertise special pants that made his ass look like it had been sculpted from Carrara marble? That video?

"I've better things to be doing than wasting my time watching dumb videos."

Tina laughed. "Struck me dumb, all right. If ever there was a reason to waste your time, watching that video is it." She headed off, visions of hot hockey butts dancing in her eyes.

"The video's archived on my feed," Theo said slyly. "Of course, Aurora and the Tarts have been spreading the word."

She suspected she was going to regret this. "What about your parents? You don't talk about them."

"My mom died when I was in high school—drug overdose—and my dad was never in the picture."

"Oh, I'm sorry. That must have been really tough for you." Yet here he was, a ray of mothereffing sunshine who didn't seem to let anything get him down. Where did he find the energy? "You don't talk to your dad?"

His brow darkened, and for a moment he looked harsher. Anti-Theo. "He knows about me but he's not interested. I was raised by Aurora and didn't even know that Candy was my mom until I was older. Thought she was my sister."

Holy wow. That was a heckuva lot more family drama than she expected—and she knew family drama.

"I didn't handle it so well when I found out and ..." He looked at his beer bottle, obviously ill at ease. "So, I understand about deadbeat dads, about parents who don't step up. But I've also seen the other side: a family that's built on love and strength. Aurora did that for me." He lowered his voice. "I'm ready to be whatever you and Hatch need."

His honesty toppled her. Someone who went through life stripping his heart bare to all and sundry was such a stark contrast to the dark secrets she worked hard to keep in place. It gave her hope that their baby would inherit Theo's open, carefree nature.

"Hatch? You've already nicknamed it?"

"I can't keep calling it Blobby. That was my first thought, but it seemed kind of generic so I thought about dinosaurs and how much they mean to us"—he winked—"and did you know baby dinosaurs are called hatchlings, so Hatch seems like a cool name, don't you think? Now I'm not trying to pressure you, I swear. I just want you to be aware that I'm prepared to do this and—"

"Okay."

He nodded and released a world-weary sigh. "Yeah, I get it. Shut up, Theo, right?"

"No. Well, yes, but also, okay. Let's ..." She couldn't here. He'd go nuts and she had rules to lay down. "Could you step into the back for a second?"

She sent a pleading look at Tina, who waved her off again, completely over her drama. A minute later, they were in the pub's office.

"If we do this, Theo—"

He cupped her shoulders and gripped tight. "Do you mean—are you saying—Ellie, are you agreeing to do this? To have a baby with me?"

"Lower your voice, you lunatic. We need to go over the ground rules."

"Sure. Rules. Let's sit down." He guided (manhandled) her into the swivel chair, then grabbed a step stool and opened it so he could sit on it. His grin was joy itself, and she prayed he'd never lose that feeling. "You want to have this baby with me?"

"I think I do."

"Okay, that's good. Better than good. Amazing. And do you feel pressured to do this? Has anyone been giving you a hard time? Jordan? Hunt?" He looked horrified. "Me? Is it because of my sad sack upbringing story?"

It didn't *not* help, but she had decided before that. "No, I'm making up my own mind. I think we should do this, but you don't owe me anything. Those were my faulty condoms and this is on me."

"Not going down that road. We're both on the hook here and I will be 100% involved. Now, let's run down these rules of yours."

The rules. She had to protect both the baby and Theo, so rule number one was going to be a doozy—and she suspected he wasn't going to like it.

She inhaled the deepest breath of her life.

"I'd like to keep it a secret. At least until the baby is born."

THEO HAD EXPECTED Elle would be difficult. The woman was

like an opposing forward line barreling toward the Rebels defense while they were a man down. Liable to check you hard and knock the wind out of you. But this was completely bananas.

"Have you forgotten I'm famous?"

"Insta-famous. Which is like fake famous, isn't it? Besides, you're going to be so busy with the games and if you guys make the playoffs and the finals, that's what? Early June? I'll be five and a half months by then. If it's easier, I could go away somewhere so I'm not distracting you."

She'd insulted him about five different ways there.

Maybe she was embarrassed to be carrying his kid. That had to be it. Sure he was hot and talented, so the child would win the genetic lottery for looks and athleticism, but he wasn't the sharpest blade on the ice. Your typical jock. Hell, he knew that. Nick Isner had known it, too. Elle was a blazing smarty-pants, so hopefully the kid would get her side for intellect.

"You want to keep it secret?"

"I just don't want all your hockey butt-adoring fans to start hating on me. It won't be good for the baby."

He'd do anything necessary to keep her feeling calm and stable during the pregnancy. At this early juncture, it was easy enough to agree, especially as it was something he might not be able to control after a while anyway.

"Okay, we can do that, but eventually we'll have to tell people. Babies are kind of hard to hide. They're loud and stinky and messy. Not to put you off or anything because I'll handle all that. Diapers and feedings and everything."

Her skepticism knew no bounds. "While you're on the road?"

"You could come with me! Or maybe I'll hire someone to

help you. That might be a better plan. I just know I'm going to miss yo—the kid when I'm on the road."

Suffering Jesus, he was already forming some sort of attachment here—and not just to the hatchling.

"We've time to figure all that out," she said, very businesslike. "But for now, let's carry on as normal. You do your thing, I'll do mine, and we can do check-ins to make sure we're both handling it okay. And it's not as if you don't have anyone to talk to about it. Hunt knows."

"Yeah, he's going to love the bro-chats about babies. The guy hates me for knocking up his precious baby sister."

"Which I'm not."

"Tell him that! The guy is super protective of you and while that's nice to have in your corner, I can take care of everything from here on out. Anything you need, anything you want, and I'll be there."

She narrowed her eyes. "Why do I get the impression you're talking about more than sour patch candy and foot rubs?"

Oh, she got that, did she? He fell back on his other skill set—the art of seduction. "Whatever you need, baby."

"Back to the ground rules."

"Aw, hell—I mean, Elle." He grinned.

"No funny business."

"I can't tell jokes?"

She sighed impatiently. "Sex, Theo. We're not going to get busy. Together. I mean, you can—I'm not going to stop you from enjoying yourself."

"Sounds like a trap. I don't want you having sex with anyone else while you're carrying my kid, which means I won't be either. You need a man-made orgasm, you call me."

Color heated her cheeks. "Theo! You can't just stop me

from seeing other people. Or offer to provide a dial-an-orgasm service."

"You seeing anyone right now?"

"Uh, no. But using you to scratch an itch seems—"

"Smart?"

"Tacky."

"It's not. Just think of me as a one-stop shop. Foot rubs, ice-cream, insomnia cookies, funny videos, Llamas classes—"

"Lamaze."

He knew that. "Right, I was checking to see if *you*'d heard of it. And the service includes orgasms. As much oral as you need. No need to reciprocate because you've probably got a killer gag reflex going and sucking my dick might not be good for you. That's okay, I can make that sacrifice for a few months. I will not be sleeping with anyone else and neither will you."

Shaking her head in wonder, she folded her arms. "You're a lot bossier than I remember."

"Oh, I can be bossy in bed, too. All part of the service." He grinned, knowing he'd scored major points here. So the secrecy bothered him. Aurora would eviscerate him if he didn't fess up ASAP, but for now he just needed to get Elle past the point of no return.

"We're really doing this," she said, her voice tinged with awe.

He curled his hands around her much smaller ones. They felt rough, like she'd worked her ass off for a long time. From now on, he'd be taking care of her. She wouldn't need to work so hard anymore.

"Yes, we are. And it's going to be epic."

14

Theo parked his SUV in the parking lot of the Riverbrook Medical Clinic and turned to a fuming Elle.

"This can't be good for the baby," he observed.

She slid a sharp glance at him. "You're the one making my blood pressure go through the roof. I don't know why I'm letting you bully me into this."

"Because I've compromised on your stuff so you need to compromise on mine. This OB comes highly-recommended. I've done the research."

"But it's such a waste of money. I already have healthcare as a veteran, so why are we paying out of network to see some fancy doc?"

"Because this is my kid, too, and if I want to spend my money this way, I will." Before she could respond, he hopped out of the car and around to the other side. She was already out and glaring at him for daring to be chivalrous. Sometimes there was no winning with Elle.

He still liked being her baby daddy, though.

"You saw all the great reviews," he said.

"I did. But—"

"Elle." He placed his hands on her shoulders. "I want to be involved. I want to be here for you and Hatch, and I can't think of a better use for my bash-a-puck cash than ensuring our peanut has the best possible start in life. Can you indulge me on this?" He pushed her hair behind her ear and used the moment to cup her neck. Her skin was so soft there.

He didn't imagine her shiver.

"It would be better if you put the money you're spending on an expensive OB into a trust fund or something for the kid. Something I can't touch."

What a weird thing to say. It wasn't the first time she'd raised the possibility that she might be perceived as a gold digger. Odder still was Elle's desire for privacy, which felt way out of proportion. He understood she was wary of his fans and the media, but there was something hinky about this whole situation.

"That's next."

"It is?"

He cradled her elbow and steered her toward the clinic's entrance. "I'll be talking to my lawyer. You'll both be fine, no matter what happens."

"No matter what happens? What does that mean?"

"If the team bus crashes or I have an allergic reaction to Jorgensen's herring or another brain aneurysm strikes me down."

"Is that likely?"

"Jorgensen *does* like his herring."

She stopped and faced him. "No. The brain thing."

"I get scans but you never know. Rest assured, you and the baby will be taken care of. I've no plans to go anywhere so you and me? Forever linked by this kid." He rubbed her stomach because this seemed like the one moment he might have a chance to. The baby was at approximately eight weeks now, and there was a slight curve to her belly. The books he'd read said it was too soon to feel a baby bump, but his hands knew better.

She placed a palm over his, and it felt nice to be connected even for this briefest moment. "Just worry about the baby, financially and all that. I don't need anything. I can provide for myself."

"You're kind of a package deal."

Her frown conjured storms in her blue-gray eyes. "We're not. Any money you put in trust or aside for the baby, just make sure it's handled by lawyers. They pay all the expenses directly. It shouldn't go through my hands."

Maybe she'd grown up in a religious cult, where money was the root of all evil.

"Let's not worry about it. Right now, I want to see if this kid has the makings of a good D-man."

THIS KID, future D-man or not, was going to end up costing a fortune.

The OB Elle had seen for the confirmation appointment a couple of weeks ago should have been fine, but oh no! Not good enough for child of *The* Theo Kershaw. This pricy doc better have gold-plated stirrups to justify whatever she was charging.

As Elle got ready in the exam room, she thought about what Theo had said. *Or another brain aneurysm strikes me down.* How could he be so blasé about his future? And why the hell was he playing a game where he could get knocked over and hit his head, suffer a concussion, or get so worked up a bubble in his brain might pop? She didn't care about his money, she wanted him to be around for their baby.

Dr. Patel came in, her smile big and white against her brown skin.

"Eloise?"

"I prefer Elle, actually. This is Theo."

"Elle. Theo. Lovely to meet you both." She shook hands with her, then with Theo. While she washed up and turned on the gadgets, she chitchatted, asking questions about how Elle felt and what she was eating.

"She thinks Cheetos are a vegetable, Doc," Mr. Perfect said.

"Snitch," Elle muttered, to which Dr. Patel merely smiled.

"Let's see what we have here." She rubbed the clear goo onto Elle's abdomen.

Elle caught Theo staring at her stomach, across which the skin was starting to stretch taut. Remembering that this was the first time he'd seen so much of her since Christmas, she fought the blush climbing her cheeks. This shouldn't be awkward but she didn't feel attractive anymore—not like how she'd felt when Theo had slid inside her in the dark, whispering how sexy and beautiful she was. Nothing illustrated the change in her hotness levels than the extra poundage she was carrying around.

"I know, it's a little cold," Dr. Patel said, misinterpreting Elle's reaction. She jiggled a few buttons on the screen. "Here we are. Okay, you've got a spirited one there."

"We do?"

It was hard to make out, to be honest, just a black and white blur. *We can put a man on the moon but we can't show ultrasounds in color yet?* But then Elle started to see the outline of a head, legs, and butt. This was a real, live baby.

"Everything looks to be in normal range," the doc said, her eyes still on the screen.

"Are you sure?" Elle asked.

"Oh, yes. Very healthy with a strong heartbeat."

Elle had avoided looking at Theo, worried the emotion of the moment would overtake her. Would make her feel things she wasn't ready to explore. Looking up, she found him staring in wonder, and that lovely longing in his expression was something she'd remember for the rest of her life.

Theo Kershaw was a very emotional man. She couldn't have chosen a more suitable donor, and that was exactly what he would think if he ever found out who she really was.

Only when he loosened the grip on her hand did she realize it had been so tight—or that he'd been holding it at all.

He didn't let go completely. That felt right, too.

Struck by a quirky notion, she turned back to Dr. Patel. "So, Doctor. You don't think that maybe the baby's butt is a bit too ... big?"

Theo snorted.

Dr. Patel looked confused. Clearly no one had brought this concern to her attention before. "I'd say the baby's butt is within, uh, acceptable size ranges."

"Thank God for that," Elle said, catching Theo's sparkling green eyes. "There's genetics, you see. The dad has a rep for it. Most famous ass in pro sports."

"Jesus, Ellie," Theo muttered, but she could tell he was enjoying her teasing. It had been a while since they'd kept it light like this. All their conversations since the news had been weighted with worry: who to tell, what to eat, how to handle it.

Dr. Patel's eyes brightened, catching on at last. "Ah, I see.

Well, usually that kind of thing doesn't manifest until the child's older. Plenty of time to inherit Daddy's butt."

"Me and my butt are right here, y'know!"

"Has a Twitter account, too," Elle said, ignoring him. "SuperGlutes. You should check it out, Dr. P. Hours of enjoyment."

"I might just do that!" She gave Theo a closer look and her sly glance at Elle was one of congratulations for landing that fish.

Theo squeezed her hand, his smile big, warm, and completely infectious. He winked. "Knew you missed my ass, Ellie."

She had no response that wouldn't sound like a complete lie.

15

Day one of the playoffs! Can the @ChiRebels handle the bite of the @BostonCougars in this crucial opening game? Stick with @HockeyGrrl for all your round one analysis!

"Morning, Rebels lovers! Just checking in with my favorite people to gauge excitement levels for the game tonight. We're in the playoffs. Woo to da hoo!"

Elle couldn't believe she was still doing this: sneakily checking out the father of her child's videos on Instagram because it was safer than having to deal with sexy, in-person Theo. A cascade of hearts and thumbs-up symbols floated over the video as Theo's collective fandom made their feelings known. These people were obsessed. (And no, she wasn't like *them*!)

"Oh, you like the playoff beard?" Theo rubbed his jaw, which looked to have about four days of scruff. Heat bloomed between her thighs because all hail the hottie-in-chief, that was some fine facial hair.

"Yeah, I'm trying, but man it's hard to beat Burnett's.

That guy just has to exhale and he looks like a Grizzly bear-fighting survivalist. Now I'm heading into the gym for a little warm-up before morning skate. Let me turn the camera around."

Seconds later, the camera was pointed at the gym at Rebels HQ. Elle recognized the players in frame: Petrov, the aristocratic Russian captain with the sexy tattoos raised an eyebrow in Theo's direction as he lifted the bar on some complicated piece of equipment. Hunt scowled as Hunt was wont to do. Erik, the goalie, gave a friendly wave. That guy was such a sweetheart, one of her nicest customers, and always making eyes at her.

Theo talked over the filming. "So this is what Playoffs Day looks like, guys. Pretty relaxed, but I imagine the nerves will kick in later." The camera angle switched back to Theo. "I'd better change into my shorts and ... what's that? No, I'm not going to do that on camera! Gotta keep some mystery, people. Catch you later!"

End video.

Theo in shorts. That would have been nice.

Elle scanned the comments. From the avatars, it looked to be a mostly female fan base, which wasn't surprising. What *was* surprising was how graphic some of these comments got. People had all sorts of filthy-minded opinions on his pecs, his biceps, his abs, his ass. Of course, it was what he was famous for.

Frankly none of this bothered her—much—but it did help with her cover story. As long as Theo's fandom was as rabid as hyenas in heat, she could use it to justify maintaining secrecy about the pregnancy. When really she was protecting him from her freak show of a family.

From the real her.

She scrolled through her messages, stopping on the ones from Theo, who had taken to checking in every morning. At first she'd thought it too much. A lot of what Theo did or said was too much.

Then she realized that because they weren't spending time together like a regular couple, this was necessary for him to feel involved. She loved that he was finding a way, fighting the tide of Elle.

Sometimes he sent a joke—Dad jokes he called them. *Getting a head start!*

On other days, he sent a link to an article about nutrition in pregnancy or a think piece about playing music to the hatchling.

However, this morning he'd checked in with: *Hey, can we talk later?* Sort of serious and subdued with not a smiley face in sight.

Unease shivered through her while she waited for him to come over after morning skate. Had he found out something about her? Surely he had people who looked after his money, proxies who would be rightly skeptical of this blow-in with her claims on Theo's fortune. The first thing he should have done was run a background check.

The buzzer sounded and she jumped, holding a hand protectively to her stomach. At almost four months, she had started to show, though anyone who cared to ponder it would never in a million years think a superstar pro-athlete's genetic material was responsible.

The heavy clop-clop up the stairs got louder.

"Hey!" His smile was big and bright against that sexy beard. Her nipples hardened at the sight of him and a warm, dangerous wriggle started up in her core. Horny, hungry, and hormonal, the trifecta of trouble.

"Good practice? You guys ready?"

"Yeah, it was good. As for ready? Who knows."

"That doesn't sound like *The* Theo Kershaw. Something wrong?"

He scrunched up his mouth, as if surprised she'd even ask. Was she that tuned out to his wellbeing that such a query was weird from her? She needed to be a better partner.

"It's kind of a big deal. We haven't made the playoffs in three seasons. The last time I came close was in LA, but I missed out."

When his aneurysm ruptured. Not how you want to leave the ice.

She stepped back to let him in. "You're not worried about it happening again, are you?"

Given what she knew about survival rates and recovery, Theo Kershaw was a walking, talking, skating miracle. Recurrence was relatively rare, and she imagined someone with Theo's resources would be getting amazing follow-up care.

"No, not really. I'm all good." He grinned at her tilted head response. "As far as aneurysms go."

"You're worried about letting the team down if your ass decides to throw off your center of gravity." She checked him out as if joking, but y'know, *not joking.* You could park a cup of coffee on that shelf of perfection.

Abandon that line of thinking now, Butler.

"No one likes to let anyone down, Elle-oh-Elle," Theo said drolly.

So not exactly the most incisive of comments, but she wanted to be a good friend to him, just as he was to her. He'd been nothing but kind and considerate.

For the baby. He's a friend because he's a decent person and

he wants to ensure the baby's health, not because he's truly inter-
ested in you.

Proving her point, he held up a Whole Foods shopping bag. "How about I make you a smoothie and lunch?"

"Oh, if you must."

This was a common occurrence over the last eight weeks. Theo often came over to feed her breakfast smoothies before his morning practice, then stopped by for lunch after when he wasn't on the road. He did her grocery shopping, filling her fridge with all manner of healthy greenery (*making up for all those stolen sandwich fixins, Ellie!*). She'd already stashed the goldfish snacks and popcorn in her bedroom before he came over.

Now, he was in her kitchen slicing up mangoes and strawberries. She enjoyed these visits, the quiet domesticity, the ease of being with him. He was usually such a restless person that it was fascinating to see him in a calm—or calmer—state. Drawn to his hands, she found herself mesmerized, imagining them as he rubbed her belly then wandered—north or south, she wouldn't mind.

He looked up and smiled in a way she felt all the way to her toes.

Rather than encourage him with a smile of her own, she asked, "What did you want to talk about?"

"Do I need a reason to visit my baby incubator?"

"*Hi*-larious! You sent me a text with no emojis or jokes or links to cat videos, so I'm guessing something is up other than the need to feed your progeny."

"Progeny," he murmured. "God, I hope the kid gets your brain and not mine." She was about to tell him not to be so down on himself, when he said, "So, I was reading a meta-analysis about night work and pregnancy outcomes—"

"Reading a what?"

"A meta-analysis? It's a type of academic review article that systematically captures all the medical evidence to answer a particular research question and comes up with a clinical bottom line." She must have looked flabbergasted because he added, "I asked the team doc."

"Oh. I see," she said though she didn't.

"This article said that night work can result in premature births, low gestational birthweight, and possible depression in the offspring. And while I think those preemies are cuter than buttons and we can always get therapy for the kid, maybe we could avoid all that drama by getting you off your feet at night."

She could think of sexier ways than giving up her job, most of them involving Theo and the sofa not ten feet away. This wouldn't be the first time he'd insinuated that bartending was beneath the mother of the golden child.

In full flight now, he continued making his case. "You could take more classes. Maybe enroll in something full-time and work towards a degree, like you planned before."

"And how do I pay for rent? Or groceries?"

He held his hands out, palms up. "You could let me help."

"I can't take money from you. For me."

"This would be for both of you. For your health, the baby's health, and so you can plan your future as a hotshot investor or a Fortune 500 CEO that makes us all a shit-ton of money. This would get you on the road to your next level sooner."

But at the expense of owing someone before her future had even begun. Her universal ledger of balance would be completely out of alignment.

"I'm not overdoing it when I work. Standing is better

than sitting in front of a computer all day. I'm taking breaks, drinking plenty of water, eating right."

He shook his head at her stubbornness, but he knew better than to get her riled over this. Instead he smartly changed tack. "So what I really wanted to talk about was the game. Come tonight. As my guest."

Surprise clotted her throat. She turned to the fridge so he wouldn't see how much his request affected her.

"I have to work."

"I checked with Tina. She said she'd give you the night off if I can get a temp bartender in, which I can. But if you don't want to come, I understand. You're not a fan."

"Kershaw, quit it with the guilt trip," she said to the leafy contents of her fridge, annoyed he'd already talked to her boss about it. Still, she kind of liked the idea. She wanted to support him as much as he supported her, and time was the only thing she had of value. "Maybe I could sit with Jordan in the press box like last time."

"On the night of the first playoffs game? The box would be full. You could probably hang with the WAGs, though."

The wives and girlfriends? "That might get the rumor mill grinding."

"Is that such a bad thing? People have to know some-time." His perfect eyebrows slammed together. "I hate lying to my gran."

She faced him. "You're not lying. You're just not … telling her. Yet." Even she knew it was a lie. After all, she was an expert. "People wouldn't believe it anyway."

"Why?"

She cocked her head. "Kershaw. Come on."

He had the decency to look handsomely baffled.

"I'm not really hockey WAG material, am I?" She'd done her research. The Rebels wives and girlfriends had all graduated summa cum laude from Supermodel College. "They'll take one look and ask 'how much alcohol was involved?' or 'how dark was the room?'"

"So you had to draw the blinds and get drunk to sleep with me—"

"Theo!" She laughed, shaking her head at his efforts to be kind. "We both know that given a do-over, I would not be who you'd choose to be your baby incubator."

He nodded vehemently. "Correct. I'd find someone pliant and cooperative and who eats her vegetables. How about the owner's box with the Rebels management?"

"The owner's box with the what now?"

"For tonight's game. Try to keep up, Elle-oh-Elle."

Oh, that sneaky mother pucker. "You've already arranged this, haven't you?"

"Might have." He grinned as he pressed the button on the blender—the one he'd bought specially to ensure his spawn was pumped full of nutrients. He stopped, poured, and passed over a dreamsicle-colored mess. "I'd like you to be there. For you both to be there, so ..." He trailed off.

"So what?"

"So I can tell the little one he was in the house at the start of a title run."

"He? Could be a she or a they. And *they* won't remember a thing!"

He gave an embarrassed shrug. "But I will."

Oh. This was really important to him. Coming from the army, she should have understood better the art of compromise, but she was just getting used to doing things her way that it was constricting as all hell to have to consider the wishes of someone else.

Two someone elses. She absently ran a hand over her abdomen, only to see Theo track her movement.

"You okay?"

"Yeah. The second trimester is a breeze so far." She was still feeling nausea, but she'd taken to keeping it to herself. It would be too easy to lean on Theo for both her physical and her mental well-being, to fall into the comfort of those lovely arms, hard chest, and delicious, just-showered man scent.

She'd done that before. Relied on someone, or tried to, and got burned for it.

Tale as old as time. Boy meets girl. Girl falls for boy. Boy finds out girl's parents are bottom-feeder scam artists looking for a score. Boy tells girl to take a hike.

She didn't blame Preston Carter the Third, or PC3 as he was known seven years ago. The guy was going places, the scion of Miami's elite. And even though her family had promised they wouldn't interfere or bring their usual torrent of destruction, even though they'd promised her *this one thing* she could call her own, it hadn't gone her way. Preston's family ran a background check, had even put a private detective on the case—and why not? She was a potential fox in the henhouse of his glittering future.

She'd insisted that she didn't want his money. She'd sign anything he put before her, fork over any future rights, prove that while she might have tainted blood in her veins she was more than what nature had given her. She was Elle, the fun waitress Preston had flirted with the night of his brother's bachelor party. She was Elle, the girl he'd taken ice-skating on that magical weekend to New York.

She was Elle.

But that girl wasn't enough, not when she came with all that baggage. When Preston said his family would never accept her, he'd meant *he* would never accept her. He'd always be looking over his shoulder waiting for the knife to plunge between his shoulder blades. He wouldn't fight for her and she wouldn't beg. No guy was worth that level of humiliation.

But she'd learned one thing. She did better on her own. She'd enlisted in the army because it was the easiest way to get away from the clan, her version of "get thee to a nunnery." They couldn't use her there, and in the meantime, she could even out the harm they were doing to the universe in whatever con they were running.

Those painful memories immunized her against the virus of feels attacking her body. She looked up to find Theo staring at her, waiting for her to say yes.

THEO STUDIED ELLE—SOMETHING he found himself doing a lot—trying to puzzle her out. He knew so little about her and he was trying not to go full-scale Theo on her very fine ass. But having her at the first game was important to him.

The secrecy was really starting to piss him off. Since finding out about his sister/mom, and then having that shit show compounded by Bio-Dad being a complete asshole, Theo had determined his life would be lived out in the open. No secrets. No hidden agendas. Yet Elle wouldn't let him be, well, *Theo*. He understood that he might not be her ideal mate. She was probably embarrassed by him—he got that. Sometimes he said the wrong thing or blurted out the first notion that entered his brain. He was trying to do better, make her less ashamed to be associated with him.

Only now she was giving him this BS about no one believing they'd be a couple by choice and booze or bad lighting had led to them getting busy. Never mind that every morning he woke up dreaming of slipping between her gorgeous thighs and burying his cock balls-deep. Christ knew he'd rather be fantasizing about someone who might *actually* be interested in him and wasn't so anxious to hide their connection.

Take today's dick-springing look, a light blue T-shirt with a low-plunging V. It shaped her breasts snugly, probably because they'd increased—in his professional opinion —by at least two cup sizes since she'd become pregnant. Lush and ripe, they were the perfect spank bank material. He'd be making a withdrawal later for sure.

His cock stirred in excitement, and that annoyed him. Infuriated him, to be honest. Because she was standing there thinking and saying ridiculous shit about not being in the same league as him.

"You remember Christmas Eve? Remember what happened?"

"I'm not likely to forget."

"Well, that happened because I thought you were the sexiest woman on the planet."

"Theo—"

"Hear me out, Ellie. You seem so sure no one would believe I'd be with you, yet it happened. *We* happened. The sex was amazing. Hot and dirty enough to earn a T-rex rating." He pointed at her. "Which is a sex rating scale I just made up! What I'm trying to say is that you turn me on. Then and now. I understand you don't want to complicate things with sex but I just need you to know that Blue Balls City is not a great place to visit."

She licked her lips. *Jeez. Us. Stop.* "I—I know you must be frustrated." She sounded pretty frustrated herself, but maybe that was wishful thinking. "If you need to ... with someone else ..."

That was her takeaway from his gut-spill? "Told you I wouldn't."

"Yes, you said. But ..."

"Don't you get it? I don't want to be with anyone else. I'm dealing with it. Solo."

"Oh. I see." Did she? Did she see that his dick was making a herculean effort not to punch a hole in his sweatpants? And did her nipples just pop like nubs of sweet candy against her bra?

"You're staring," she murmured.

"Your breasts look fantastic." Yep, he'd said that, but it was the God's honest truth. Her tits did look amazing, ripe and plump and the prefect shape for his mouth. Just looking at her was enough to place his boner on his top five boners list. He opened his mouth to apologize, then clamped it shut again. Why should he apologize for telling it like it is?

"They do?" A breathy gasp. She looked down at them. "They're sore." She bit her lip, and was that his imagination, but did she squeeze her thighs together? Give him strength.

Boner list, climbing to top three.

He moved in closer. "You okay, Elle?"

"F-fine." Her breathing had picked up.

"You sure?" He fisted the kitchen island counter, either side of her. His dick was cocked and loaded but he leaned back so as not to touch her with any part of his anatomy. Let her see what she did to him. "I saw you rub your thighs together. I can see your beautiful nipples poking through that too-thin shirt. They must be so hard and sensitive to be visible through your bra."

"Cheap material," she muttered, her tongue darting out for a quick swipe of her lips.

Boner now making a run for the gold medal.

"What do you need right now, Ellie?"

"Need?" She took a juddering breath. "You've got all my needs covered, Theo. You're so good to me. Too good."

He shook his head. Slowly. Then inclined his mouth closer to hers. "There's so much more I can do for you." Her breath was a hot puff of want against his lips. "So many needs I can fulfill." But more than just physically. He was beginning to realize that Elle needed verbal assurance that she was worthy of his attention, his care, and his all-consuming desire. "I meant what I said before. You turn me on so fucking much. This hard-on has your name on it, no one else's."

She moaned against his mouth, her lips parted, and he took what belonged to him. For a second, he wondered if he'd made a mistake but she clutched his shoulders and opened for him, giving him a taste of the sweetest, most forbidden fruit.

Elle Butler's kiss.

So much had passed between them since the last time. A life had been created, their worlds had collided and joined. A ragged, uneasy union.

With his hands on her hips, he guided her back to the sofa, a few feet away in the open-plan living room.

"Theo, are you sure you want—"

"Yes, I'm sure. Right now, I'm just going to make you feel good, Ellie. This is all about you." He hooked his fingers in her pajama bottoms and inched them down. "But you need to ask for what you want. I'll give it to you, but I need you to tell me clearly what you're desperate for."

Confusion marred her features for a moment, bafflement at being given a choice. He'd seen that same expression the day she told him about the baby. Somehow she was used to being railroaded into decisions without heed to her desires.

Not today.

She pushed her flannel PJs down and sank into the sofa. "I need your touch. I need—"

The words cut off as his fingers found her wet and wanting. She closed her eyes, gave a short head shake, then finished, "I need ... that."

She'd been about to say something else, something more revealing. No problem, he could wait.

His fingers delved, swirled, sought her secrets. *Who are you, Elle Butler? Why am I so drawn to you?* He knelt in between her legs and pushed her thighs wider. All that soft, pink, soaking flesh pulsed beneath his fingertips.

"Scoot forward a bit, Ellie."

She did, a couple of inches, her thighs falling open and providing even more access. Avidly, his fingers separated the folds of her sweet, pretty pussy. He thumbed over her clit and got a gratifying surge of her body in return.

"That's too—too—"

"Too much? Too soon?"

She nodded. Perfect, because he wanted to make it last, edge her pleasure, before flinging her off the cliff. Mostly he wanted to watch as she tumbled over.

He resumed touching her everywhere but that bundle of sensitive nerves. Her hip swivel was sexy. Her little moans were sexy. That lip bite ... so sexy. Everything about her was making him harder than the ice he'd be skating on tonight.

"Take off your shirt, Ellie."

She peeled it off, and his balls filled at the sight. Gorgeous, ripe flesh overflowing the cups, the dusky pink nipples half exposed and begging for his mouth.

"Jesus, you're so beautiful. I've been dreaming of this." Silky wetness flooded his fingers. "Pop one of those pretty tits out. Get it ready for my tongue."

Just a flick of her hand was enough to free her breast from the cup, and she held the spilled, abundant flesh, almost in wonder that it felt so good to offer it to him.

His mouth closed over the nipple, and she groaned her pleasure. "Theo. Oh, God, that's ..."

Yes, it was. He stroked over her clit, softly at first, then with more pressure. She grabbed his shoulder for leverage as she came all over his hand. Her body bucked as he sucked her breast and finger-fucked her to earn a second, longer orgasm.

After a few seconds, she opened her eyes, blinking slowly like she was coming back after a long trip away from reality. He was glad he could do that for her.

He collapsed on the sofa beside her. She reached over to rub his erection through his sweats.

He groaned at her perfect touch. "You don't have to."

"Yes, I do," she said, a gentle ferocity in her tone. She looked a little undone, one lovely tit uncapped, the rosy nipple still damp and peaked. Her hand around his cock was the definition of care and pleasure. But the nicest thing about it was her warm gaze, face to face, connecting in a way that told him this wasn't his imagination.

While she stroked, getting rougher at his urging, he cupped her jaw and drew her in for a kiss. She tasted like sweet cream and strawberries, like soft woman and strong warrior. It didn't take long. He exploded in thick, ropy bursts over her stomach and breasts, marking her as his once more.

A while later, he asked, "Okay if I nap here? I usually do around this time."

"Sure." She pulled a throw blanket over their bodies and wrapped an arm around his torso. The press of her breasts against his side was exquisite, all warm, willing woman. He loved that she cuddled him without hesitation, as though this was her first instinct. One she'd been fighting since the beginning.

"You want us at the game tonight, Theo, then we'll be there. For every game you need us."

Us. The sweet sound of progress. He closed his eyes and passed into untroubled sleep.

16

"Hey, how did you get in here?"

Elle turned sharply at the sound of the voice, only to find a grinning Jordan.

"Hey, lady," Elle murmured, then lowered the volume even further. "I've been invited to the owners' box by Theo. He said he wanted his kid to be here at the start of any potential cup run. You know, idiot dad stuff."

Jordan's mouth curved. "Ah, that's so sweet. He's going to be the fun parent."

"Yeah. I'll be the horror-freak disciplinarian. I already see how this is going to play out."

"So, how are you feeling, friend?" Jordan squeezed Elle's arm.

"Good, actually. Great." She leaned in. "So, can you tell I'm carrying a genetically-enhanced super child?" She'd worn her baggiest hoodie, but she felt like everyone *had* to know with even the most cursory of glances.

"Not at all. You look—"

"Hi, Jordan."

They both turned to a woman who looked vaguely

familiar: dark-haired with pink overtones and green eyes glittering with humor.

"Hey, Violet," Jordan said. "This is Elle Butler. She has an invite to the executive box tonight. Elle, Violet Vasquez-St. James is one of the team owners."

"In name only," Violet said. "Normally, I wouldn't be here, but Bren's pretty excited that the Rebels are back in the playoffs, so I'm doing my bit for team spirit. Ra ra." She smirked at Elle. "I'm not a big hockey fan."

"Neither am I," Elle said, taken off guard.

Violet sized her up, and Elle got the impression she was suddenly more interesting to the woman before her. "Sounds like there's a story there. Let's share our hockey hate in the box together. Later, Jordan. Go do whatever you hockey lovers do."

Oh, nuts. Elle had now drawn attention to herself in the worst possible way. A grinning Jordan took her leave (snake!) and headed into the press box.

"I mean, of course, I like hockey," Elle said, scrambling to amend her previous statement. "Actually, I'm a friend of Levi Hunt's. We were in the army together."

"Grumpy Hunt? Nice. And you were in the military? Sounds like you're one tough chick."

The owners' suite was crowded, but a man of the exceptionally hot, bearded, and tall variety came forward the moment they stepped inside. Gathering Violet close, he landed an X-rated kiss on her mouth.

"Nessie," Violet murmured when he let her up for air. "I was only gone five minutes."

"Seven," he said, oblivious to Elle. Must be nice to have a guy who was blind to everyone but you the minute you walked into a room.

She mentally punched that thought back in its box. She

didn't need that. Though waking up in Theo's arms a few hours ago had been about the sweetest moment she'd ever experienced. Even better—by a smidgen—than the feel of that sexy beard against her jaw.

"Elle, this is my husband, Bren St. James, former captain of the Rebels. Bren, this is Elle, who can't really decide if she likes hockey or not."

"I'm a bartender at the Empty Net. So I see all the players and the games all the time." *Why, brilliant, Eloise!*

Bren stared at her in understandable confusion. When Elle didn't enlighten him, he asked politely in a distinctive Scottish accent, "Would you like a drink?"

"A ginger ale? If you have it."

"Got it." He smooched his wife again.

"Scotch and soda for me, Nessie."

He raised an expressive eyebrow and walked away.

"Come sit over here," Violet said, already steering her to a row of seats near the windows.

Looking around, Elle recognized a few of the big shots. Harper Chase, the oldest sister and CEO of the team, cozying up to a broad-shouldered guy with startling blue eyes and well-worn laugh lines. Isobel Chase, the middle sister who sometimes drank in the bar and was married to the team's captain, the hot Russian, Vadim Petrov. Some of the other faces looked familiar from TV interviews she'd seen while she worked.

Once they were seated, a gorgeous guy in a gorgeous suit who looked like something out of *The Godfather* approached and kissed Violet on the cheek.

"Behaving yourself, *tesoro*?"

"Not likely." Violet smiled at Elle. "Meet Dante Moretti, the Rebels' general manager. Dante, this is Elle."

Dante assessed her with mild curiosity. "Theo's friend?"

"Right. He's a friend. Good friend." Damn. She should have told Theo to organize this through Hunt. And why did her tongue turn to vulcanized rubber around exceptionally hot men? This guy should be a model, promoting those fancy watches as big as her face or espresso machines that broke after producing one solitary cup. Elle remembered now—Dante was married to Cade Burnett, one of the Rebels defensemen.

As she had no scintillating conversation to offer, he refocused on Violet.

"Bren said you were sick this morning. Feeling better? Can I get you something?"

"He's getting me ginger ale because I can't drink for five more months! I must have been crazy to agree to this."

The back of Elle's neck prickled. "You're pregnant?"

"Yeah, but as is so often the case with this family, it's anything but straightforward. Meet one of the fathers of my children." She gestured to Dante. "I'm merely a vessel for the royal bambino. The Italian Stallion here is one of the daddies while Cade's the other."

Oh, she understood. Maybe. "And where does Bren fit into all this?"

"He's paying the bills." She laughed, then laughed more at Dante's hot frown. "My handsome, understanding husband is on board and is taking very good care of me."

"We all are," Dante said. "Or trying to." He stroked her cheek and muttered something in Italian before checking a gold pocket watch—*who were these people?*—and stepping away to talk to Harper.

"That's a really nice thing you're doing," Elle said.

"Cade's my bestie and Dante's up there, not that I'd ever

tell him. We have a frenemies thing going on. They needed someone to donate an egg and carry the kiddo, and I figured, why not?"

Pregnant by choice to help out two friends? What Elle wouldn't give to have her life *that* together.

Bren appeared with two glasses of ginger ale and handed them off. "I need to find Franky. She said she was going to head down to the locker room."

"Want me to come with?"

"You stay and visit." He smiled at Elle and went on his way.

"Franky's Bren's youngest daughter," Violet explained. "She's thirteen and allergic to everything except much-too-old-for-her hockey players. Bren's pretty protective of her. Of all of us." She rubbed a hand over her stomach.

Must be nice to have that safety net. Not just her husband, but her sisters, Dante, and Cade. A big network she could rely on—or who could fail her. But Elle suspected no one in the Rebels family would let each other down. The bonds were strong. Unbreakable.

For now, she had Theo, but for how long? This life with uberfans and the threat of injury and trades at the drop of a hat was so uncertain. She felt as though she was out on a sinking raft, buffeted on all sides by waves she had no control over.

She forced a smile for Violet. "So, how's your pregnancy going?"

"Not too bad. A little nausea."

"Sour patch candy works well. Or so I hear."

Violet smiled. "I'll give it a shot. So, I thought you were here because you were a friend of Hunt's, but Dante said you were with Kershaw."

"Oh, not with him. He's just ..."

"Another friend?"

Elle could feel her smile crumbling around the edges. All this secrecy was taking its toll. "I'm a good bartender. And hey, look at the perks. Here at the hockey match."

Violet grinned. "Yep, here at the hockey match."

17

AFTER SHOWERS AND PRESS, Theo headed to the player lounge, where the management wanted to give a pep talk, congratulating them on a good first game, a 4-2 win. All Theo wanted to do was check in on Elle.

The lounge was filled with people from all over the org: players, staff, and front office with Rebels alums rounding out the party. Theo spotted Remy DuPre, the smooth-talking Cajun who was married to Harper, and Bren St. James, the dour Scotsman and former captain, who frankly intimidated the shit out of Theo.

"Hey, cap," Theo said.

"Not the captain anymore," Bren observed drolly.

"It's like a presidential title. Once one, always one."

Bren's mouth twitched as someone wheeled in a big sheet cake with what looked like "Congratulations" and —*holy baked goods*, was that a baby made from fondant?

Theo's throat went dry. "What's going on?" he asked Bren cautiously.

"My wife's having another man's child. Actually two other men."

Okaaaay. Theo spotted Elle near the door talking to Jordan. Something she said made Jordan laugh, and Elle joined in. Just seeing her light up made him warm. Getting a taste of her this afternoon and a chance to nap with her—crucial game preparation he didn't share with just anyone, he might add—had given him hope that maybe she was softening toward him.

Cade and Dante stood close to Violet Vasquez, the youngest Chase sister and Bren's wife. "She's having a kid for those guys."

"Yep."

"And you don't mind?"

"Have you ever tried stopping a determined woman from doing whatever the hell she wants?" Bren shook his head. "Wouldn't have wanted to anyway. It's what brothers do for each other."

Theo identified intimately with the "determined woman" comment, though he couldn't imagine being close enough to any of his teammates to be cool with that kind of arrangement. Knowing Elle, she'd probably do it to spite him!

Dante cleared his throat. "Hey, everyone, it's a good night and I'm glad we're not drowning our sorrows after a bad first game because this celebration would be pretty awkward. You all killed it out there and we couldn't be prouder." Cheers went up and Dante waited for them to subside. "Now for something a bit more personal. Some of you know this but consider this our official announcement. Cade and I are going to be parents soon, and it's all because of this amazing woman here. I just wanted to say a few words of thanks to Violet for doing this for us. For her generosity. For loving us this much. For so much more that if I was to list it all, she might start crying, and then she'd have to kill me later."

"I would!" Violet's response drew hearty laughs.

Dante kissed her cheek. "You were a friend before, now you're our family. Grazie, Violetta."

Everyone raised a glass and hooted and hollered. All Theo could think was: *don't look at her. Do not look at her.*

He couldn't help himself. Magnets drew his gaze, and he found Elle staring right back, her face creased in discomfort. Theo's first instinct was petty. *Good.* Let her feel bad that people—normal people—celebrate this kind of thing, but *she* needed to be different. Because of what? She was ashamed of him? Anyone else would be thrilled to be carrying his kid.

He moved away before his mood ruined this celebration of a Rebel baby. An official one, because his was just a dirty secret he couldn't share. *He* was just a dirty secret.

He needed air.

Slipping outside the lounge into the corridor, he tried to fill his lungs. When he was a kid, he used to suffer from anxiety in social situations. He was long over that, but back then, it was Candy who used to give him his strength. The woman he'd thought was his sister would take him aside, cocoon him in her arms, and tell him he was the best kid she knew. How she was so proud to be his sister.

All that time she'd been lying to him.

Elle wasn't lying but what she was doing was just as bad because he *felt* just as bad.

A movement at his side made him turn. Gunnar Bond stood there, his bearded, bruiser face watching him curiously. "You okay, Kershaw?"

Theo blanked his expression as best he could. "Yeah, just taking a break. You?"

"They're a young team," Gunnar said, which sounded off-topic except ... all this talk of babies must be tough on him. That's what he meant. A young team with kids on the way and futures so bright.

Just over two years ago, a couple of months after Theo's brain blew up, Gunnar lost his wife and four-year-old twins in a car crash in California when their car went off the road into a ravine. Pinned in place in the overturned SUV, Gunnar had watched his family slip away from him, one breath, one heartbeat at a time. A broken man, he'd left hockey and gone off the grid. Only now was he starting his life over with the Rebels, on the roster but not yet playing.

Theo's problems were nothing compared to Gunnar's. At least he had a healthy baby on the way. So he couldn't tell anyone about it and his baby mama wasn't falling over herself to be anything else, but his life was moving along instead of in limbo like Gunnar's.

Gunnar's dark blond brows drew together. "Kershaw, I know when you're in a mood. Is it something to do with that brunette you can't take your eyes off of?"

"Maybe," he said sheepishly. "It's complicated. She's ... complicated." He threw a glance over his shoulder, checking they were alone. Should he confide in Gunnar about something so sensitive?

He took a chance. "She's pregnant with my baby."

So Hunt and Jordan knew, but this was the first time he'd said the words aloud, had told someone what he wanted to shout from the rooftops. *I'm going to be a dad. Woo hoo!*

Gunnar's smile stretched the skin around his scar taut. He rubbed his beard. "You want this baby?"

"Yeah. I do. But Elle—that's the momma—she doesn't

want any attention. Wants to keep it a secret. I'm not even sure she likes me all that much."

"You still watch *Days of Our Lives*, Theo?"

Back in his LA Quake days when Gunnar was his captain, they'd both been fans of the show. "Salem forever, man."

Gunnar's lips curved. "Well, if there's one thing we've all learned from *Days* is that a baby can never remain a secret for long and a baby's parents usually can't stay away from each other. It's soap opera law. And man, between your parents, your crazy gran, your aneurysm, and now this, your life is more dramatic than *Days* during fucking sweeps."

"Hey, I'm not responsible for all that!" He'd forgotten how much he'd shared with Gunnar back when he was a rookie in LA. He'd also forgotten how much his former captain had been there for him.

"No, you're not. But you are responsible for how you handle it. You gave us quite a scare a few years ago. I can't believe you came back from that, yet you're out on that ice as strong as you've ever been. I know it wasn't easy. The rehab. Relearning everything." Gunnar squeezed his shoulder. "What I'm saying, T, is that you're gonna get through this because you have a deep well of inner strength and you're a fighter. Always have been."

Theo inhaled, glad of the assurance from this man he'd always looked up to. Since Gunnar's acquisition, Theo had been holding back on getting in the weeds with the guy, realizing that his friend needed space to adjust to being back in the pro mix. "G-Man, I really missed you. Sorry I didn't reach out sooner."

"You were in rehab," Gunnar said gruffly. "Had enough on your plate."

Theo could have made more of an effort once he was

back on his feet, but by then, Gunnar was skinning squirrels in a cabin somewhere in Bumblefuck, New Hampshire. Or so went the rumor.

"It's great to have you here in Chicago. For real."

"Thanks, man. And anything you need, come to me."

THEO'S EXPRESSION when Dante announced he and Cade were going to be parents had cracked Elle's heart in half. In it she saw censure, but mostly hurt. Hurt that she'd caused by denying him the chance to do what Theo did best: be the hero. He was happy about the baby, and his inability to celebrate that with the full range of Theo-joy was killing him.

She'd looked away, unable to face him and what she was doing to him. When she turned back, he was gone.

She had to find him. "Back in a sec," she said to Jordan, who wasn't paying attention anyway, too agog at the juicy news stories her reporter eyeballs were witnessing in the flesh.

Outside the lounge, she found Theo talking to someone oddly familiar.

"Hi, there."

"Hello, again," the stranger said.

Theo divided a look between them. "You know each other?"

"Not really," Elle said. "We exchanged a few words in the press box a while ago."

"Gunnar Bond," he said, which sounded like a superhero. "I'm one of Theo's teammates."

"Oh, I thought you were a reporter. I'm Elle Butler. Nice to meet you officially." She turned to Theo. "You okay?"

"Just taking a break."

"All right then, I'll leave—"

"See you later, Kershaw. Elle." Gunnar left, walking down the corridor instead of going back into the lounge.

"Is he okay?"

"Not sure," Theo said, staring after him. "I don't think he's used to being around people yet."

"Why?"

"Long story. So what's up?" It sounded sharp.

She leaned her back against the wall, so they were side-by-side. "Great news about your buddies, huh? Sounds like babies are the must-have accessory this year."

"What? Oh, yeah."

It was weird to see Theo so subdued and out of sorts. She needed to be honest—or as honest as she was capable in this moment. "Can I ask you something?"

He looked surprised. "Of course."

"Hockey players move around a lot, get traded, have to settle in a new place at the drop of a hat, right?"

"It's the nature of the job." He frowned. "Is that what's got you so skittish? Are you worried I'll leave you here holding the baby, literally?"

If only that was the problem, but it did bear thinking about. She'd worked hard to exercise some modicum of control over her life, yet here she was subject to the whims of an omnipotent pro-sports franchise. "Theo, lots of things could separate us," she said. "We're not a couple so we're not obliged to be joined at the hip if you're traded out. I won't be following you around like some groupie."

"Hardly a groupie. You're the mother of my kid."

"That's just biology. But this biology has consequences and I'd like to be assured of the logistics up front."

"If I'm traded out, I don't have much say in that."

She moved closer, her arm touching his, seeking the

words to make him understand something she wasn't quite sure she understood herself. "I know. I need assurance that you won't try to take the hatchling with you if you have to move. You have money and fame, and with that comes influence and a massive organization behind you. I don't want to be a cog in the machine of your life. I've been there before with my family. A pawn, no agency. This baby—he or she belongs to us both. I know I might not be a good mom at first but I'll learn. I'll eat better, I'll read every article you send, watch every video. I will, Theo."

Her voice pitched higher, sounding like it came from someone else. Someone scared. Until she'd started this line of thought, she hadn't even realized it was a concern. That the threat of Theo taking the baby was possible or that she'd care so much.

He'd be a better parent, anyway. He's not descended from criminals.

"Elle." He placed his hands on her upper arms. The scent of him both buttressed and made her swoon. He smelled like naughty nights and dumb jokes and the guy who had all the answers.

She wanted more naps with this guy.

"This is a joint operation," he said. "If I have to trade out, it won't be for a while. As long as I'm valuable to the team, I'll be here, and as soon as they decide my value lies elsewhere, then we'll talk about what that means for us as a family. We won't be a traditional one living under one roof but in every other way, we will be. In every way that counts, we will be. Decisions made as a team."

"A team," she repeated, the word sounding foreign on her lips. Teamwork was the foundation of her time in the army, but in her personal life, she'd always been more of a lone wolf because her original pack was so dysfunctional.

"Yes, you and me. Together for the baby."

Ah, yes. The baby.

"I know you have goals—school, dreams, a life you want to start. I can't stop you from moving somewhere else or taking our kid with you. But I want to be part of my kid's life. I won't be one of those deadbeat dads who only sees their kid twice a year or not all."

His vehemence about deadbeat dads struck home—she'd heard that before and it made him sound like a different person. But mostly she noted that it was assumed she'd have primary custody. Whatever happened, she would be in charge of where they—she and their baby—lived.

Imagine what her family would say to that. *Bleed. Him. Dry.*

The trust he was placing in her not to do that—because she wouldn't, she couldn't—was shocking. But of course, he didn't know what she was truly capable of.

"I think I've been in denial," she said. "Trying to act like this is normal and nothing will change. I thought if I could keep it under the radar for as long as possible, we could maintain some sort of fiction of business-as-usual."

"It's happening, all right. We're having a baby, Ellie." He smiled like this wasn't a disaster, and she smiled, too, because maybe it wasn't. Maybe being shackled to Theo Kershaw wasn't such a terrible, frightening thing, not when she could be pinned in place and bathed in that sunshine grin.

"A baby? You guys are having a baby?"

They turned to find a gaping Erik.

"Another baby?" he repeated with a glance over his shoulder to the lounge he'd just exited.

Theo immediately stepped in front of her. "Listen, Fish, this is not—"

"Hey, guys!" A few more players chose this inopportune time to leave. "There's something in the water. Theo is having a baby, too. With Elle."

Travis Perez, another Rebels player, gave Elle a hard look. She didn't know him well, though he'd always seemed nice enough when he ordered drinks. Now his expression said it all: Gold digger.

So it begins.

"Congrats, man," he said, recovering his composure. Two guys beside him, players she didn't know, grinned and moved forward to shake Theo's hand. Like he'd performed this amazing job impregnating the local bar wench. She stood half-behind him, somewhat protected, but she couldn't stay there forever.

"Listen," Theo said. "We're trying to keep it on the down low for now. Don't want to steal Cade and Dante's thunder. We'd appreciate it if you could keep the lips zippity-zipped until we're ready."

Murmurs of assent went up, and then the guys were gone, leaving Theo and Elle alone.

Theo checked his phone. "I'd say everyone will know in about fifteen minutes."

"Fifteen minutes? But, that's ridiculous."

"They'll use the text chain." His phone buzzed and he winced at what he saw. "Yep, there we go."

"I thought you said we had fifteen minutes!"

He frowned. "You knew it would have to come out eventually. What I really need to do is call Aurora because she will flay me alive if she doesn't hear it from me. You probably should tell your parents, too, if you haven't already."

"I thought we had more time." Before the vultures descended—and she didn't mean the press, his fans, or his grandmother.

"Are you really that ashamed to be connected to me?"

Her pulse rate spiked. "What? Why would you think that?"

Discomfort lined his handsome brow. "I know I'm loud and obnoxious, not what you had in mind at all. Just a dumb jock—"

She grabbed his arm. "I don't think that at all! You're amazing, Theo. And you're going to be an amazing dad. I've been trying to protect you from ..." She rubbed her forehead, searching for the words to describe her motivation for secrecy. "I would never be ashamed to be connected to you, but you might be if you knew more about me."

"What does that mean?"

The lounge door opened again and Hunt popped his head out. "Hey, you two."

Theo did that protective move again when really Hunt was the last person she needed protecting from. "Hunt," he said tersely.

"Where is he? Where the hell is my bro-in-expectation?"

Hunt stepped aside to allow someone else to charge into the corridor: Cade Burnett, one of the fathers of Violet's baby.

The Texan's hazel eyes fired into whiskey golden bursts on seeing Theo. "Are you kidding me, Kershaw? You and Elle are taking this magical fucking journey with us?" He grabbed Theo by the shoulders and shook him. "Why didn't you say anything?"

Without waiting for an answer, he shoved Theo aside and wrapped Elle in a hug. "This is awesome! Congrats, I'm thrilled for you both. And Violet will have someone to commiserate with."

A pregnancy gripe circle. Yay.

Despite Elle's reservations, it felt lovely to be welcomed

with such generosity. She glanced at Theo, who was watching her closely. His expression was hard to read, which was odd because he was usually so open. He was probably wondering what the hell he'd gotten himself into.

"Thanks, Cade," he said, switching on the bro-charm. "We didn't want to crash your party."

"Bullshit. Man, the team's PR is going to make a five-course meal out of this. When are you due?"

"Mid-September."

"We're at the beginning." Cade's eyes were bright as buttons as he split a gaze between Elle and Theo. "Just in time for the new season. We'll be setting up a Rebels daycare next."

She laughed because it was a cute idea, then caught Hunt's eye. His expression asked, *are you okay*? She smiled to let him know she was, surprised that she meant it. Maybe this wasn't going to be so terrible after all, especially if she was part of the Rebels family.

That's what these people were to each other, a family bonded by friendship, respect, and love. Was there really room here for someone like her?

Cade gripped Theo's shoulder. "Come in and celebrate with us, the both of you. Plenty of cake to go around."

Theo opened his mouth, and Elle knew what he was going to say. *We're keeping it quiet. Carry on without us. Maybe later.* All the excuses he'd been making for her.

Her excuses.

Time for her to own this. She got there first. "We'd love that. Thanks, Cade."

And then she took Theo's hand and led him back into the lounge.

18

@TheTheoKershaw Baby Daddy in the house! Oh, yeah. Won our first playoffs game which is awesome, but ... BABY! #RebelsBaby #PlayoffsBaby #TheoBaby #DinoBaby

"Hey, guys! It's been a whirlwind 24 hours. If you haven't heard, I'm having a baby!"

Elle put her hand over her mouth, wishing she could put it over his. Theo was back to his daily Instagram live check-ins and doing what he did best: blabbing for his country.

"Yeah, I don't know how I managed to keep quiet about it because as you've probably figured out, I'm not known for being quiet about anything! I'm a total attention ho but Eh —the mother of our baby—she's a private person so I'm hoping people can respect that."

The comments section was filled with affirmations and congratulations. A couple of them observed that his baby mama was so lucky to have Theo as her main squeeze, and Elle had to admit: if she was going to get knocked up by anyone, Theo Kershaw wasn't such a bad prospect.

Prospect. That sounded a little too close to "mark."

The guys had been mostly discreet at the impromptu reveal party, but it wasn't enough. She woke up to several text messages from Jordan telling her that her name was all over social media. No pics, but everyone was speculating on who she was and how she'd managed to snag a fine piece like Theo.

Her phone rang with a number she didn't recognize, but as the location ID read Saugatuck, MI—Theo's home town —she answered. Someone was already talking. Loudly.

"ELLE? Elle Butler, this is Aurora! THEO'S GRANDMOTHER!"

"Oh, hello, Mrs. Kershaw."

"Please! There isn't nor ever has been a Mr. Kershaw. It's Aurora. Now I KNEW there was something about you."

Elle's muscles solidified to cement. "You did?"

"As soon as my Theo mentioned you at the holidays I knew you were THE ONE."

"Um, Mrs. K –I mean, Aurora, this wasn't planned and we're really just trying to take it a day at a time. Theo's great. Lovely, really, but we're not a couple in the traditional sense..." Where was she going with this?

Aurora picked up the slack. "I just want you to know that you are part of THE FAMILY. Now, what about your parents?"

A chill seeped into her bones to go with the cement muscles. "My parents?"

"When can we meet them? Theo says he hasn't had a chance to talk to them yet."

"Oh, they're ... traveling right now? On business." Probably true, they were always moving from Point A to Point B to bilk someone out of their life's savings. "They're really pleased."

"OF COURSE THEY ARE! Maybe they can come to

Chicago for one of Theo's games. Okay, I have to go. Someone just came in and he looks like he's got cash to spend on that nice print of the lighthouse surrounded by ferrets. I'll send a care package of lotions and brownies soon and we'll set up a weekly—maybe twice-weekly?—check-in. SOUND GOOD?"

"Uh, okay."

Hurricane Aurora rang off. Damn. Elle was going to have to get her story ducks in a row regarding her parents and why they would always be traveling. She also needed a backup plan for if/when Theo found out about them.

She checked her oh-shit fund, knowing already the balance to the penny and knowing also that it was not enough to start over. Would it ever be now that she had another mouth to feed? And if the kid had Kershaw's appetite ... No matter what happened, Theo would provide for the baby but she refused to take more than her due.

Her phone rang again. A dreadful shiver slithered down Elle's spine as Amy's silvery laugh echoed in her ear. "Elle-Belle, you naughty girl."

"Hey, what's up?"

"You little minx. So that's what you've got going on. And I thought you were the good twin."

"This isn't a con, Amy. This is a real situation where I accidentally became pregnant."

"Maybe you didn't plan it," she said, her voice thick with disbelief, "but now it's happened. How are the financial arrangements?"

"Anything Theo provides will be in trust for the baby." She assumed. "No one will be making a profit from my kid, okay?" She was surprised at the titanium tone her voice had taken on.

"Okay, calm down, preggo. Sheesh, you sound deranged over there. When can I visit?"

"What? No, you can't."

"Oh." Amy actually sounded hurt. "I thought you wanted to mend fences but I'm guessing you don't need us now you have your new, rich friends."

She didn't need the drama. Surely, Amy saw the difference.

"He doesn't know about any of you."

"That we exist or that we exist by our wits?"

Her family loved to talk about their business as if it was a noble calling. "I'm not letting you get your hooks into him, Amy. He's too nice."

"Ha! You like him. You actually like him!" Her smug tone indicated such an accidental slipup would *never* have happened to a pro like her.

"I do like him. A lot." Call it hormones or weakness or just needing to be honest with the person who knew her best, but she had to share her feelings with someone. "He's an incredible guy. And if he finds out who I am, where I come from, he's going to think I tricked him, Ames. He's going to be really hurt and I can't do that to him."

"Aw, Elle," Amy said sympathetically. "He doesn't have to know anything. I'll stay out of your hair and I'll do my best to keep George and Dee away. Tell them you're working the con and it's better you do it alone. They'll be so proud of you."

Great, exactly the sort of pride she wanted to instill in her parents. *Here's your trophy for best little scam artist, darling!*

"I still plan to earn my way and not take a dime of Theo's money."

"Hmm, pity, because I could do with some of that cash right now."

"Ill-gotten gains running low?"

"Must be nice to land in a big pile of legit money *by accident*." She snatched a breath. "Sorry, I'm just jealous. Don't worry, I'll figure it out. I always do."

There it went again, that ping on Elle's twin radar telling her something was wrong—other than the usual.

"Amy, are you in trouble?"

"I *am* trouble, Elle-Belle," she said in her sexy vixen voice.

"Seriously, what's going on?"

"Oh, Jackson's people aren't too happy with me."

Elle had to dig deep. "Jackson? Is that the guy you were going to marry? What do you mean they're not happy?"

"They're connected, Elle. And they didn't like being made fools of. I've been lying low but I'm not sure how long that's going to work."

Her sister sounded worried. Amy *never* sounded worried. "Connected? Like ..." She lowered her voice, though she was alone in her apartment. "Mob connected?"

"Not that bad. Just a little import/export stuff. They've got a nice front with their shipping company but it turns out they're not as understanding as I'd hoped they'd be. And with you blabbing the family's secrets—"

Elle's stomach dropped. "Hey, wait a second. Don't think you can blame me for trying to scam the wrong people." The prospective groom had seemed so nice when she met him, a really sweet guy. It was why Elle had butted in. His family were some sort of criminal enterprise? "That mark was not our kind of people. He was too nice for you."

"You don't think I know that? He's not in deep with all

that but his family is. And they're not pleased that we made their baby boy look like a fool."

Her skin felt clammy, her head spun. "Are you lying, Amy? Is this just a way of getting Theo to cough up something for the cause?"

"No! You think I'd lie about this? I've been totally downplaying it with Mom and Dad so they won't worry. Not like they would, hyenas that they are. And I'm not asking you to pump the jock for cash."

Guilt pinged her. "I'm sorry, Ames."

Her sister heaved a sigh of discontent. "Don't worry about me. I'll do my best to keep George and Dee out of your business. And, Elle?"

"What?"

"Congratulations. You're going to be a great mom." She hung up.

Would she be a great mom? Only if she could continue to keep her before-Theo life separate from her present. Her parents had yet to check in, which meant they were scheming their best play. Amy might be able to hold them at bay for a while but soon they'd turn up like the bad pennies they were. Angling for box seats, special treatment, a place to stay so they could be close to their future grandchild. Then they would insinuate themselves into Theo's life, gaining his trust, eventually asking that he help out with this debt here, invest in that scheme there. Theo would want to do the right thing by his baby's grandparents.

She needed to come clean and head the problem off before it blew up in her face.

~

THEO SHIFTED his big frame on the tiny blue sofa. Carefully,

because he suspected that any sudden moves might send it
—and him—crashing to the plush carpet beneath his size
twelve feet.

Seated beside him, taking up approximately three
square inches of space and looking like she could buy and
sell him fifty times over, Harper held up a tall fancy pot with
blue flowers on it. "Coffee, Theo?"

"Sure, Ms. Chase. Thanks."

"It's Harper. I'm on a first-name basis with your grandmother after all."

He grimaced, not liking where this was going. Aurora
was none too pleased to be out of the loop. Then she called
Harper and started in on her—as if the team's CEO was to
blame for one of her players getting a girl knocked up and
not telling his grandmother. Now he was seated in the woman's
swanky office at Rebels HQ after a royal summons.

"I didn't tell Aurora or anyone because Elle wanted to
keep it under wraps for a while." Forever, if she had her way.
"Sorry you got caught in the crossfire."

"Sugar?"

"No, just a little cream."

Harper handed off the coffee on a saucer. Milano
cookies were whispering sweet nothings of temptation, but
he didn't indulge.

"Don't worry about your gran calling as much as she
does. I think she's glad you're back in the game, so to speak,
even if the consequences are not what she imagined."

He pinched the bridge of his nose. "Why do I get the
impression you're not just talking about hockey?" At Harper's grimace, he blew up. "You mean she talks to you about
my sex life?"

"You're her pride and joy, Theo, and she wants to think
you're happy, healthy, and—"

"Tapping plenty of ass." He winced, expecting his face would lock in that position by the time this heart to heart was done. "Sorry, that was out of line."

She waved it off, a gesture that said nothing could faze her. No doubt she'd heard it all. "Why I really asked you to stop by this morning is to let you know that we're here to support you and Elle throughout the pregnancy. I know it's really none of my business but someone said it was a surprise to you both?"

He nodded, and she smiled sympathetically. "The team's here for you. And with Violet in the same boat, we can share resources. We want to help."

So did his gran. He thought back to the conversation he'd had with her at two in the morning. She'd been upset not to hear it sooner but mostly she wanted to be sure he was okay with it because it brought up memories. Of Candy, and the guilt he still carried for not being the best son he could be when he found out who she really was to him.

He wouldn't let Elle or the baby down.

"I appreciate it, Ms. Ch—uh, Harper. Right now, Elle's biggest concern is that certain business decisions made by Rebels management might affect the ability to see my kid."

Her shrewd green eyes narrowed. "Are you angling for trade gossip, Kershaw?"

"Who, me?"

She smiled. "You're safe for another year, at least. You bring something special to the team and our defense wouldn't be the same without you. Now if Elle's worried about you being traded does that mean you're not a couple?"

"Right. Is that a problem?"

She considered that. "Not for us, though team PR or your publicist would probably prefer if you were. You might not think it but players are role models for younger fans. As

long as you're doing the right thing by Elle and your baby,
Theo—and everyone sees that—then your love life is not
our concern."

The right thing. There were several ways to parse that.

Harper went on. "Now if you need any of the team's
professional services, in particular, legal, then don't hesitate
to ask."

"You sound like Tommy. He'll be here soon to stick his
nose in."

"It's what agents do. Just make sure that you protect
yourself, Theo."

Did everyone think he was some sort of putty-hearted
dick-on-two-legs who couldn't spot a gold digger at fifty
paces?

"I don't need protection, Harper. I can handle myself and
I'm going to do right by Elle and my kid."

She studied him for a long beat. "Never doubted it for a
second."

Three hours later, Theo was faced with another person
in his life acting like they knew best.

"She's late."

Theo checked his phone to verify his agent's statement.
Elle was indeed late, but he'd dropped this meeting on her
last minute.

After their conversation last night, he'd recognized that
she was feeling insecure. He wanted to keep her calm and
centered during the pregnancy, so he'd decided to be more
up front about the legalities. Surely she wouldn't object to
ensuring their baby's future was financially secure.

They were meeting in a fancy law office in downtown
Riverbrook. His agent, Tommy Gordon, had flown in unin-
vited from New York to make sure it was all above board,

and right now he was fidgeting two seats down at the conference table.

"A hundred bucks says she brings her own lawyer," Tommy said.

"What's your problem, man?" The minute Tommy heard that Elle was pregnant, he'd gone into shark mode.

"You think you're the first player who's found himself in this situation? You should be waiting for a paternity test."

"The baby's mine."

"You don't know that." Tommy tapped the table with one of his manicured fingernails. "You're an athlete in your prime, a rich mark, and now you're handcuffed to this woman unless we can think of a way to uncuff you."

Theo shook his head. "Not everyone is trying to rook me, or you, for that matter. Have a little faith."

"You won't even let me do a search."

"Like that stopped you."

Tommy grinned, which would probably look attractive to women susceptible to well-dressed reptiles.

"Of course I did. Unlike you, I care about where my clients' money is going." His grin faded. "Didn't find anything useful. No college. Four years in the army, honorably discharged. Before that she waited tables at a couple of places in Miami."

She'd never mentioned living in Florida. Wasn't her family from New York? Theo's curiosity burned bright, and his silence rewarded him with more revelations from his tight-fisted agent.

"Mother and father run a financial consulting firm in Long Island. Twin sister is—"

"Twin sister?"

Tommy's eyes ignited with the pleasure of discovery. "And why don't you know this?"

Why, indeed. "I know she has a sister but she gave me the impression they're not close." A twin? That seemed like an essential piece of information he should have in his possession.

Unease shivered through him. His kid shouldn't grow up under a cloud of secrets, not knowing where he came from or who his mom or his mom's family was. His gaze flickered to the sheaf of legal documents on the cherrywood table. According to the lawyers, the settlement for their child was generous, but it was just ink on paper. A contract wouldn't tell a kid he was loved.

"Maybe this isn't enough," he said, picking up the papers.

Tommy's eyes flew wide. "Are you kidding? You're settling a fucking fortune on this kid and ..." He waved a hand, searching for the name but not looking disappointed when it refused to come to him.

"Elle. She's carrying my kid, Tommy, so you'd better start remembering her name."

"Sorry." His agent sounded anything but contrite. "So she's carrying your child, but what else do you need to give her?"

"My name." He didn't have that as a kid. His father's name. In fact, he didn't even have his mother's—not really. Not when she'd rather go off partying with her friends than be a mom. Maybe it would have been different if Nick had stuck around. Maybe his mother would have felt like she wasn't alone.

His child wouldn't suffer that fate. He'd make sure of it, and the best way to make sure of it was to offer Elle the kind of security a woman in her precarious position needed.

"I'm going to marry Elle."

19

SHE'D CHOSEN A VERY interesting time to walk into the office. Theo had just announced his intention to marry someone called Elle.

Oh, wait. That was *her* name.

"Sorry I'm late."

Ever the gentleman, Theo stood on hearing her voice. The guy in the sharp navy blue suit remained seated, but one equally sharp look from Theo brought him to his feet.

"Hey there!" Theo said, and her heart melted at his obvious pleasure in seeing her. Maybe it was an act for the suit but she didn't think so. "This is Tommy Gordon, my agent. Tommy, this is Elle Butler."

"Nice to meet you, Elle." It pleased her to no end to hear him practically choking on her name. He shook her hand, the grip warm and firm. Testing. She squeezed and let go.

"So what are you guys talking about?" She raised an eyebrow at Theo.

He turned to the suit. "Could you give us a minute?"

"Might be better if I stayed."

"Thomas, out," Theo said, all steel, and God, was that sexy.

The agent appeared to nonverbally plead with Theo for a split second, though Elle questioned whether he'd ever begged anyone for anything. Maybe the gods to not allow bird crap to fall on his Porsche or a barista to accidentally— or given this guy's attitude, purposely—decaf his triple-shot Americano. His message was clear: *don't let her take you in.*

In that moment, Elle actually respected the suit. Perverse, perhaps, but he was doing his duty, looking out for soft-hearted Theo, and she appreciated that he was in the guy's corner. Theo needed to be protected.

Don't worry, Tommy boy, I'll do my part.

Once his agent had left, Theo took her by the hand and led her to a seat.

She spoke first. "I'm not marrying you."

"Hear me out, Elle-oh-Elle."

She folded her arms to indicate she meant business.

"I told you a little about my mom. How I thought she was my sister when I was growing up."

She nodded.

"When I found out, I felt betrayed. Unwanted. I had Aurora but it wasn't the same. My real mom had been living in the house with me all this time, pretending not to be connected with me, pretending not to be my mom."

Her heart panged for that hurt little boy, but the situations weren't comparable. "Our kid will know who both his parents are, Theo." At least on the face of it. She could never be truly knowable by these people. "Getting married wouldn't change that or make it better. It wouldn't make us love our kid any more."

She touched her stomach. She already adored this child

and a piece of paper or an expensive ring wouldn't change how she felt.

"It's not just about the hatchling," Theo went on. "I want you both to feel supported. I want the world to see I'm there for both of you. Not just with money. Anyone can throw money at a situation, Elle. Sure, it sets my kid up for life but it's not the same. I want him or her to feel we gave it our best shot."

Shock washed over her. He was serious. She'd never seen him so earnest.

The fear she'd heard in her sister's voice was still with her. Marrying Theo would give her a chance to help Amy, but where would it end? And if Theo heard about the kind of people her family were mixed up with ...

She couldn't give in, though the thought of being Theo's wife gave her glorious tingles. For a moment, she let herself imagine, not the paper or the ring, but a true partnership, a meeting of minds, a happily-ever-after.

But nothing good came from a house built on such a rocky foundation. An unplanned pregnancy, a tissue of lies, and parties not even in the same league on either hotness or economic levels.

"Parents don't have to be married to give their kid the best start in life, Theo." Hers were hitched but it certainly didn't make her upbringing in their den of thieves any more stable. "I know you didn't have that, but a ring doesn't fix anything."

She wasn't sure money did, either. How much was he planning to settle on their child? She hoped it was the bare minimum. She hoped it didn't make her feel any guiltier or beholden than she already did.

He cocked his head, waited a beat. "So you're saying no

to my incredibly romantic marriage proposal in this lawyer's office conference room?"

She laughed, glad he could see the ludicrousness of it. "Theo, it's lovely of you to consider it and I understand your reasons. But it's not necessary. We're both going to be here for the sprog and we don't need to be married to each other to do it. This is the twenty-first century, dummy. Now, where do I sign?"

His brows slammed together. "You should get a lawyer to read it so you feel protected."

Huh, like she was paying another leech to review what she could see with her own eyes. She picked up the papers and started flipping through them, looking for numbers. "You're setting aside some green for the kid. That's all I need to—holy fucking hell!" Her eyes bugged out. "That's a lot of money for gold-plated rattles." Anxiously she scanned the rest, finally landing on a financial statement attached to the end.

Wuthering Christ. Her lungs went on hiatus and she had to cough to get all her internal organs started again.

"You earn this much money? For playing hockey?" So much for being the redheaded stepchild of pro sports.

"My contract is common knowledge. The rest are endorsements. Underwear, aftershave, skincare, Instagram influencer stuff. It adds up."

She swallowed, but the lump in her throat refused to budge. "Theo, you're a millionaire. Multiple times over." And his skin really glowed. That shit must work.

"Have you been living under a rock?"

"No, just the army, and I don't keep up with the sports pages." She put the contract down, feeling as though it had burned her fingertips. Her blackhearted soul.

That he was richer than the average guy she understood,

but she'd had no idea that he had this much wealth, and now it looked like she'd landed this huge fish through ... carelessness!

Fucking army-issue condoms. *Never mind funding for better armor for combat units, senator. Think about the unplanned pregnancies!*

She should tell him everything. About her parents. About Amy. About how Tommy the asshole agent was actually his best friend in the world right now.

"I don't want your money, Theo. I appreciate the amount you're willing to settle and I'll happily take maybe, a quarter of that amount for Baby T because I'll be contributing as well."

"You want less?"

"This is too much."

He blew out a breath, shaking his head in wonder. "My lawyer put in the legally-obligated minimum and I tripled it. Can we just compromise on that? I'll be stashing money in an account for the kid anyway. Whether you touch it or not, you don't really get a choice."

Just tell him. He should know the nest of vipers he's falling into.

"Theo, we need to talk."

"Isn't that what we're doing?" He chewed his lip. "Okay, there's something else in the contract. Something to give you ... an out."

Her body chilled. "An out?"

"You said before that this kid was going to change your life. Tie you down. Upend your plans. So, if it gets to be too much, you can bail. I told you about my mother. Well, I found out when I was eleven and I was pretty hard on her."

Bail? Her heart bled for him. "You were eleven. You were hurt."

He looked like that excuse wouldn't cut it. "She didn't want to be a mom, and I get that not everyone has it in them. I didn't understand it at the time, but I do now. Hindsight and all that jazz. If you want to surrender parental rights, you can do that. I won't judge you, Elle. I just want to you to be happy."

He meant it. "And who the hell would look after the baby when you're on the road?"

"Aurora? She'd love to have the little ankle-biter around the house. And the Tarts would be all over it." He patted her arm, kind of condescendingly, she thought. "I just want you to know you have options."

A different sort of panic washed over her, her own words coming back to haunt her. He wanted to take her baby away from her. That agent douche probably put him up to it.

Was Aurora in on it? Was that why she wanted to do her weekly—no, twice-weekly—check-ins? Maybe they were a test to see if she was mother material.

Oh, God. If Theo found out about her family, about whatever shit her sister was tits-deep in, it would be evidence against her in some custody suit. If he knew the swamp she came from, she'd be thrown right back into it.

Her hand fell to her stomach, a protective grab of her rights and the rights of her baby. Too many people wanted her to fail—even Theo, though he didn't realize it. He thought he was doing the right thing in giving her the option to bow out gracefully. He was thinking of the baby.

This was a complete disaster-piece.

But it didn't have to be.

She might not have Theo, but she had this baby. Theo couldn't learn about her family origins, which meant she needed to become more serious about this. Too much was on the line.

"I want this baby." While not the first time she'd thought it, it was definitely the first time she'd said it aloud in such definitive terms. Before, it had been a "hey, let's do this, fellow baby maker." Now, she needed to be clear(er) about her intentions.

Theo must have recognized something in her tone. He didn't mock or make a joke. He merely murmured, softly yet firmly, "I do, too."

It felt like they were making a vow. Like this was the marriage ceremony he'd asked for earlier and they'd just committed to this life-changing thing. Not only a commitment to the baby but to each other.

I'll be the best mom I can be, those words said.

And in his eyes, she read his intent: *I'll do everything in my power to be a dad that steps up.*

Theo Kershaw had never been sexier to her, though his "offer" to give her an out should have made her furious. Theo saying "I do," even if it was in relation to his kid rather than her was sweet, powerful, and hot. Oh, how she wished her own father had cared even one iota this much instead of seeing her and Amy as pawns in his schemes.

Recalling her father set her mind back on track. She touched the legal documents.

"You'd better have something about a paternity test in here."

"You won't take one?"

"You need to be *insisting* I take one, or no dice." She knocked on his forehead. "Don't be a handsome baby, Theo. Listen to your lawyers. Listen to that shark in Armani, who is doubtless pacing the hallways out there, wringing his baby-soft hands, praying that you'll come to your senses and not get taken for a ride."

He scoffed. "You're not taking me for a ride."

"And you know this how? Because my pie-hole is mouthing the words? You have all this money and I see you buying rounds for strangers at the bar and handing over checks for charities that probably don't exist."

"It's just money."

Said the guy who had so much he could settle the GDP of a small country on a baby.

She waved the contract between them. "Can you bring in one of your lackeys so we can make a few changes to this?" The first thing would be the removal of this "bail-out" clause.

Poor Theo looked whiplashed. Good. He needed some sense knocked into him.

Looked like she'd have to be the one to do it.

20

@ChiRebels vs. @BostonCougars in Beantown in the 4th game of the series. Battle of the two best defenses in the league. @HockeyGrrl and @ChiSportsNet have got you covered.

ONE OF THE things about impending motherhood is that it's supposed to make you more, well, maternal. Or, that's what Elle had assumed before she walked into Bren and Violet's house to watch an away game on TV. Now she was questioning this supposed wisdom because: So. Many. Children.

Rather than spending the night with drunken fan boys at the bar, she was hanging with the WAGs and their genetically-blessed offspring.

"Ola! You made it." Violet ushered her inside, pulling off her jacket as she did so.

"I brought cookies." She'd stopped at a gourmet bakery and spent a fortune because she suspected Oreos wouldn't cut it with this crew.

"Fantastic. You didn't have to, but that's really nice."

A dark-haired boy of about four or five—maybe ten?

Elle had no idea—crashed through the entryway followed by two lurching blond girl toddlers. Baby zombies.

"Aunt Vi, they won't leave me alone," the first kid said, sounding very put out.

"Can you blame them, Max? You're very handsome."

Max sighed in acceptance of this undeniable fact while one of the vixens grabbed his hand. "I want to show you something," she intoned like Dracula's Bride.

"Satanic etchings?" Elle murmured, drawing a laugh from Violet.

A tall, curvy woman appeared from another room, all smiles. Like so many of these people, she looked gorgeous and familiar. Elle needed flash cards. "Hi, there, I'm Addison."

"Mom!" Max attacked the woman and clung to her thigh. He gestured to her to hunker down to listen to his whispered concerns.

"You can hang with Franky," Addison assured him. "She said she has a new slug to show you."

Max beamed. Apparently slugs beat out the forced attentions of a couple of aggressive romantic interests every time.

A couple of minutes later, Elle had been given the brief tour of the beautifully-appointed house in Lake Forest where Violet lived with Bren and his two teenage daughters. In the kitchen, Olympic medal-winning hockey player Isobel Chase was taking out what looked like pizza bagels. For the kids, probably. Elle eyed them enviously.

Isobel removed her oven glove and thrust out her hand. "Hi, Elle, I've seen you around, but great to meet you officially. You're brave to show your face at one of these shindigs."

"She was in Special Forces with Hunt," Violet said, while

she handed Elle a ginger ale from the fridge. "Think she can handle what we're bringing."

Elle's modesty kicked in. "I wasn't in Special Forces, but I did communications and support stateside."

"Hey, don't downplay it," Addison said. "That's the kind of stuff that saves lives. So, if you don't mind me asking, what's your bra size?"

A sip of ginger ale went the wrong way down Elle's throat.

"Jesus, Addy? Already?" Isobel shook her head. "Give her a chance to settle in." To a coughing Elle, she said, "Addison has her own lingerie line, so that's her way of making friends."

"Selling me bras?" She recognized her now. Addison Williams, famous lingerie model and designer, was married to right-winger Ford Callaghan.

"Oh, I was going to give you something pretty, as a gift. We have a new line in sexy nursing bras, too, for when the time comes. Congrats, by the way."

"Thanks. I'm usually 36C but lately ..." She gestured to her chest to indicate that all bets were off.

"Oh, I hear you. Mine exploded when I was pregnant with Max and the things nursing did to my nipples..."

Isobel made a sound of disgust. "Do you mind? We're eating here. Have a pizza bagel, Elle."

Elle didn't need to be invited twice. Observations about pregnancy-ravaged nipples wouldn't ruin her appetite.

"Okay, time out on the crusty nipple and loose vag talk," Violet said with a grin of solidarity at Elle. "Puck's about to drop, so I'm going to check on the kids to make sure no one is bleeding, on fire, or married against their wishes."

"Poor Max," Addison said. "Popular like his dad."

Bren's daughters, Cat and Franky were babysitting so the

adults could watch the game and swear with abandon. Ten minutes into the first period, and the Rebels were already down two goals.

"Nice to see Gunnar's getting some ice time," Isobel said. "I hope he can get back to a hundred per cent."

Gunnar Bond, scarred and bearded brute, press box savior. "What's his story? Injured?"

"He lost his family a couple of years ago," Addison said. "Wife and twins in a car crash. He took some time off to recover, but how do you get over that?"

Everyone allowed themselves a moment of silence to echo those sentiments. Something Gunnar had said to Elle that first time she met him replayed in her brain. *I recognize the signs.* He'd known from one look that she was pregnant.

That poor man.

"Kershaw's off his game tonight," Isobel mused.

"Yeah, I wonder what's up," Addison said.

Three sets of eyes turned to Elle.

"He was fine the last time we talked." She bit her lip, slightly embarrassed. "And if something was bothering him, he probably wouldn't tell me."

"Theo?" Violet smirked. "Considering he never shuts up, I'd think he couldn't help spilling all his problems. He's so honest on his Instagram. I find out more about the team's psychology there than talking to anyone else."

Was he so honest? Elle wondered if that was true. Theo had said it was an act for his fans—some of it was his natural good humor but he wasn't as open a book as everyone seemed to think.

"He asked me to marry him and I said no." Elle couldn't believe the words had dropped fully-formed from her mouth.

"What?"

"Are you kidding?"

"No way!"

"He only asked because he thought it was the right thing to do. He's kind of sweet and old-fashioned. We're not even a couple—like that."

"You think that's what bothering him—your rejection?" Isobel's gaze was suspicious.

"I doubt it. He laughed it off. Even he knew it was silly." Didn't he?

This morning he'd sent a video of a monkey washing a cat with the caption: *Who needs parenting classes when we have YouTube?* He'd checked in by text when he arrived in Boston, though she'd never asked him to do that, and insisted on a recounting of what she'd had for lunch.

"Nice to be asked, though," Violet commented, her sharp green eyes missing nothing.

"Even when it's out of obligation?" Elle knew Theo's history, how his mother had kept her identity from him, how his father didn't want to know him. He was determined to be the opposite of a sperm donor and it colored every interaction between them. Not trustworthy by nature, Elle was always going to look askance at any offer like that. Theo wasn't looking for a bride. His interest in Elle was half-sexual, all paternal—meaning the baby was the prize.

"Maybe there's more to it," Addison said. "Solid relationships have been based on less."

"Like anonymous mutual orgasms on adjoining hotel balconies with the hot stranger next door?" Isobel offered a pointed look at Addison.

Elle's jaw dropped. "Excuse me?"

Addison flushed, but recovered enough to tell the story of how she'd met Ford, a tale right out of high-quality porn.

The first period ended, the Rebels still two goals in the

hole. Addison went to check on the kids, Isobel opened her iPad to analyze the game's plays, which left Elle to help Violet with the next round of snacks in the kitchen.

"This was really nice of you to ask me over even though I'm not officially one of the WAGs."

Violet's expression was kind. "What's official? A ring? I think a bun in the oven is about as official as it gets."

Something about Violet gave Elle hope that maybe she could make it through this. She got the impression that the youngest Chase sister was once as much an outsider as Elle herself. "Theo said you didn't grow up with your sisters. That you didn't even know about them until a few years ago."

"Oh, I knew about them because I knew about Cliff— that's our dad. But he wasn't interested so I didn't connect with my half-sisters until after he died. They'd found out a couple of years before and Harper tried to make the effort but I wasn't up to building bridges. And when I did come visit, I only stayed because Cliff's will required I pitch in with running the team to get my cut of the inheritance. I mean, me running a hockey team. Laughable!" She shook her head, amused at the memory. "I didn't need a new family and frankly, I felt kind of guilty because my mother had gotten pregnant on purpose."

Elle froze. "Are you kidding?"

"No! Here I was, ready to collect, and I had to get to know the marks."

"Did they know about that? About your mom's plan?"

"Eventually. I felt guilty, so I told them. But really I was telling them to make them turn on me. I didn't like how much I was falling for them. For Cade. For Bren. For his girls." She smiled. "You know how sometimes you're not sure you deserve to be in the place you've ended up in, especially because it feels too right? And all your life, your instincts have been out of whack so you can't trust them?"

Hell, did she. She nodded.

"That's how it felt. Like I was in the right place, with the right people, in love with the right man, but I didn't trust it. Sometimes we don't want to believe the good when it feels too perfect."

"Waiting for the other shoe to drop." Elle knew what that was like. That draft on the back of her neck was the ghost of her past catching up to her. Trusting that this might be her future—that Theo would be around for the long haul —required more faith than she was capable of conjuring.

"Yup. It's the worst feeling in the world—uncertainty."

It was up there, but Elle could think of worse.

"Game's starting again," Isobel called out.

"Elle," Violet said. "I don't want to force my busybody friendship on you, but you're always welcome to hang out here with me and the girls anytime. I'm not trying to turn you off motherhood—"

"Bit late for that."

She grinned. "But it has its perks, at least in my position as wicked stepmom. And this one ..." She rubbed her stomach. "She'll grow up with Cade and Dante but I want to be part of her life. We're all pretty tight-knit around here, but that doesn't mean we can't add a couple of inches to the Rebels quilt. Theo's one of us, so that makes you one of us."

Elle's chest tightened at the thought of her circle widening. Violet grabbed the tray of cookies, the one Elle had brought. "But like I said, if you feel it's all too much, then just tell me to fuck off. We can be awfully overbearing."

"No, you're all lovely, really. It's just ..." She swiped at a tear. "These hormones."

Violet squeezed her arm. "I know! We're a mess. I really

miss Bren, then when he's here I want to kill him whenever he opens his mouth. And the man hardly speaks. God knows how you're standing to be around Kershaw. Good thing he's pretty."

Elle sniffed. "He's kind of a saint, to be honest. I keep pushing, looking for his limit."

"The men must be tested, their balls of steel forged in the hell-fire of their pregnant womenfolk's fury," Violet intoned before she added with a grin, "Cookie?"

Elle enjoyed the company for the rest of the game, though she wished it could have gone better. The Rebels lost 4-3, putting them behind 3-1 in the series. Afterward, the ladies' phones blew up with texts, the players checking in with their loved ones.

Everyone's phone but Elle's.

Wanting to give them privacy, but really not wishing to stand out like a sore thumb, she stepped into the kitchen and stared at her screen.

So she didn't know anything about hockey. She would probably be the last person Theo would contact for comfort after a hard loss. But that didn't mean she couldn't make the first move.

So far, Theo had been making all the moves.

She hovered over the screen, trying ... just trying.

Bad luck tonight

Sorry you lost

Wow. Bummer, man.

Finally, she settled on: *How are you, Kershaw?*

A few seconds passed, then a few more. Finally the telltale dots of an incoming reply appeared.

And disappeared.

Her phone lit up with Theo's handsome face, a shot of

him grinning with his Santa hat on. She answered with embarrassing haste.

"Hey!"

"You texted, Elle-oh-Elle. You never text first."

"That's not true." It was. "I'm sure I've texted first in the past." She had not.

"Takes a shitty loss to make you come around, I see."

"Sorry about that. The game."

"Well, them's the breaks. We'll get 'em next time, etcetera, etcetera."

That was strangely fatalist. "What's going on?"

There followed a pause, in which she could hear Theo readjusting the phone to his ear. "Ah, nothing. Just in a mood."

He was allowed to have them, of course, and his team had just suffered a stinging defeat. She wanted to be there for him just like he was for her.

"If you want to moan about it, my bar's always open." Her legs and heart, too, if she wasn't careful.

"I'll be fine. This is me we're talking about! So what are you wearing?"

"Really?"

"I just lost a game. It's the least you could do." Another voice echoed close by, and Theo answered with a "yep." "We're heading to the airport now, so I'll take a raincheck on the phone sex. See you tomorrow?"

"Sure. Safe travels."

"Night, Ellie."

21

THE HOCKEY GODS GIVETH, the hockey gods taketh away.

Their season wasn't over—yet. But they'd lost both games in Boston and were on the butt end of a 3-1 score in the series. The Cougars defense was a many-horned beast and Chicago couldn't make enough of an impact to come out ahead. The plane back was quiet, everyone preferring to process the loss in their own way.

"You want to come over for a beer?" Erik asked Theo as they got off the bus in the player's parking lot at Rebels HQ.

It was almost four a.m. but it wouldn't have been the first time Theo'd drowned his game-day sorrows in an early morning booze-up. But right now, he needed something stronger.

He needed Elle.

He wanted to crawl into bed with her and inhale her scent when he buried his nose in the crook of her neck. His memories of that early Christmas morning had fueled plenty of fun-times with his right hand. It wasn't just how good it had felt to slip inside her in the dark. He'd felt connected to her, and he'd thought she felt it, too.

Wishful thinking, said the devil on his shoulder. Without the baby they wouldn't even be talking to each other, even with the mutual orgasms of a few days ago. He'd been given this opportunity to team up with another person, ostensibly for Project Hatchling, but they could be so much more—if she'd only let him in.

"Think I'm going to call it, Fish. I'll see you tomorrow."

Everyone went their separate ways, and Theo drove until he found himself on the main drag in Riverbrook. He parked a block from the Empty Net. The town was quiet—not as silent as Saugatuck—but still barely awake.

He opened up his phone and checked the text he'd received this afternoon from Nick Isner.

Good luck tonight.

Brief and impersonal, yet three words he'd have killed to hear the night before his NHL debut just four years ago. To have heard before his first NCAA game at Vermont. Today those three words had done nothing but throw him off his game in Boston and made him second-guess the most basic of decisions on the ice. Did Bio-Dad really want a relationship after all these years? Theo wasn't sure he had the bandwidth to deal with this right now.

He opened up Instagram and searched for a profile: @Dekeiii. Most kids used Insta for comments or contest entries, but not his half-brother Jason. He actually posted photos. Also, his account was open! Theo really should talk to Nick about that.

The photos here weren't the posed, sanitized family pics that Alderman Nick posted to his Facebook. These were the real thing. Jason scarfing down Gino's East pizza, his face half-covered in sauce. Older brother, Sean, looking like he'd just woken up annoyed. Was that their usual sibling dynamic? A ten-second video of them trying to teach their border collie to jump on his hind legs. Nick appeared at the end, laughing proudly at their efforts.

Theo played that one over more times than was healthy.

It was too late for him and Nick, but he wouldn't mind getting to know his brothers. Maybe they'd enjoy being uncles to the hatchling. While Theo had never felt an absence of love, he wanted his son to have every possible family connection. The more the fucking merrier.

Shutting his phone down, he looked down the street, taking in more details. How long had that light been on in the Empty Net?

He clambered out of his SUV and put his face to the glass windows in the big oak door. What he saw did not please him.

Elle. Dusting liquor bottles. On the top shelf.

The top shelf.

His fists balled and moved toward the door before he realized that pounding the oak might give her a fright and make her fall from the stepstool she was perched on. Instead, he continued to watch, getting angrier and angrier until she finally descended to safety. Then he connected a fist with the door.

She jumped, squinted, and came forward. "Theo?"

"Open up."

She did—a little slower than he'd have liked, but finally that big, wooden barrier was no longer between them. "What are you doing here?"

"What am I doing here? Want to tell me what *you're* doing here at four thirty in the morning?"

She looked over her shoulder for an answer, and not finding one, she faced him again. "I couldn't sleep so I thought I'd do a little cleaning."

"On a ladder where you could just—just—fall off!"

"It's three feet off the ground. Two and a half."

"Are you kidding me with this?"

She tilted her head. "Listen, I know you're upset about the game but—"

"I am not upset about that. I'm upset that the mother of my child is working at all hours on a fucking ladder in this shitty dive bar when she should be getting rest and looking after herself. What did you eat tonight?"

She blinked at him. "Eat?"

"For dinner. What did you eat for dinner?"

"We had snacks at Violet's place. Pizza bagels. Hummus with celery and carrots."

Okay, that was something. "Did you eat all the vegetables?"

"Most of them. Not really a fan of carrots. Theo, you need to stop worrying. Dr. Patel said the baby's fine and everything is developing as expected."

"Does Dr. Patel say anything about how much sleep you're getting or how you're on your feet for ten hours at a time or how dusting bottles of Grey Goose is probably not good for your health?" Or his sanity.

She placed a hand on his arm. "I'm not an invalid, I'm pregnant. And I need to feel I have agency over my body and this situation."

Everyone wanted that, but when a kid was involved, you didn't always get what you wanted. He inhaled a deep breath. Anger leeched out of him, slowly, with curiosity moving in like a gentle wave to replace it. "Is that what the army was like? No agency? Always following people's orders?"

"I didn't mind that. I signed up for that. To give back, to do something good."

He was ready to ask more but for once, she continued

without prompting. "Before, I didn't always feel like I was in control of my decisions. My family has a certain way of doing things. Expectations for how I should contribute." She smiled, beautiful yet forced. "And now, I want to contribute *my* way. Be a good person. Raise a good person."

So she considered herself a bad person? She'd hinted at that before, that she might not be worthy in some way.

"You're going to be a great mom."

Her face crumpled, her eyes filled with tears.

"Ellie." He gathered her into his arms, gratified when she sank into him. For the last couple of months, he'd felt helpless, like all he could do was throw money and smoothies at the situation because she insisted on doing it her way. He had so much more to offer. Comfort. Strength. His body.

Holding her tight yielded a sob against his chest.

"Hey, now, it's okay."

"You—just—got—through—telling—me—I'm—a —screw—up!"

"No, I didn't." He held her back so he could look her in the eye when he asked, "When did I say that?"

She wiped at her eyes, more anger in them now than sorrow. "You accused me of not eating all my vegetables!"

"You're right. I was a jerk."

All the fight seemed to go out of her. "You're too nice, Theo. I really don't deserve you. I mean, look at you. The hottest athlete on the planet. And a decent person, too!"

"You'd rather I was a jerk?"

"It wouldn't hurt. Or if you were a touch less hot."

He thought on it. "You want me to complain about my problems, maybe put on a few pounds. Anything else?"

"A zit might work. Eat more fried foods and do less of the skin care regimen."

He hadn't broken out since he was a teen. He was blessed with beautiful skin that not even a French fry could threaten.

"Not sure I can be less hot but how about I work up the jerk stuff?"

She looked hopeful. "Really?"

He moved in, crowding her against a low table near the bar. "Sorry I'm so handsome." He nuzzled against her temple and whispered, "Sorry I'm so perfect." A nip of her ear sent a shiver through her. "Sorry I'm such a goddamn saint." His lips found a sensitive spot below her chin.

Slowly—so slowly—he worked his sainted way around her jaw, to the corner of her mouth, where he nibbled and sipped. "So. Damn. Sorry." And then he apologized some more with his mouth stamped over hers, contrition in every luxurious swipe of his tongue with hers.

He'd intended—in as far as he was capable of forming intent—to be tender with her. A minute ago, she'd been sobbing, highly vulnerable. Now she was kissing him with a need he felt all the way to his dick.

She pulled back, licking her lips. "A jerk wouldn't apologize. A jerk would just take what he wants."

Parting her thighs with his knee, he stepped between them and dragged her flush against his erection. "Like this?"

Her breath hitched. "Yes. Like that. He'd punish me for ... for not eating my vegetables."

"You naughty girl. I'm going to make you suffer and then I'm going to make you eat ... kale."

He placed a hand over the V of her T-shirt, so his palm covered her upper chest, the heel nestling in her bountiful cleavage. With his other hand, he squeezed her ass and lifted her onto the table.

She moaned, soft and yearning. He cupped the back of her

neck and positioned her for the plundering. She clearly liked the power he exhibited, the jag-off dominance he was showing. He should feel silly but he didn't. It felt good to take control. But then she had a mouth that would make anything feel right.

Her tongue twined with his, and the sweetness of it—of her need for him to be anything less than a gentleman—fired him up. She was looking for less than perfect. He would give her the illusion of it, because it would be perfect all the same.

He yanked down her leggings and flirted with the edges of her panties.

"These come off," he growled.

"They're not ..." she panted. "Sexy."

"I'll decide what's sexy." Who the fuck did she think she was telling him her underwear wasn't sexy? They were currently on her body, next to her skin, standing between him and sweet oblivion ... *nothing* was sexier in this moment.

Except, he must have been rusty because he was having the hardest time de-briefing her. He pulled at them, tugged a little more. No go. "Are these things welded on?"

"They're a bit tight. I've put on weight."

Probably because she hadn't bought any new underwear, given that she was so adamant about not spending a dime on herself or taking his money. Her too-tight, bonded-to-her-skin, chastity-belt underwear was a symbol of everything that was wrong here!

She probably would be happy if he fucked her on this table, then headed out once the deed was done. No after-care. No cuddling. Nothing.

Not on his watch. He pulled back, furious with where his brain had gone.

"What's wrong?"

"We should be in a bed. I should be m—"

"Don't say it," she growled.

"Making love to you. You're the mother of my child, not some floozy in a bar."

She thumped his chest. "I can be both, Theo Kershaw. I can be sexy and wanton and lusty and still be the woman who will give birth to a future hockey champion or maybe a Math nerd or an artist. Who knows? Because people can be multiple things."

She was right. He was overthinking this, trying to be respectful when the most respectful thing he could do was honor her wish to be banged in a bar. Ladies' choice.

"Whatever you want, Ellie."

Her smile was everything and she threw her arms around him. "Tell me what you're going to do, Kershaw."

"I'm gonna fuck you, Ellie. I'm gonna do you so hard you'll see stars. Then you'll beg me to do you again, maybe from behind."

Her mouth hooked up in a mischievous curve. "That dirty mouth suits you, Theo Kershaw. Suits me."

Suits me. Sexier words had never been spoken. That's what he wanted here. To match her well. To be her mate. To exist at her level. And he didn't think he needed to come down to get there because she was already a queen in his eyes.

He let his fingers converse, his mouth lead the way. He rolled down her panties and resituated her on the table. Stepping back, he stripped off his shirt and pulled down his sweats.

She brushed a hand across his abs, then stroked his cock, a long delicious pull. "You're so sexy, Theo. Every morning I look at you on your stupid Insta feed and I can't believe you're real. That this is real."

Ha, knew she was a fan. Digging his fingers into the hem of her T-shirt, he lifted it up and made fast work of her bra. His mouth watered as her breasts spilled free.

"God, your tits are gorgeous, Ellie. I dream about them every night." He cupped one, enjoying the weight of it, the feel of the nipple under his thumb as it hardened to an inviting peak.

He RSVP'ed with a lusty suck.

He coasted a hand down her stomach over the life they'd created until his fingers landed in a thatch of curls. Another couple of inches found her hot and slick.

"Open your legs, Ellie. Give me room to work."

She parted her thighs.

"Wider."

She followed his instructions, giving him the access he craved. He rubbed his dick along the slick seam, watching as it became more and more coated with her desire. Her head leaned on his chest, her gaze locked to the dance below.

"Tell me you want this, Ellie. That you want me."

"Oh, Theo." She sounded sad. "How could you doubt it?"

He wasn't about to unpack that. Everyone had doubts, and while he was sure she was sexually attracted to him, he was looking for more. He wanted *this* to mean *us*.

"Please. I can't take any more." She grasped his ass and guided him to her entrance, then hooked her leg around his hip. With a full stroke, he thrust deep inside.

"Ellie, you're—oh, Christ." That velvet grip tightened around him, milking him good. She tunneled her fingers through his hair, her breath hot and fast against his lips.

He withdrew a couple of inches, every second outside

her torture. Only inside, deep, tight, wet, did he feel at home. Each long, slow, consuming stroke bound him closer and burned away their problems.

She dug her fingers into his ass and he felt her tighten, the moment of her release. He joined her on one final thrust, yelling out his climax and probably cracking a couple of those top-shelf liquor bottles while he was at it.

22

THEO WAS dead to the world, but not to Elle. To her he was very much alive as she took a moment to appreciate the beauty of this naked man in her bed. He'd even unconsciously done a solid for her eyeballs by turning over on his front so she could admire that perfect ass.

So much for her *no sex, it's complicated* rule. Theo's efforts to be a jerk had merely revealed another perfect side to him —his willingness to respect her and give her what she needed right now. She'd tried dragging him down to her level and he'd only succeeded in giving that dirty old level a spit-and-shine.

"Take a picture, it'll last longer." He turned his head, his inky lashes blinking his gorgeous green eyes awake. "Though, my stamina has never been in question."

"Just admiring the view before it's ruined when you open your mouth."

No sooner had she uttered that cheeky retort, Theo had her pinned beneath him. Those pro-athlete reflexes.

"So I should use my mouth for other things." He nibbled

her ear, finding a sweetly sensitive spot she'd never known was so sweet or so sensitive.

"You're in a good mood. Better than when you arrived last night."

"Well, I had reason to be cranky, Ellie. You're going to give me a heart attack before this baby is born."

"I don't mean to be so difficult."

He scoffed, so she pinched his bicep.

"Honestly. I'm just not used to having anyone be so ... kind." The girls last night, the new friends she was making, the man in her bed.

"Well, get used to it. You will be pampered and cosseted and cared for as long as I'm around to do it."

That was all well and good but she didn't want to be a leech. "Kind of goes both ways. Want to tell me what your week's been like?"

"We're one game from being bounced from the playoffs and last night I played like shit."

"That's all?"

"Isn't that enough? Then there's my constant state of arousal because my baby mama is so damn sexy and I've been a good boy keeping my hands off. Mostly."

"Theo." She stroked his perfect cheekbone and rubbed a thumb along his full bottom lip. A Theo move. "You've listened to every one of my gripes. Tell me what's going on. Really. Last night you seemed more out of sorts than usual."

She watched as he waged some internal battle. Finally, he said, "A few weeks ago, I talked to my dad for the first time in seven years, and yesterday he texted me before the game."

Not expecting that. "Really?"

He blew out a breath and rolled off her, pulling the sheet over his half-mast erection.

"I told you how he didn't want to know me. He's aware I exist but he's not interested in any relationship with me. The first time I met him was just after I got into college on my hockey scholarship. I'd done this cool thing. Was pretty proud of myself. I wasn't looking for money or anything. I wanted to reach out to him once I had something to show him. My talent."

Her heart melted for him, then and now. As if Theo the great kid wasn't enough, he had to bring gifts to the reunion party with his asshole sperm donor.

"What happened? Back when you met him?"

"I went to see him in his offices here in Chicago. He's a lawyer, but he was about to make a bid for alderman. He said he didn't think it was a good time, he wasn't sure if it would ever be a good time. The love child showing up on his doorstep wasn't the best optics. It hurt, but I moved on."

She cupped his jaw. "And then he got back in touch? After all this time?"

"He texts every now and then, just to let me know he's alive. When I was in recovery from brain surgery, he sent a fruit basket and a get well card." He rolled his eyes. "Then, a couple of months ago, one of his kids showed up for a tour of the Rebels locker room."

Her jaw dropped. "No way!"

"Yes! I couldn't believe it, Elle. It was like looking at me when I was his age, but he had no clue. His mom was there and *she* had no clue. The kid entered some contest because he's a fan. Of me."

"That's ..." Wild.

"Right? The next day, Nick called and practically accused me of setting a trap for his kid. Like I had some say in who gets picked. That's what my publicist is for!" He looked away, clearly embarrassed that he was so emotional about it. But that's what she loved about Theo. No one would ever accuse him of being a brooding automaton. "Said maybe it's time we got together. I shut it down because ... I don't know. It felt off, like he's doing it because his worlds are colliding and his hand is being forced, not because he really wants a relationship with me. Maybe he's trying to get ahead of the situation before it blows up in his face. Yesterday, he texted me good luck before the game and it freaked me out. Why do I have to do this on his schedule? And my brain's running a thousand miles a minute because I can't help building it up to be this thing it can never be. So stupid."

"No, it's not. It's not stupid to hope." She knew all about hope, how it gathered you up in its soft arms before the claws came out and slashed your dumb dreams to pieces.

"Wonder if he knows about the baby," he said distractedly. "Maybe that's his play. Thing is ..."

"What?"

Emotion clouded his eyes. "I don't care about him, not really. But I have brothers. I always wanted brothers and I wouldn't mind getting to know them better. Unfortunately they come with Nick."

Just when she thought Theo couldn't impress her more, he raised the stakes. Of course he wanted to be the best big brother, just like he wanted to be the best dad. This man had so much love to give. How lucky was she to be under his giant wing span.

"I've been checking them out on Instagram. One of the kids—Jason, the same little dude who came to visit—is pretty active there. They have a dog." He screwed up his mouth. "That's messed up, isn't it? Me stalking them?"

Oh, Theo. "Not at all. It's natural to be curious. In fact, I have a confession to make." She stroked his chest with her fingertips. "I'm a bit of a stalker myself. Of you."

His mouth formed an O. "Knew it! For how long?"

"A while. Not that long. I was just filling time while I drank my morning Joe!"

"You like me."

She pushed at his unyielding chest. "I like *looking* at you."

Those strong Instagrammable arms wrapped her up and held her tight. "I won't tell anyone that you've got a crush on me, Ellie." His lips brushed the top of her head, and she rested her head on his chest and allowed herself a moment of peace.

"We don't need him, Theo. We have Aurora. The team."

"And your parents."

Right. She remained silent, wishing she had it in her to be as honest as him.

After a long beat, he asked, "Did they hurt you? Is that why you won't talk about them?"

"No, nothing like that." Though she supposed it was a different kind of hurt, leaving wounds that hadn't healed as quickly as she'd have liked. She'd grown up feeling used and unworthy to be their daughter. "We're not all that close, that's it. They'll come visit eventually but don't expect much, okay?"

"What about your twin sister?"

Had she told Theo Amy was her twin? "We kind of fell out but we're finding our way back to each other."

"Maybe you should invite her to visit. Once the season is over, we'll have some down time."

Elle wanted her sister to turn over a new leaf. What better example than surrounding her with kind people? They hadn't experienced a lot of kindness in their lives.

"Maybe. I'll think about it."

He curled a hand around the nape of her neck and drew her lips to his for a kiss. "The sharing thing goes both ways. I'm not just a smoothie-making sex machine, I'm also a good listener when I'm not talking about myself. So you don't want to tell me everything, but we can be honest about this. About desire. About comfort. About friendship. It doesn't have to hide behind me role-playing as a jerk. We haven't had enough sex to need to spice it up that way yet!"

She giggled. "Maybe I just wanted to see how far you'd go to get some."

"Pretty far, it seems. I'm so hot for you, Ellie. And I like you. A lot." His eyebrows dipped. "Well, would you look at that."

She followed his gaze to her nightstand where she'd placed the small plush dinosaur Theo bought for her the day after she told him she was pregnant.

"It's cute," she said by way of explanation. *I like you, too. A lot.*

"And it's the last thing you see before you fall asleep and the first thing—"

She growled. "Don't make a thing of it, Kershaw."

"Wouldn't dream of it." He had never looked smugger. He cupped her jaw and rubbed her nose. "I know you're not sure about me but be sure of this: I think you are gorgeous and smart and funny and I want nothing more than to slip inside you on a regular basis. How's that for honest?"

Not bad. Really good, in fact. Rather than think too hard on that, she kissed him and let herself be adored.

23

READY TO CHILL after morning skate, Theo took a seat on the ass-dented sofa in the player lounge. He should really be over at Elle's making her lunch, but she'd promised to help with inventory at the Empty Net, saying it was a chance to earn some extra cash.

Jesus, she pissed him off. He thought they were getting somewhere between the best sex of his life and opening up to each other yesterday morning. She'd even brought up her sister without prompting.

Gunnar sat beside him and turned on the TV. "It's a very special episode of *Days*, Kershaw. Kristen's about to get her comeuppance."

In classic *Days* style, Kristen DiMera was currently wearing a Mission Impossible-style mask of Nicole Walker while running around causing havoc. Bonus: she was also married to her own brother, Tony.

"What I don't get," Levi said. "Is how Brady had sex with her and didn't realize it wasn't Nicole. Hell, Kristen's fifteen years older and wearing a latex mask!"

"Brady has the IQ of a pistachio," Theo said. "Heads up, John and Hope are about to figure it out."

Two minutes later, John had made a speech worthy of Hercules Poirot and de-wigged Kristen in front of all of Salem. Nice. And ... commercial break.

Theo took a bite of an energy bar. "I'm worried about Elle."

Hunt, aka Bodyguard to the Hockey Star's Baby Mama, snapped, "Why? What's wrong?"

Theo shot a glance of *this guy* at Gunnar, who merely grunted. "She's still working at the bar. I know she's not an invalid, probably because she's told me, oh, a million times. But she's on her feet all night, eating on the go, getting to bed late, and having to deal with drunks hitting on her."

Theo would never dream of telling any woman what to do. Caveman tactics weren't his style, not when he had a beautiful smile and sparkling green eyes that did the work for him. But then he'd never met a woman like Elle Butler.

He wished she'd let him take care of her.

Which he knew was a real old-fashioned attitude, but it couldn't be helped. When it came to protecting what was his, he was an old-fashioned guy. And he didn't think there was anything wrong with that.

"She can handle it," Hunt said. "Though it sounds like the drunks hitting on her bothers *you*."

"Have you not been listening? It *all* bothers me." When neither of them said anything, he added, "It's not like that, anyway. We're not a couple. Not in the real sense."

Another indistinct sound from Gunnar.

"Do you have something more intelligent to add, Double-O, or is this the extent of your contribution?" Double-O because his last name was Bond. Like all Theo's nicknames, it was a work-in-progress.

"Soap opera law, T. You say you're not a couple but you guys can't keep your eyes off each other."

Other things, too, but he didn't need to know that.

"I'd like if we were on a more stable footing. Would make things easier."

Levi said, "For your kid?"

"It's better when both parents are involved with the kid and each other." He didn't have that and he turned out all right—didn't he?—but he would have liked to have a mom and dad in the picture. Or maybe he was just looking for another reason to get closer to Elle.

"I still haven't met her parents. She hardly talks about her family. Tommy did a background check—I didn't ask him—but there are no red flags. She doesn't seem interested in introducing me which makes me think ..."

"What?" Gunnar asked.

"That I'm not good enough for their daughter. She said they didn't approve of her going into the army and that they expected her to contribute in some way she wouldn't." He turned to Hunt. "Remember when she showed up here in November. We thought then that she was running from something."

Hunt looked thoughtful. Sometimes it took him a while to pronounce. "So she's got some stuff about her family she doesn't want to share. Maybe they're like the DiMeras on *Days*. Maybe they're toxic and she doesn't want that around her baby or you. People put too much stock in the past as predictive of the future. Just be there for her now."

"Is that what you did with Jordan? Ignored the past and embraced the future?" Theo knew for a fact the past had gnarled Hunt's world view when it came to Jordan, his best friend's widow.

"I'm just saying that she's a smart girl and a good person,

Theo. Let her know you think that and she'll start to feel safe around you. Trust has to be earned."

While Theo agreed with all this in theory, he was impatient to get Elle on the same page. If he got traded out, he wasn't leaving her or the baby behind.

He let that sink in. Was this about Elle or the hatchling?

"So she's running from something," Gunnar said. "All that matters is who or what she runs toward."

That was all well and good. "You don't think it matters what's going on in her past, with her family? You don't think that's going to have to be dealt with eventually?" He'd tried that with his father. It didn't work out but at least he hadn't ignored it—bottling up past hurts never boded well. If Elle couldn't be honest with him or even herself, what hope did they have?

Gunnar drew his brows together. "I think you'll find that it'll come to a head eventually. A person often meets his destiny on the road he took to avoid it."

"What's that? Plato or some shit?"

"Kung Fu Panda."

Hunt coughed out a laugh, then turned up the volume of the TV. Bro-bonding break over.

THE NIGHT before game five at home against Boston, Theo's grandmother descended on Cavalero's, a nice Italian restaurant in Riverbrook, in a swish of shawls, red lipstick, and Chanel No. 5. Kind of like a geriatric Stevie Nicks (or just Stevie Nicks who was herself geriatric by now). She'd given a wrapped rectangular package to the server and told him to "guard it with his life," then ordered a dirty martini with Tito vodka and three olives.

"Darling," Aurora said to Theo, "did I tell you what the Saugatuck Players are doing this summer? *CATS!*"

"*Cats,*" Theo repeated, like the word was a foreign language. "The musical?"

"They're putting it on for the July 4th holiday weekend. And I have a MAJOR PART."

"Let me guess. One of the cats."

Aurora smiled indulgently. "Yes, Theodore. One of the cats."

"Because nothing says Independence Day more than people dressed in cat suits singing about ..." He turned to Elle. "What do they sing about?"

"Memories," she said. "It's pretty much responsible for ruining Broadway musicals."

Theo pointed at his grandmother. "See? And this is what you're contributing to?"

Aurora waved off any criticism. "We're looking for extra kitties in the chorus. You'll have time when the season is over."

"You should do that, Theo," Elle said. "You have a lovely singing voice."

"He does, doesn't he?" Aurora gazed at her grandson fondly, blind to any faults, because he had none.

"No chance." From his stern tone, Elle got the impression Aurora had "convinced" Theo to participate in sketchy activities in the past.

"Oh, well," Aurora said easily. "I'll make sure to set aside two tickets for our opening and closing performances."

"Same night, I hope," Theo muttered.

"Front row, please," Elle said, enjoying the dynamic between the two.

"Every summer she's got something going on," Theo said. "The year before last, it was a performance art piece where she got naked and covered herself in chocolate sauce and peanuts."

Elle gaped. "You mean you performed naked? In front of your grandson?"

"Like that was the first time," Theo said with a withering look at Aurora. "As soon as I realized what was happening, I covered my eyes and didn't peek until the curtain fell. Thirty minutes of torture, listening to her rolling around on the floor while she talked about being "Snickered" as a stand-in for feminism."

Aurora cackled while Elle covered her mouth. "Oh, that's just cruel."

"This is what you're getting yourself into, Ellie," Theo said. "Not too late to make a run for it."

"Oh, she's made of stronger stuff!" Aurora declared. "So, Elle, tell me all about *your* family."

Maybe not the most elegant of segues, but not completely unexpected. Elle put a large forkful of spaghetti into her mouth, chewed, and chewed some more.

"Um, sorry," Elle said when she'd swallowed. "Nothing to tell, really. Mom, Dad, sister. They live in Florida."

"Thought it was New York," Theo said, tearing open a bread roll with those magical digits.

"They split their time. My father's business takes him all over."

Aurora smiled warmly. "And what's that?"

"What's what?"

"Your father's business?"

"Financial consultants. They advise people on what to do with their retirement funds, that kind of thing."

Theo eyed her over his water glass. No one cared about her family in the army. Even Hunt had never bothered to delve deeper, probably because he didn't want to divulge any secrets of his own.

Aurora was just getting started. "What do your family think about the baby?"

"They're happy as long as I am."

"And are you?"

Time appeared to stop and she felt all eyes on her. "I'm in a better place than I was when I first found out." She peeked up through the veil of her lashes at Aurora, who watched with compassion. "It's such a huge shock that at first, it's hard to see the woods for the trees. But everyone's been really great."

"Stop badgering her, Aurora."

"I'm not! I'm just curious about the competition. Who'll be the best at raspberry kisses on the baby's tummy? What am I up against?"

You'll win hands down. "You're going to be the coolest great-grandmom in the world, Aurora."

Evidently pleased with that, she turned to her grandson. "How did your doctor's appointment go the other day?"

"Doctor's appointment?" Elle barked at Theo. "Is something wrong?"

Theo narrowed his eyes at his grandmother. "No. Just a routine MRI. I get one every six months to make sure my ticking time bomb of a brain hasn't begun another countdown."

Aurora pointed a knife at him. "Oh, you joke now."

"That's what I do." But there was a hint of uncertainty about those words.

Elle caught Aurora's eye and saw her own concern reflected back at her. Not just that, but an understanding: *we both care about him so much. We'll do what it takes to keep him safe.*

Elle spoke up. "He has doctors at his beck and call, 24/7. Short of an overdeveloped Broca's area which makes him *never shut up*, he's the picture of perfect health."

Theo stared at her. "When did you become an expert?"

"When I realized you're more valuable to me on that ice."

"And they say romance is dead," Theo muttered.

She stuck out her tongue, which made him smile. He reached for her hand and squeezed it.

"When he goes to his maker," Elle said to Aurora, still holding Theo's hand, "it'll be because I killed him in a pregnancy-induced rage."

Aurora said, "It's a vulnerable time for a woman."

"Sounds more vulnerable for a man if I have to watch my back," Theo said.

Elle smiled. "Don't fret, Kershaw. Any violence will be to your face. Literally and figuratively."

That made him smile again. "Lucky me."

Abruptly, Aurora grasped Elle's hand, a tight, but friendly squeeze. Then Theo's, completing the hand-holding circle.

"Just go with it," he murmured.

"Dearest Venus, goddess of all that is lovely and good, bless these astoundingly beautiful and breathtakingly fertile youngsters as they embark on this amazing journey. May their baby be healthy, their happiness assured, and their sex life unusual, for variety is the spice of life."

"Jesus, Aurora."

"And may the Rebels beat the tar out of those Boston fuckers."

"Amen," Theo said with a wink at Elle.

24

After their shocking come from behind series win in round 1, can the @ChiRebels shut down the tremors the @LAQuake are bringing in round 2? Join the conversation with @HockeyGrrl and @ChiSportsNet #Playoffs #ChiRebels #Round2

"What did you do to Tommy Gordon?" Violet asked.

Sitting at the back of the owners' box, half-watching the first game of the series while Violet filled her in on all the team gossip, Elle met the knife-sharp gaze of Theo's agent. They'd crossed paths infrequently since that day in the lawyer's offices but anytime they met, she shriveled under his eagle-eyed scrutiny.

"He thinks I'm playing Theo."

"He's such a dick. Hot, though."

Elle looked away. "Guys in suits do nothing for me. Give me a—"

"Guy in a jock strap?"

She cocked her head at Violet. "Am I missing out on the fantasy opportunities afforded by jock straps?"

"Ask Theo to wear one some night," Violet commented.

"You can get a lot of sexy mileage out of a cup. Bren has one I like to call the 'meat lover' ..."

"Baby, don't tell all our secrets," a thick Scottish burr cut in. Bren nodded at Elle, his color high above his facial hair. "Elle, how are you?"

"Good. Getting quite the education about sports equipment. Missing everything, especially beer. My back is sore, but that might be my mattress, and ... oh, you weren't really expecting that level of detail."

Bren smiled patiently and Violet laughed. "Think I'll go get some food. You need anything, Elle?"

"No, I'll get something in a minute."

She kept her eye on the TV screen, pleased to see that Theo was on fire tonight. He'd blocked several passes in the zone, had spent more time on ice than anyone in the first period, and was clearly having a good game.

Her phone buzzed with a text from Amy. *You busy?*

"I need to make a call," she muttered to Violet who was busy whispering to Bren.

Outside the executive box, she called her sister. "Hey, everything okay?"

"Just wanted to hear your voice. I've been thinking about you a lot lately. Your guy seems to be doing well." Amy sounded oddly muted.

"He is. I've been thinking of you, too." She checked to make sure no one was near. "How's that problem?"

"Oh, that," she said, with far too much casualness. "They want the engagement ring back, but I already sold it."

"How much is it worth? I have some savings."

"That's not why I called. I've been watching those goofy videos he does. Your guy. He seems so sweet and I can tell he's thrilled about the baby." Her voice was wistful, maybe even tinged with regret.

If there was the slightest chance Amy could break free of her old life, Elle had to take it. "I want you to meet him. Come stay with me for a while."

"What? Oh, no. I don't want to screw things up for you."

Amy's usual confidence had clearly deserted her. She sounded like a shadow of herself. "That's just it. I think it's going to be okay. It's early days but Theo and I have an understanding."

Amy hummed. "Oh. Shit. You're thinking of telling him, aren't you? About the fam?"

Until Amy said it, she hadn't been certain. "I am. I figure I can trust him to be cool with it. I thought that maybe he would try to take the baby if he knew but he won't. It's better he knows."

"Is it? Remember what happened with that guy back in Miami?"

Preston. "This isn't the same. I'm not looking to be in a relationship with Theo." *Liar.* "He's too nice for me, but he deserves to know the truth about his baby's grandparents."

"You're in love with him."

Was she? No. Perhaps a little. She definitely cared about him. Was that why she wanted to tell him? Either to test his resolve or push him away?

"No—maybe. You've seen him on those videos. That's his personality. He's impossible not to fall for. He lives this open, honest life, so opposite to people like us, Ames. He's good to me because he's worried about the baby. That's his primary concern. He and I don't have a future but I want only good things for him."

"Oh, sis. That's just it. You're not like us. You got all the good genes. I wish—God, I wish I could be more like you. Maybe Jackson and I could have ..." She choked on a ... was that a sob?

"Jackson? You mean—oh, Ames." Her sister had fallen for her mark, the most egregious mistake a con artist could make.

"I didn't mean for it to happen. He's a really nice guy, completely opposite to me, and I really hurt him. By the time I'd figured it out I was already in too deep."

Tell me about it. "I'm so sorry. Have you tried talking to him?"

"He won't take my calls. Now I'm dodging some slimy associate, a so-called spokesman for his family, who says I owe them."

Jesus, would this never end? "I have about nine grand in my savings account. Maybe you can pay off your debt with that."

"Your oh-shit fund? No way." Her voice became stronger. "I'm rooting for you two, the hockey hunk and girl with the biggest heart of anyone I know. I'm hoping you won't need that money because it works out for you. Hoping that it works out for one of us. Good luck, Elle-Belle." She sniffed and hung up.

Elle shut her eyes, her heart in turmoil. She wanted to help her sister, but Amy was right—she might need her emergency fund because Elle really had no idea how Theo would react when she told him his child's grandparents were criminals. He put on a good front to the world, but after everything he'd gone through with his mom and dad, he had to have significant trust issues. Telling him she'd lied all this time was a huge risk.

What if she gave the money to Amy and depleted her savings? Elle would have to rely on Theo until she could go back to work. She had no doubt he would help but the idea of dropping all this on him shredded every last nerve.

"Hello, Elle."

She turned to meet a set of soulless shark's eyes set in the face of Tommy Gordon, because this shit always comes in threes: Amy, her imminent confession, and now this. A voice in her head told her that this guy had Theo's back. They both wanted to protect him even if they were going about it differently.

"Tommy." She could barely muster enough politeness for even that. Had he overheard her conversation with Amy?

"How are you feeling?"

"Pretty good." She felt like a bug under a glass. "Something on your mind, Tommy?"

"Elle, you seem like a nice girl—"

"Emphasis on 'seem,' right?"

His jaw clenched at the interruption. "Theo's a great guy, one of my favorite clients. And he needs to be protected from people who will try to take him for what they can get."

"You saw the agreement. I don't get a penny." The notion of having to defend herself to this douchebag made her ill, even though she understood his heart—if it could be called that—was in the right place.

Her head was spinning. Amy was in trouble and completely downplaying it. Elle needed to psyche herself up to tell Theo about her family, about all her lies and deceptions.

Tommy was still talking. *Please shut up, I'm thinking.*

"I underestimated you, Elle. You're more subtle than I gave you credit for. A multi-point plan, I suppose. Why go for a lump sum when the cash cow keeps on giving? What are your intentions here?"

Her intentions? "Who the hell do you think you are? Lady Catherine de freakin' Bourgh? My intentions are none of your business."

He raised an eyebrow at her outburst but a second later, his eyes widened with concern. "Elle, are you okay?"

It wasn't just her head spinning anymore. The walls looked like they were attached to a treadmill. "I'm—I'm fine. I just need to—"

Fall down.

~

THEO BARGED through the emergency room doors at River-brook Northwestern Healthcare and stopped at the front desk.

"My ..." *My what?* "My fiancée was brought in earlier. She's pregnant."

"Her name?"

"Elle. Elle Butler." He shook his head. "It might be under Eloise."

"Theo."

He turned at the sound of a familiar voice—Bren St. James stood behind him with his wife Violet. They must have been sitting in the waiting area when he thundered by.

"Is she okay?"

Violet nodded quickly and patted his arm. "As far as we know. Just a dizzy spell. The doctor and her parents are in with her now."

"Her parents? Are you sure?"

Violet slid a glance to Bren. "Yeah, apparently they had just shown up at the Rebels Center when it happened."

Bren squeezed his shoulder. "She'll be okay, Kershaw."

Five minutes after hitting the locker room, Dante had pulled him aside and told him Elle had fainted outside the owners' box. Dante had driven him over and was off parking the car.

"Theo." Tommy stood behind Bren, his expression grave. What the hell was he doing here? "I was with her when it happened."

"You?" Tommy's opinion on Elle hadn't changed—Theo knew that much—but he was careful to keep it to himself. Only, Tommy's face right now ... "Did you upset her in some way?"

"I'm sorry." He looked stricken. "We were talking and I might have been a little harsh."

"A little—" His step forward was halted with Bren's hand in his chest.

"Go see your girl, Theo. Plenty of time to deal with this later."

He nodded, inhaled deep. He turned back to the nurse at the desk. "I need to see Elle Butler."

A switch of recognition flipped in the nurse's eyes. "Sure, Mr. Kershaw, I'll take you back there now."

He was vaguely aware of someone patting him on the back before he was ushered somewhere else. The nurse said something about the baby being okay, that everything was normal, and other stuff that he couldn't hear above the waterfall rush of noise in his ears. Intellectually he knew Elle was fine, but his heart hadn't caught up. His pulse trip-hammered fifty thousand miles a minute.

Seated on the bed, she looked pale and serious. Still in her regular clothes, a blue sweater and leggings, so he supposed that was a good sign. On seeing him, she smiled. A little tentative, but enough to put him at ease.

"The baby's fine," she said first thing, assuring him that the reason for their connection was still viable. He cared—of course he cared—but this wasn't just about the baby.

"I heard. What about you?"

"Me?" Surprise tripped across her expression. When

would she get it into her head that she was just as precious to him? That he loved her.

Christ, he loved this woman.

"I'm okay. Just low blood sugar."

He grasped her hand and raised it to his lips, closing his eyes as he held her knuckles there. "So you didn't eat enough today?"

"I did. I promise. I made one of those salads you brought over with the chicken breast." When he still looked unmoved—because there had to be a reason for this—she whispered, "Can you shout at me later?"

That made him smile, jockeying with his need to be very annoyed with her. "Oh, I'll be happy to."

She looked over his shoulder, making him aware that they weren't alone. Elle's parents had finally turned up.

Her mother was dressed in an elegant wraparound dress with humungous red flowers on it. Younger than he'd expected, she had big blue eyes like her daughter's, high cheekbones, and dark hair in a knot at the nape of her neck. She stepped forward and squeezed his arm, subtly checking out his biceps. Weird.

"Theo, it's so wonderful to meet you at last. I'm Dee, Eloise's mother."

He searched for those flat New York vowels, but her accent was cultured and unplaceable. Behind her stood an older, distinguished guy in a well-cut tan suit that stretched tight over broad shoulders. His trimmed goatee picture-framed a thin mouth. All-seeing brown eyes assessed Theo and flickered to warmth as he offered his hand.

"George Butler," he said.

Theo shook. "Theo Kershaw, sir. It's great to meet you at last. I didn't know you were coming to town."

"It was meant to be a surprise," Dee said. "We'd just

called Eloise to let her know we were on our way when we heard what happened. Trying circumstances under which to meet, but everything seems fine." She sounded brisk, maybe even a little impatient.

He turned back to Elle, hoping to tell from her body language if everything truly was fine. He wasn't sure if he could believe a word out of her mouth. She wasn't eating right, she wasn't looking after herself, she was keeping things from him. Something felt off.

"Yes," Elle said tensely. "The doctor checked in with Dr. Patel and wants to keep me here for another hour of observation, but then I'm free to go. How did the game go? They didn't tell you until after—I told them to wait."

She did what? "We won."

"Oh, thank God. You were playing great before ..." She waved a hand over herself. *Yeah. Before.*

"Well, my love," Mrs. Butler cut in. "We're going to leave you for now, but we'll catch up tomorrow."

"Where are you staying?" Elle asked, and there it was again: that frisson of tension.

"Oh, an Airbnb in the city. But we want to take you out to dinner tomorrow night. If you're free, Theo."

"We'll see how the patient feels," Theo said. "I can't wait to hear stories about little Ellie."

"Little Ellie?" Dee's expression was amused, and something about it bothered him. There was a trace of cruelty in that smirk. "Plenty of stories, that's for sure." She smiled at Theo and patted his arm.

Mr. Butler said, "We'll want to know all about you, Theo. Make sure you have what it takes to look after our girl."

He leaned over and kissed his daughter on the cheek. "We'll be in touch." They both left quietly.

"The famous parents," Elle said, blinking rapidly. She

looked relieved that they'd left. He had to say he didn't feel so bad about that himself.

"Tell me what happened. Exactly."

"I had just finished a phone call outside the owners' box—"

"With one of your parents?"

"My sister, actually, when I became dizzy. Next thing I knew, they're taking me here. It's all overblown, Theo."

"Tommy said he might have upset you."

She shook her head. "Tommy? We were talking but he doesn't scare me. Don't blame Tommy—he's got your best interests at heart."

Defending his asshole agent? Didn't see that coming.

"And everything's okay with the hatchling? You're sure?"

"Yes." She sent a glance toward the ajar door through which her parents had just exited.

He went over and closed it. "I'll talk to the doctor in a minute but first we need to have a chat."

"I said I was sorry about the eating. That wasn't it, though."

"You didn't say that, actually, and I'll deal with that later. For now, I need you to tell me what exactly is going on with your family. The truth."

25

I<small>F</small> E<small>LLE</small> <small>WAS</small> <small>A</small> <small>TURTLE</small>, Theo suspected she'd have with-drawn her head into her shell and stayed there until the danger had passed.

But she wasn't a turtle. She was Elle Butler, the woman carrying his baby, the woman he had fallen in love with, and he wanted an honest, forthright conversation about what was worrying her.

"You and I need to talk about the in-laws."

"Well, they're not technically—"

"Ellie. Stop. I know you're the queen of deflection, but not today. Today, we need to talk about your family and why it bothers you so much that they're here."

"I'm just trying to protect you." At his bafflement, she added, "From them."

"Okay. You're going to have to be more specific."

She swallowed. "I told you we don't get along. I don't approve of how they make their living. The thing is, they're, uh, grifters."

"Grifters." That sounded old-timey. "You mean—"

"Con artists, Theo."

Theo hauled in a breath. He'd been prepared for any number of things about Elle's people: toxicity, psychological abuse, outright disapproval of their daughter's choices, or just plain don't-get-along-itis, but not this.

"So they what? Convince people to buy pieces of London Bridge? Run Ponzi schemes? That kind of thing?"

She nodded. "That and more. They're not like other parents. They lie, cheat, steal. They've never done an honest day's work and that means I was raised on the backs of other people's hard graft, on the coattails of their pain and suffering. They move from one scam to the next, squeezing people for every cent they can get. They're consummate liars, though they'd call it storytelling. And I'm a product of them. I lied about who they were because I was ashamed and then I was scared that once you knew, you'd hate me or take the baby away. I'm already screwing up with the diet and exercise and late nights. This would be just one more mark in the ledger of bad motherhood."

Had he been so hard on her, so adamant that she get this motherhood thing right that he'd closed off all channels of communication?

"Have they broken the law?"

She nodded.

"Have *you* broken the law?"

"No. Or, not as an adult. When I was a teen, I did some behind the scenes stuff. Dodgy websites, drop-offs. An accessory, I suppose. But my parents ... I'm sorry, Theo. I didn't want you to get caught up in this."

"Ellie." He placed his hands on his hips and walked back and forth. "I wish you would have told me, but I get it. So you're ... not like them?" He needed to know everything.

"Let me tell you a story. When I was sixteen, my parents said it was time for my training. Amy—my sister— was the same age and she'd already been running games since she was fifteen. She looked older, more sophisticated. I'd hoped I wouldn't have to work the front lines. Maybe I could be behind the scenes, taking care of documents or IDs, but they needed people they could trust to hustle. I was supposed to meet a guy in a bar and steal his hotel key—that was it. No bother for anyone in the business. But he caught me. And I think I wanted to be caught."

Jesus. What a horrible thing to do to your child. "Did you get into trouble?"

"No. It turned out he was a friend of my parents, just a guy they'd asked to be the mark. They didn't trust me with a real one, so they tested me and I failed. And that's when I knew I could never do it. Could never be one of them. I headed to Miami, got a fake ID to say I was eighteen, waited tables, tried to make an honest dollar. And then I joined the army."

"Kind of a switch."

"I wanted to do something that was the opposite of the life they'd led, the life they were grooming me for. Give back. Prove I'm not like them."

Imagine living a life that devoid of trust. Not so different for him as far as his mom was concerned, but at least he had Aurora.

"This is why you wanted to hide the pregnancy. You didn't want them to know because you were worried about … me?" The relief was overwhelming. It wasn't because she was ashamed to be connected to him. So the future in-laws were hustlers, but at least Elle wasn't embarrassed by him. He'd take that as a win. "You think they want to scam me."

"You're the perfect gull."

"Gull?"

"Gullible. Mark. You're so nice and kind and you'd give the shirt off your back to anyone who asked."

He wasn't that nice—and this appearance of a threat to Elle, his baby, and the life he was imagining for himself would show her just how not nice he could be.

"Maybe I'm not as cynical as you."

"Well, that goes without saying. However, getting involved with me means that you're exposed to some shady characters who I happen to share DNA with."

"What about your sister? Is she here, too?"

Sadness curtained her expression. "No. She's lying low after a scam gone wrong. One I—I interfered in. I broke up a con she was running and now the people she pissed off are looking for her. To be honest, that's why I haven't told my parents to take a hike. I'm trying to get Amy out of the game and I need to keep the channels open while I work that."

This was ... a lot. "You've been dealing with all this and you didn't tell me? I could have helped."

"I don't want your money to solve this, Theo."

"Not just that. I could have been a shoulder for you to lean on. Jesus, Ellie!" He paced the room for a few steps but unfortunately the room was too small to get a good pace on. He pointed at her. "I have great shoulders, you know."

She bit her lip and said quietly, "I know."

"I mean for moral support. Stop objectifying my shoulders."

"You brought them up!"

He had. *Okay, think, Theo.* What else was happening here? He'd seen her fear, but it was for him. Worry he'd be scammed. He also got the impression that Elle was looking for something from her parents. Approval, support, just plain old love. We can't choose our family, and even if they hurt you, you can still want to make the relationship better. Theo knew this intimately.

"Tell me. Do you miss them?"

"Sometimes," she said. "It wasn't all bad. They love me in their own way, but whenever they're around I'm on a knife's edge waiting to see what havoc they'll wreak."

"But they can't do any harm to us because I know who they are. What they do."

If he'd expected her mood to brighten, he'd clearly over-reached. She didn't look convinced. What happened to the truth will set you free?

"This is why you're so weird about money. Why you can't take a dime from me that's not accounted for."

"I can't owe you anything, Theo. You're already paying so much and I can't have you think for a single second that I planned this. I didn't."

"Okay, we're not retreading that. I know you didn't plan this. I also know that you'd rather cut off your right arm than take a single dime from me that's not related to feed-ing, clothing, sheltering, and educating our kid. You've been pretty clear about this and unless you're playing the ulti-mate in long games, I'm going to take what you've said at face value. For the record, I don't agree with your position because I want to give you and our child—and I mean both of you—everything. I want you to feel safe and protected and valued, and sometimes money is necessary to provide those things. But I'm not going to argue with you over that now because we have other things to consider, such as whether you actually want your parents to be here."

Her eyes went as wide as pucks. "What? That's what you're asking?"

"Yeah. They're your parents. You've said they're bad role models and maybe they're shitty parents, but I'd like you to have a choice. You're an adult, this is up to you. You've told me what they're like, what they're capable of, and how different you are from them—now tell me if you'd like them to stay. If they're too toxic and are detrimental to the health of you or the baby, then I'll send them on their way. But if you've missed them, if you'd like to give them a chance to redeem themselves in your eyes, then we can ask them to stick around and we can tackle this as a team. But I reserve the right to send them packing if I think they're over-stepping."

Her eyes filled with tears. "I—I didn't expect to have a choice. Theo, are you just being nice here? Are you really furious but keeping it in so as not to upset me or harm the baby?"

"Of course I'm furious! You shouldn't have kept this from me but I'm not pissed because of the secret you kept, I'm pissed because you couldn't trust me enough to come clean. I've tried to be honest with you. I've told you stuff I've never told another living soul. Now you're telling me this because I'm prying it out of you."

She swiped away more tears. Shit, now he was just upsetting her again.

"I was getting ready to tell you, I swear. I'm not used to opening up like that. We were raised to mask everything, to keep our true feelings hidden because it signifies weakness. Gives an advantage to the opponent. And that's what my family thinks. It's us and them. I want to give them the benefit of the doubt but they're probably here to make a score, Theo."

"But now I know what their game is. We're what do you call it?"

"Forewarned."

"Right, so we can be ..."

"Forearmed."

"Finishing each other's sentences, baby! And you said it could never work." He turned grave. "Say the word and I'll kick them out on their lying, thieving, con-artist asses."

More surprise, more tears. Didn't she understand yet the lengths he'd go to protect his new family?

"Theo, I didn't expect this. I didn't expect you."

"Well, looks like we're still surprising each other." He dropped a light kiss on her lips. "You think about how you want this to play out. I'm going to chat with the doctor."

"Because you don't believe me?"

"Because you underplay everything, Elle Butler. I'll be back in a second."

He left the room, his pulse rate no calmer now than it had been going in. Elle and the hatchling were *his* family and he would protect them with everything in his power.

Before he sought out the doctor—because Elle was right, he didn't believe her—he made a phone call.

"Hey, I need a favor."

26

"A GLASS EACH OF CHAMPAGNE?" Dee wrinkled her nose at the patient server in the Peninsula's famed Lobby on Michigan Avenue where they were seated for afternoon tea. "Make it the bottle. And let's do the Dom, not the Veuve Clicquot."

Twice as expensive, of course.

"Eloise," her father said, "we've stayed away because that's what you wanted. You've made it clear you have your own path to tread."

Today, George Butler looked sharp, with his (dyed) greying goatee and Southern gentleman suit, a costume he donned when entering small towns and wholesome lives. People stopped looking further, seeing only an elegantly dressed man instead of the charlatan beneath. Despite his failings as a father, she believed he did actually care for her, or as much as someone with such loose morals could.

"Things are actually going well, Dad. The baby was a surprise but Theo is very supportive."

"And you two ..." Dee trailed off.

Elle shook her head. "Oh, we're not a couple. It's purely a co-parenting arrangement."

Her parents exchanged glances, likely assessing if their least talented daughter could possibly attract someone like Theo beyond a one-night stand and how they might use it to their advantage.

"Well, darling, it's all very nicely done," Dee said, though Elle couldn't be sure whether she was talking about the pregnancy, Theo, or the imminent score of a lifetime.

She'd not missed how Dee's eyes had glittered with knowledge on meeting Theo in her hospital room two days ago. Only two days, yet Theo was still here. He'd not abandoned her despite knowing her family's history and all the ways they could rip a life to shreds.

"I'm actually happy, Mom. Don't ruin it."

Dee managed to look affronted. "Why would I do that? I'm thrilled for you. I did worry you would have trouble finding someone because you've never been one for using what the gods gave you. So pretty, but would any man ever see it as long as you're wearing those baggy clothes and not a dab of makeup? And then the army—good Lord! I thought you must like women, not that there's anything wrong with that. In fact, it might have opened up some new avenues, but … well, this strategy of yours is as good as any and Theo seems to be hooked."

"It's not a strategy, Mom. It was an accident and Theo and I are making the best of a bad situation. Not a couple, remember?"

Her mother grimaced, then lit up on seeing the bottle of champagne appear. After the pop and pour, she raised her glass toward Elle, who had no choice but to pick her own up and clink it. Never mind that she couldn't drink it in her condition.

"What was that face for?" Elle asked.

"What, my love?" Her mother perused the tea menu. "Maybe Russian Caravan? Or should we go traditional with a nice Assam?"

"What was that pained expression for when I told you that Theo are I are doing the best we can in the circumstances?"

"Well, look at him. I'm amazed you managed to get this far. The man is gorgeous, and while I've no doubt you've learned a few tricks on your travels—we must have done something right—Theo wouldn't look at you twice if he wasn't such a decent guy."

"I know that!" Being aware of her limitations was the best play here. But she'd seen how Theo looked at her, she'd felt his eyes and hands and body as he moved inside her. It might not be complete commitment but it was close.

Only where did commitment end and obligation begin?

Her mother was in full flight. "At least this time, you have the anchor to keep him around." Unlike last time when Preston told her *adios*, she supposed. "Just ..."

"What?"

"Dee," her father warned, perusing the menu. "Let her handle this."

Dee scoffed. "Just don't keep the cuffs on him too tight. A man on the road for his work and with all that attention needs a little freedom to indulge. You'll do better if you give him latitude. Let him do his thing and you stay home, cashing the checks."

"How long are you staying again?"

Her mother mouthed *ha ha*. "I'm hoping that this can be a new start for us, Eloise. After you broke up the band with your interference at your sister's wedding, I wasn't sure we were going to be able to get over that hump."

"But now I have a bump to get me over the hump, huh?"

Dee grasped her hand and squeezed. "I want to be your friend, my love. I do. But that self-righteous streak makes it so hard. Everything we did—we do—is to help us survive. No one is going to give us a thing. But I can see that Theo means something to you. We're not here to interfere, not when you're doing so well already." She might have winked at that. "So you're not a chip off the old block. We can't all be the same and that's fine. It is!"

At an early age, Elle had recognized that she wasn't like her family and that her worth was tied up in how she could contribute to their bottom line. Maybe that was about to change. Maybe they would finally listen.

"I won't let you hurt Theo, and that includes asking him to invest in anything, lend you anything, or scam him out of anything. Are we clear?"

Her mother's eyes widened in faux shock. "We'll behave! Believe it or not, we're here for you and the baby. So we've had our differences. It's time we buried the hatchet."

Was there any point in arguing? Theo was on alert and Elle had done her best to warn him. The moment they tried anything, she'd eighty-six them back to wherever they'd blasted in from.

"So how come Amy's not with you?" She'd texted her sister, only to get cryptic replies telling her she was busy and to forget she'd even mentioned the sort-of-mob-connected former fiancé's family who were after her for the engagement ring she hocked. No biggie!

"Oh, you know how she is," George said. "Likes to do her own thing."

"She said that last score had aftershocks. I'm worried about her."

Her mother laughed softly. "Oh, we never have to worry

about Amy. She'll always land on her feet. It's you we've always been concerned with. Too soft."

All relative, she supposed.

How bad could it be? They wouldn't dare try anything, at least until the baby was born. No way would they risk endangering their pay day.

She could handle this. Manage her parents, manage Theo, manage her pregnancy. After all, what else could she do?

$\sim$

ELLE UNLOCKED the Empty Net's back entrance and headed to the office. Tina sat there, pouring over paperwork.

"Hey, how are you feeling?"

Elle leaned against the door jamb. "Well, my nutso parents are driving me up the wall, my sister isn't answering my calls, I'm carrying a pro-athlete's super-baby, I'm not eating nearly enough vegetables, I haven't done anything about taking classes, and I'm probably the worst employee ever. Other than that, peachy."

Tina laughed. "Don't worry about the bar. If you need time off, it's fine. In fact ..."

"You're going to fire me? It's okay, I have it coming."

"No, I'm not." She swiveled in her chair toward the printer and a large box on top of it. "I was going to say that Theo arranged a bar-back for tonight so you could go on your date. I really should just give him access to the weekly schedule. And he dropped this off." She handed off the box.

"Our date?"

With astonishing timing, her phone vibrated and she checked the screen.

Be ready at seven. DATE NIGHT!!!

Tina smiled. "Wish I had your problems."

ELLE CHECKED herself in the mirror. She didn't usually wear makeup but she'd stopped at the drugstore on the corner to get some concealer and lipstick, spending far too long in the cosmetics aisle looking for magic that would make her look WAG-worthy ... and worthy of the dress Theo had bought her.

For their date.

She should be terrified, waiting for the house of cards to come tumbling down. For the last couple of days, her parents had behaved themselves. Last night, Theo had finagled an invite for them to the owners' box, which was full to bursting with plenty of opportunities for her parents to do their damage. Elle had recognized a couple of pro athletes from the NBA and MLB, and combined with the megawattage of the Rebels organization, it was the perfect hunting ground. Elle had spent the night keeping one eye on the TV screen and another on her viperous family in full flight. Dee regaling Dante with some story about a trip to Sicily—Elle couldn't recall if she'd truly ever been, but she sure sounded like she had. George pumping Harper for information on trades while the Rebel Queen rebuffed him politely at every turn. Elle trusted no one would be foolish enough to be taken in and so far no damage had been done.

This might work.

Theo was going out of town tomorrow to LA for Game 3 of the series, so he wanted to spend some time with her—and only her—tonight.

On a date.

She looked in the mirror again. The whole thing had a

Pretty Woman vibe she would normally not appreciate. The dress was red, draping perfectly over her curves, and leaving no one in doubt that she was pregnant. Maybe that was Theo's intention—an assertion of his biblical rights as a father. *Behold! Look at the baby bump I have madeth!*

But what took the dress from lovely to perfect was the matching footwear: patent black wedge Nike sneakers with a diamond-encrusted swoosh. Comfortable, yet completely classy. She wasn't a bling sort of girl, but this choice spoke to her. *I want you to be yourself and look as hot as fuck in that dress.*

He had dropped it off at the bar, which was presumptuous and weird and oddly romantic. But after coming clean in her hospital room, something had unfurled inside her—a transformation of her heart.

Theo wanted her to be happy.

He cared about Elle, the woman as a separate person from Elle, the mom-to-be. He wanted her to have choices, to exercise agency, and to accept that sometimes she didn't have to do everything alone.

She opened her door to a vision of male perfection. They'd been here many times before: Theo in a towel, Theo in sweats, Theo just being Theo. Tonight, he wore charcoal dress pants and a slim blazer with a pink shirt, open at the neck.

"Wow!" Said together, which made them both laugh.

"You like the dress?"

"Yes. How did you pull it off? Somehow I can't imagine you scanning the racks at Macy's."

"I asked Casey, Harper's assistant, to get it for me. Don't worry, she was well-compensated."

The perks! "But you chose it?"

"Yeah. I wanted something that makes you feel classy

and comfortable." Which was exactly what she'd thought before he arrived. Simpatico! "We should get going," he added.

Fifteen minutes later, they walked into a beautiful restaurant downtown overlooking the lake. The dining room was packed, and several people acknowledged Theo as he walked by. A couple of people even clapped!

One eager beaver tried to take a photo and Theo's defensive and papa bear tendencies took over as he stepped to block. "Sorry, not tonight." Polite yet firm.

"What are you doing?" Elle whispered.

"You don't want that, right?"

True, but she didn't expect Theo to play bodyguard. People had been hands-off about hounding her as the mother of Theo's baby and now her family knew, it didn't seem so important.

Hand in hand, they continued on through the dining room. "You haven't been sharing as much on social."

"Trying to be more mindful of that."

"Oh?"

He leveled a serious gaze at her. "I have to be careful about who has access to my family. I know you don't want to be in the spotlight and I'd never want you to feel hassled. You're a private person, so we're private people."

My family. The words made her warm all over.

Heading toward the back of the restaurant, one diner stood out on their journey. His cheeks were flushed an ugly red, his jaw had a pugnacious set to it, and his suit looked stiffer than his spine. She would have paid him no mind but for the extra squeeze Theo gave her hand as they walked by.

Seated in a private enclosed porch, they had a fabulous view of the water. Strangely, all the other tables in the section—nine of them—were empty.

"No one's eating tonight?"

"Not with us."

Awareness dawned. "How many people's dinners were ruined because you had to have your way?"

"Me? Nice, wouldn't-harm-a-fly Theo Kershaw ruining dinners?" He grinned, though it wasn't quite as wide as normal. "Everyone who had a reservation will be accommodated another evening and will have their dinner covered by me."

She shook her head. "You'll be bankrupt before the kid is born."

"Actually, I won't. But I'll happily bankrupt myself to make sure he's got the best life I can give him and grows up healthy, well-adjusted, and loved." Theo was fairly certain the kid would be a boy. The next ultrasound in a week or so would tell them for sure.

A lump the size of the delicious rosemary-olive bread roll on her side plate lodged in her throat. She took a gulp of water, hoping it would pass.

"Who was the stiff suit out in the main dining room?"

"No one important."

"Theo."

He slid an uncomfortable glance out the window. "Alderman Isner."

His father? Hell, no! "Are you okay?"

"Yep." He wasn't, but he covered. "Don't worry, I've had great teachers, coaches, captains. I'm not interested in making nice with a guy who'd abandon a sixteen-year-old girl so he could have the full kegger experience at Harvard."

The words were quiet, forceful. This was Theo with his heart broken.

And it wasn't just because of his father. There was the relationship he was being denied with his half-brothers.

"It's okay to be angry, Theo. He let you down. They both did." On their phone chats, Aurora had filled him in on Candy and how she fell in with a bad crowd, desperate to ignore any responsibility as Theo's mom. By the time Theo was ready to accept her and the consequences of her deception, she was already too far down the path of drug addiction, which would ultimately lead to her death.

She grasped his hand, a gestured promise that she couldn't verbalize. *I won't let you down. I won't hurt you.*

Of course he had to play his part in stopping that from happening. Stop being so appealing, stop making her fall head over Nike wedges in love with him. It was getting harder and harder to resist him. Shackled for life with this man might not be such a bad thing, but only if he felt the same way. Was that even possible?

The server came, told them about the specials, and took their order for drinks.

Still stuck on how his parents had let him down, she thought about her own upbringing. George and Dee hadn't treated her as a child, more like an apprentice. She and Amy could do anything they want as long as it didn't threaten the overall enterprise.

"I guess neither of us lucked out the day the goddess was handing out moms and dads."

"Family's what you make." He reached for her hand. "We're building something. You and me and Hatch. We can choose who we have in our lives, who's privileged to be part of our circle."

It was tempting to think they could reframe everything, create their own molds for the future. "I wonder what kind of parents we'll be," she said. "There are all these books on parenting styles and I have no idea where to start."

"Don't need a book. Just common sense." He smiled,

clearly pleased to be on his favorite topic: his awesome dad potential. "TV or no?"

"Like TV as a babysitter while I take my first shower in three days?"

His lips turned up at the corners. "Sure."

"Of course. You?"

"Don't want my kid's brain to be mush."

"Already will be because of the processed foods."

He growled. "If our kid wants to get a pet, do we let him?"

"I already see myself on the hook for poop scooping and early morning walks. And you won't be around."

"We can hire a dog walker."

"Sounds like we'll be hiring an army to do all the things I don't want to do. Leaving me plenty of time to be a bad mother."

He chuckled.

"You think I'm joking."

He laughed again, and she joined in because it was sort of funny. And easy with him. All this pressure she felt—was it self-inflicted? She was beginning to think it was, that her problems with Theo came down to what went on inside her head and not what was going on between Theo's ears or in the schemes of her parents.

She wasn't sure if that was a comfort or a curse.

"So this one is for an older kid," he said, having no heed to the turmoil bubbling in her chest. "You suspect they have a false ID and are drinking. What do you do?"

"Rip them a new one because threatening them with you will be useless. You'll be too nice."

"Not about underage drinking!"

"You'll want to reason with them. Be their friend. And they'll hate me because cool Dad isn't around and mean

Mom is trying to limit their freedom of expression. I already suck at this and the kid's not even born."

He curled a big hand around her fingers. "You said 'they.'"

"What?"

"You said 'they'll hate me.' Plural. Like we're having more than one."

"I meant the gender-neutral pronoun. I'd rather not impose societal rules on them until they can choose their own path."

"Don't think so. I think you want me to fill your belly with more babies."

She shook her head. "One child with us as parents will be enough. The poor kid will have my neuroses and your lack of filter. I shudder to think what we're creating."

He leaned in closer. "Sometimes I worry that I'm going to pass on something weird, some genetic weakness that makes his brain blow up."

"Theo, it's not genetic."

"That's what they say, but who knows? Who the fuck knows anything?"

She thought about his father, out there in the dining room. She thought about her parents and the pain they'd caused her all these years. "Let's worry about what we can control. We can produce a kind, curious, well-adjusted little human and make sure he's safe and sheltered and loved so damn much. He'll never have to live for his parents. He'll be his own person. And no matter what he wants to do or turns out to be, we'll support every choice. As long as it's legal and not just plain dumb. Deal?"

"Deal." He grinned. "I have something for you."

"You mean more than the bountiful seed you've already

given me, Kershaw?" And all this terrifying hope for the future, she didn't add.

His smile took her places. "It's not much." From inside his coat pocket, he extracted a jewelry case, bigger than a ring box, but still—had her mind gone there? So dangerous.

"Theo, you didn't have to do this."

She opened it with fumbling fingers. A silver-linked bracelet lay on a velvet bed, a couple of twinkling charms winking at her. She plucked it from the box, her mind racing as she examined the details. One charm was of miniature dog tags representing her army service. Another was a crossed set of hockey sticks fashioned into a heart. The final one was baby feet. Her heart skipped several beats, and she pressed hard on her breastbone, seeking to return it to its regular rhythm. As if the choices he'd made weren't enough to rip her heart to pieces, the fact that there was room for more punched her in the feels.

"I can return it or get you something else—"

"No. I love it. It's perfect." She wasn't usually a jewelry person but she would treasure this forever. "I didn't get anything for you."

"You did." He squeezed her hand. "Best gift ever."

She burst out crying.

"Ellie! You have got to get those hormones under control."

She dabbed ineffectually at her eyes with her napkin, thankful that Theo had done the tacky thing and booked an entire restaurant section.

"Christ, if you're going to be hormonal, you should be channeling it into getting orgasms instead of all this emotional fuckery."

He was teasing so she wouldn't feel like a blubbering fool—and it was working. How did he always know what to say? His emotional intelligence was off the charts and she couldn't wait to see him being a dad.

She only wished he could be more because she'd done the dumbest thing and fallen in love with him. She didn't expect him to feel the same way and no number of date nights or charm bracelets could convince her otherwise. She just hoped she'd get over him eventually.

27

DINNER WAS PERFECT, and Theo didn't even seem to mind that she ordered extra mashed potatoes—probably because he insisted she choke down three florets of broccoli and show her open mouth like an asylum patient proving she'd swallowed her meds. On her way back from her third visit to the restroom (her bladder was the size of pea these days) she spotted Theo's father approaching. She searched for the resemblance. It was there around the eyes but there was a harshness to his mouth that he hadn't passed on to his son.

As he walked by her, he fronted a careful blankness that rubbed her the wrong way.

"You going to pretend you don't know who I am?"

He stopped. "Sorry, are you speaking to me?"

"You know who you're speaking to, Alderman. And a man in your position would make it his business to know what his son is doing so it won't come back to bite him."

The polite mask fell away. "What exactly can I do for you?"

Elle knew this guy, or guys like him. Would-be Masters of the Universe, with small minds and smaller dicks.

"I just wanted you to know what a mistake you've made cutting Theo from your life."

He opened his mouth, then closed it quickly. "This isn't really the time or place."

She felt drunk, though she hadn't touched a drop. Call it a mashed-potato induced rage. "You didn't want to step up, Alderman. I'm just letting you know that you're missing out on knowing a wonderful man. A good son and grandson, a stalwart friend and teammate, the best damn defenseman in the NHL. He's going to make a great dad, a stand-up parent, and a wonderful partner to me. I will never have to worry that he won't be there for me, my baby, or any of the people he cares about because Theo Kershaw is a good person. The best person. You're not worthy to share his DNA, Alderman. And I'm sorry for you. Sorry that you have to lie to yourself and the world about this wonderful person you produced."

The alderman's color was hellfire-hot. "I don't have to listen to this—"

"No, you don't. But there will come a time when your other sons are old enough to know who you are. To see the chips in the veneer you wear so well. They should know their brother and he should know them. You can make that happen or—"

"Or what? What are you saying?"

She shrugged. "I won't tell them. But secrets don't stay secret in the same way these days, Alderman. Home DNA kits, genealogy trees. Wouldn't you rather control the mess—?"

"Elle!"

Theo's sharp voice cut her off. He closed the gap between them, tucking his hand under her elbow. "Let's go."

The alderman's brow furrowed, his expression one of

yearning toward his son. Dark silence clung to them as they left the restaurant.

THEO WAS FURIOUS.

True, Elle should not have taken it upon herself to lecture dear old Dad about his parental responsibilities, but he wasn't mad about that. No, he was furious that she'd had to even breathe his self-righteous air.

They took the elevator down to the second lower level of the parking garage, the descent similar to the drop of his heart five minutes ago when he came across Elle defending him. Telling his father what he was missing out on. How great a man Theo was and how great a father he would be.

The elevator opened and Elle stepped out ahead of him. As she rounded the corner to where they were parked, she pivoted. "Theo, I'm sorry. I didn't mean to—"

He stopped her apology with a kiss. She looked so gorgeous in that dress, so curvy and tempting. All good reasons to kiss a woman, but not his reason now. He kissed her because words were useless to express what he felt right in this moment.

"Theo—" She tried again.

He kissed her more. Deeper. Truer. Stealing her breath helped fuel his lungs and find the words. "I can't believe you did that for me. Talked to him like that."

"Why not? You're amazing and that fucker needed to know." She shook her head, wonder creasing her pretty features. "Don't you have any idea how remarkable you are, Theo? How proud I am to have you be my baby's father?"

"Proud? Really?"

"Proud, blessed, overwhelmed. I wouldn't want to do this

with anyone else. I can't *imagine* doing this with anyone else."

He worried about doing something unmanly then. Sobbing, perhaps. Whimpering, even. Instead he poured all that emotion into a kiss, sliding his tongue into that sweet, velvet clasp and tasting her fury and fire. Coasting greedy hands down her hips, he grasped her ass, so round and inviting.

It was easy to bunch the material in his fists. Pull it up inch by inch so he could remove another barrier. He was as hard as the granite beams holding this parking structure together, and he wanted her to know. Grinding his cock against the fork of her legs, he made his case.

"Theo," she gasped between sensual assaults on her mouth, her neck, the hollow below her ear. His favorite spot. She tasted so sweet there.

"Turn around, Ellie."

"What—here?"

He couldn't wait for her to catch up, he was too far gone. Too hopped up on need and desire and an unmistakable well of feeling that seemed to overwhelm him whenever he was near this woman.

Her panties were an improvement on the last ones. These beauties covered her glorious ass in silky black fabric with a pink lace trim. With a more unhurried deliberation than the situation really called for, he ran his hands over her perfect curves like he had all the time in the world.

"Theo, please. Touch me."

"Patience, my gorgeous girl." He continued his exploration, his palms smoothing over the cheeks, squeezing, testing her limits. "These are pretty."

"Addison gave them to me."

Callaghan's wife designed underwear and Theo had to

say he appreciated the connection. He slipped a hand around the front, between her legs, and cupped her. Pressing his palm against her pussy, he absorbed the damp heat of her desire.

"Take 'em off, Elle."

"Are—are you sure?"

"Yep." He pressed against her, whispering in her ear, "Need you now. Need to be inside you."

Her breath hitched, her hands fell to her sides, and she pushed those sexy panties down. All that lovely, gilded skin came into view, each inch sweeter than the last. She stepped out of one leg, and that's all the access he needed. His palm returned home, spreading her wide, stroking through that sensitive flesh until he earned a moan.

Then another.

"There's no—no time," she gasped, though it felt like they had all the time in the world. A future that had opened up when he'd overheard her defending his corner.

She grabbed his hand and pushed against it. That made him chuckle.

"Bastard."

And that made him harder. His prickly little peach. With the hand not bringing her off, he unzipped his pants and readied his cock, not that it needed much encouragement. He rubbed between the cleft of her ass, dipping into the moisture-filled crevice, seeking entry to paradise.

She hinged her hips, tilting her ass up to meet the slide of his cock which zeroed in on its target with a will of its own. It met no resistance, only a warm, wet welcome.

"Yes, that's—oh, God, Theo. Yes, that's it."

He withdrew a few inches, and with another thrust, she clamped hard, tightening greedily around him. He dug his fingers into her hips and held her in place for each rhythmic stroke. She balled her hands into fists against the gray wall, anchoring her body for his invasion.

No more words, just the smooth push and pull, the erotic slap of flesh on flesh. Her body was made for his, the fit so right. One tender press to her clit sent her over. The tension peaked to an exquisite torment, and he gave himself over to the sweetness of it as he emptied into her.

∼

THEO SALUTED VICTOR, the doorman to his building, as he walked in.

"You played a barnburner last night, Mr. Kershaw. No mistake."

Mr. Kershaw. No matter how often he tried to get Victor to use his first name, the old-school guy was having none of it.

"I had a good night."

Game four of the second-round series against the LA Quake had gone the Rebels way, pushing them over the top and making them division champions. Theo wasn't so modest as to deny his part in it. Something about the progression of his relationship with Elle had opened up a new path inside his brain, inspiring him to be freer on the ice. He'd mentioned it to Hunt on the plane home last night —not the specifics but the feeling.

Your planets are aligning, Kershaw, was Hunt's crunchy-granola—for him anyway—response. The big guy said it had happened with him and Jordan. Like a dam had broken open, and that river of honesty had liberated any blockages.

Theo understood what made Elle's walls so thick, and now he had the sledgehammer to deal with it.

"Mr. Kershaw, you have a visitor." Victor gestured to the

lobby sofa behind him. George Butler sat there, dressed in a sharp suit set off with a blue tie and red rose. Very dapper, but then he usually was. *All the better to con you with, my dear.*

For the five days before the LA trip, he'd done his best to support his woman. He took the Butlers to dinner, invited them to an executive box at the Rebels arena for the second game, had played the perfect host to the family who would be in his kid's life, for better or worse.

Theo was still trying to puzzle George out. What kind of man forced his family to exist on the edges like this? Theo didn't know how much Elle had told them about his insider knowledge. There was definitely the sense that they were feeling each other out, seeking an access point to an opponent's weakness.

Theo had the best defense in the business. Nothing was getting by him.

"Theo!" Elle's dad stood and approached, hand outstretched.

"George." They did the manly handshake where attempts were made to break fingers. "What brings you here?"

"Oh, just thought I'd stop by for a chat with the father of my grandchild. Not a bad time, is it?"

"Not at all. I was about to have lunch. I make a mean sandwich, if you're interested." Usually he'd have gone to Elle's but she was out for pedicures with her mom. A dual front from Team Butler.

"A sandwich would be delightful."

They headed up to Theo's apartment. George looked unimpressed, which made Theo smile to himself.

"Would have thought you'd have something a little bigger, Theo. Not much room for a family here."

Theo walked through to the kitchen and opened the fridge. "This is pretty standard for the new additions to the team, especially the single ones, until they figure out where they want to end up. I'll be looking for something bigger in the summer for Elle and the baby."

"I hoped you'd say that. She seems happy. You make her happy."

Theo kept his smile pinned on, then realized it wasn't such a chore after all. He *was* happy. "I just want to take care of her and the baby. They're my primary concern here." He gestured to the gouda. "Cheese?"

"Sure."

A moment later, Theo passed the sandwich over along with a beer (and look at him, in a glass!). He stuck with water for himself.

"I'm glad you've been here for my daughter, Theo. She's going to need your strength in the coming months." George took a bite of the sandwich, chewed, swallowed, and declared it "perfection!"

"That's what I'm here for," Theo said.

"Good, good." George took another bite while they chatted about the game and Theo waited for him to get to the point.

George dabbed at his mouth with a napkin. "Her mother —well, her mother doesn't want to bring her down, but ..." He inhaled one of those breaths you take to stave off tears. Pinched the bridge of his nose. Sniffed loudly. Looked down. Shook his head. The Saugatuck Players would have been proud.

"George, is everything okay?"

"Dee. My Dee. She's not well. I don't want to stress Elle out, with the baby and all. She's so fragile right now."

"Sorry to hear that," Theo murmured. "I think Elle would prefer to know, though."

"Oh, no." George said, horrified at the notion. "I saw how fragile she was during that hospital visit. I just wanted to be sure she's being taken care of."

"Can I ask what the trouble is with Mrs. Butler?"

"She needs a small operation, but you know how these things get magnified. You hear things. What's routine isn't always so. And well—I wanted to be sure that my daughter was in good hands while we're away for that."

"You won't have to worry about Elle, George."

The man met Theo's eyes, perhaps surprised at the vehemence in his tone. When Theo had learned what George Butler was capable of, he'd expected that the man would act shiftily, unable to hold the gazes of the people he was about to cheat. Like Nick Isner or your standard politician. But George was more of a pro than that. He had a way of looking at you: sharp, shrewd, like he knew exactly what you were thinking. All your decisions would be foretold. Nothing left to chance.

"Glad to hear it. With her mother needing ..." He waved off that unpleasant topic. "We'll be in Mexico. The healthcare is cheaper there, though still quite beyond our range. But we'll manage and I'll feel better knowing that my daughter is doing so well." He took another bite of the sandwich. "Excellent vittles, Theo."

"You really should tell Elle about her mom. I don't think she'll like it if I have this knowledge and she doesn't. We don't keep anything from each other."

Something flickered in George's eyes. "I didn't think you knew each other that well. A one-night stand, I'd heard. Sorry if that's indelicate."

"We've become quite close. Expecting a child together does that."

Again the flicker, before he shut it down. "Close? I see," George mused. "So the manner of your connection might not be orthodox but lots of people are thrown together and come out of it stronger. Your baby will be better off if you two are committed. In this together."

Now they were getting somewhere. "I asked her to marry me." Just as George's thin mouth curved into a self-satisfied smile, Theo delivered the punchline. "She said no."

George's jaw muscles bunched, the first indication of his true self since Theo had met him. Definitely not pleased with his daughter.

"She's always been so independent. It can be a curse as well as a blessing."

"Don't I know it! But she was right. We don't need a piece of paper or a ring to make this official. Elle's only concern is that the baby be taken care of and I've made sure of that. Financially."

"Good to hear. You've made this old man very happy."

"I'm happy to do what I can while Elle's mom is unwell. Still think you should tell her."

George looked pained. "I wouldn't want to upset her. We have to do everything in our power to keep her and the baby in good shape, uh, health. I may not be able to visit as often as I'd like over the next few months. The trips add up, you see."

Theo had had enough with all this pussyfooting around.

"I've had my lawyer do a little digging, George. If you want money, you may as well come right out and ask for it."

The man's smile was feral. "I'm not sure what you mean. Your lawyer?"

"Cards on the table."

George became more alert. "Has Elle said something to you?"

Even now Theo didn't want to destroy Elle's relationship with her family. While he thought she'd be better off without them, he was resigned to having her make the call herself.

"No, Elle has kept all your secrets. You don't have to be concerned about her loyalty."

"Yet ... she tried to warn you in her own way, I assume. Yes?" Whatever George saw on Theo's face was enough. The man was clearly a master at reading body language. "Congratulations on getting access to her heart."

Theo had no more access to Elle's heart than this man did, but he was making progress. The flattery was likely another part of the game. Nothing George said could be taken at face value.

At Theo's instruction, Tommy had produced the gory details: the bank accounts drained, hearts broken, lives destroyed. Sure, Theo had given her the choice to let them stay, but he wasn't sure that she could be objective when it came to her family. What she didn't seem to realize was that her parents' mere presence was threat enough.

"Is Dee really ill?"

"We're none of us well, are we, Theo?"

Anger flared. The time for pretense was over. They understood each other at last. "You've really done a number on Elle, George. And I don't appreciate what you're trying to do here. I'd hoped that maybe you'd visit for a while, take the hospitality on offer, and not push your luck."

"Pushing my luck is how I've survived so long, my good man." He chuckled. "To look at you, I wouldn't have suspected such cynicism beneath the Captain America exterior. Could my Eloise be rubbing off on you?"

As if Elle had tainted Theo instead of opening up his life to possibilities. The man was as toxic as they come, all the worse for never having given his daughter a chance to take another path. Instead, she had to slash her way out and find that road herself.

A man who would lie about his wife's health would lie about anything. Theo had overestimated his ability to trust that Elle's family would be benign, harmless influences in their lives. He had to act to protect Elle and their baby. To protect his family.

"George, let's talk man to man."

28

SURE, hockey paid good money. Elle just hadn't realized it paid mansion-on-the-lake money. She got the memo loud and clear as Theo drove them up a long drive to what Violet had labeled "Stately Chase Manor."

Elle had thought she was kidding.

On seeing the home that wouldn't have looked out of place on the set of Downton Abbey, Elle came over in a cold sweat. When her parents saw this, there would be no getting rid of them.

"Maybe we should turn the car around."

Cowardly? Oh, yes.

Theo chuckled. "You know these people. They want to see you."

"Yeah, about that. Don't you think it's kind of weird that Violet would include me in this? Inviting us as guests is one thing but a joint baby shower—that's just crazy, isn't it? I barely know her and all these people are going to wonder who the hell that bitch is, hanging on the Chase coattails-slash-ballgown trying to act like she's one of them."

"Elle ..."

"Also, people throw baby showers at the end of the second trimester not in the middle of it. Why aren't we waiting until the season is over?"

Theo stopped the car about half way up the drive, the same drive they'd entered about an hour ago and had *still* not completed. Ludicrous.

He turned to her and took her face between his hands. She loved when he used his strength like that—to protect, to soothe, but mostly to tell her to calm the fuck down. How had it come to this, where Theo Kershaw was the one displaying all the Zen?

"First, they want to celebrate us getting to the conference finals for the first time in four years. That's huge! Also Violet's a little further along so the timing makes sense to her. And finally, Ellie, my sweet, they are including you because they love *me*. This isn't about you at all, so quit being so self-centered."

"Oh, shut up." She giggled, loving that he always knew the perfect way to cap her crazy.

He leaned in to kiss her, soft at first, then deeper, sexier.

"Besides, you'll be getting another one when Aurora and the Tarts give you a baby shower back in Saugatuck."

"Which would be all for you as well," she muttered.

"You're going to have to face it. I'm the popular one. The fun parent. You have your good points but you'll always fade in the spotlight of my sun." He grinned and nuzzled her nose. "But seriously, isn't it kind of nice to be the center of attention?"

"Nice for you."

"These are good people who want to get to know you better. There's new life being created, new hope for the team, new futures being crafted. Let's celebrate the fact that we're alive on this earth, our baby is healthy, and it's a glorious spring day."

How could she object to a single word out of his mouth? Seeing the world through Theo's rose-tinted viewpoint was a revelation. It was impossible not to feel hopeful around him.

To feel more.

"There'd better be a chocolate fountain."

"That's my girl."

THERE WAS a chocolate fountain all right. And balloons. And party favors shaped like teddy bears. Not to mention an entire roster of burly hockey dudes looking like they wished they were anywhere but there.

Most of the women present had already birthed a couple of kids—and they had stories.

Sore breasts. Cracked nipples. Ripped vaginas. Pooping at the wrong time in the wrong place, usually when doing your utmost to expel a seven-pound bowling ball from your body.

Theo's rosy-eyed view underwent some dark tinting as the afternoon wore on. Pris Perez held the men in horrified thrall as she recounted in excruciating detail the birth of her second child.

Then she brought out the video.

Granted, the evidence wasn't funny but the effect was magnificent. These tough, battle-hardened men, who had lost teeth and dislocated shoulders and suffered kicks in soft places, all looked positively green at the gills.

"The miracle of birth," Violet murmured, placing her arm though Elle's and leading her away. Theo was too involved in the horror-around-a-campfire to even notice.

"Thanks for including me," Elle said to Violet for at least the fifth time.

"Are you kidding? You're doing me a huge favor. Harper is driving me up the wall and Izzy's useless because she hasn't got a maternal bone in her body. I need someone who understands."

"Doesn't Harper have three kids?" Gorgeous, blond daughters all under the age of four.

"Hatched in a tube."

"Really?"

"No, not really, but I should start a rumor. Harper does everything perfectly so all the births were less than three hours and each kid slid out singing arias and performing ballets. I just know this one is going to be trouble." She rubbed her stomach. "Look at their fathers. All that drama."

Elle's gaze landed on Cade and Dante, who were busy listening intently to one of Harper's Stepford children and not being dramatic in the slightest. "So which one is it?"

"We don't know. It's a Tex-Italian mix with my Boricua egg. The kid's already so far ahead of the game." She picked up a marshmallow and dipped it in the chocolate, then pointed at the bracelet on Elle's wrist. "That's pretty."

"Thanks. From Theo."

"That guy is such a sweetheart. Quite the front."

"Front?"

Violet's smile held for a brief moment while she decided if Elle was worthy of her confidence.

"I find it hard to believe that anyone who plays like he does, with all that aggression, doesn't have a bit more going on."

Elle had seen other sides to Theo, humanizing sides that revealed him to be more than a sexy doofus drama queen. "Everyone's got more going on," she muttered in his defense.

"Yeah, they do," Violet said pointedly. "You know, if you ever feel you need to talk about what's bothering you, I'm here for you. We all are."

Elle swallowed her surprise. In all this time while she was watching other people, she hadn't realized that someone might be watching her.

"I don't want to hurt him," she said quietly. "I think I have the capacity to do that." As always when she thought about the ways people could hurt each other, her parents took pole position in her brain. She looked around, wondering where they were. It wasn't like them to miss out on a chance of free booze and mingling with the upper echelons.

She'd thought they were the true threat, but no. Theo knew what they could do—or enough—and he was still as optimistic as ever. It was all too perfect. So now, in typical Elle style, she was waiting for the next disaster to strike.

"Maybe just let yourself be happy for a while," Violet said. "You've earned it."

Elle looked over to Theo who was laughing at something Erik had said, but seemed to sense she was looking his way. He caught her eye and squinted enough to ask her if she was okay.

She smiled. Because maybe ... she was?

Harper appeared, looking harried. "Ladies, time for a game."

"Do we have to?" Violet whined, then winked at Elle.

"This is a fun one." Harper rushed off, calling out, "Couples assemble!"

"Oh, God," Violet muttered.

The next few minutes were spent convening couples for the diaper game as Harper termed it. (The poopy game, according to Violet.) The goal was to see who could "diaper" a baby using cloth diapers and safety pins in the shortest time without piercing the poor infant. As using actual infants was considered too risky, balloons were substituted.

And it had to be done blindfolded.

Up first were Remy, Cade, and Theo. As his trusty assistant, Elle tied a bandana around Theo's eyes. "This is giving me some fun ideas," she murmured against Theo's chin as she knotted the fabric.

"Would prefer not to do this with a hard-on, you witch."

She giggled, then led him to the table. The partner was supposed to guide the diapering party to success, advising what to fold and where to put it. Elle thought it would be more fun to lead her man astray, but he caught onto her game quickly and generally forged ahead doing the opposite.

"GO, BABY BOY!" Aurora was on hand to be the support Elle wasn't.

A heart-stopping pop twenty seconds in signaled that Cade had pricked his poor spawn, who now lay in ragged remnants of latex.

"Cade's meat hook hands have been his downfall," Elle said excitedly. "You can do this, Theo!"

"If only I had a baby mama who was helpful," he quipped.

Remy's years as a stay-at-home-dad came in useful as he expertly set about wrapping and pinning the balloon, including the addition of diaper rash cream—show off—without blowing it up.

"Come on, Theo, you're neck and neck with Remy!" He

wasn't, but she figured it was her job to encourage. Better late than never.

Remy completed the task before Theo could get his balloon into position. And there was a sentence she never imagined she'd be thinking or saying.

"And the winner is Remy!" Harper cheered as she made the announcement then whipped off Remy's blindfold.

"All that practice," he said, kissing her sweetly. "Makes me think it might be time to make more."

The crowd roared their approval while Harper blushed to the roots of her blond hair. "If we win the Cup ... maybe."

Theo removed his blindfold and peeked at the diaper supplies. "So close." Not close at all, but the man lived and breathed optimism. "Beaten by the old timer."

Remy nudged him with his shoulder. "This old timer can teach you a thing or two, Kershaw, on and off the ice." He winked at Elle. "You need any childcare services, Ellie, just drop your little one off with our brood. I can change diapers in my sleep."

"Oh, that's kind of you." They were all so generous that for a moment, Elle was overcome. Also, another person calling her Ellie. This was her new life. A new Elle. Maybe she could trust that it was real.

Theo held up the blindfold. "Let's see how you do with the balloon." He lowered his voice and added, "Or without it."

"Or we could just open presents?" Violet commented with perfect timing.

Theo's eyes lit up. "Presents? I love presents."

"They're for the baby, Kershaw," Harper chimed in as she click-clacked by.

Elle laughed. "Same difference."

She wondered how the gift-giving would work for Violet,

given that she wasn't keeping the baby. But people had been thoughtful with their presents, many of them for her instead of the kid, so she wouldn't feel left out. Spa packages, foot rubs, that kind of thing.

"Oh, this one's for Baby Kershaw!" Violet passed over a wrapped gift—the first of many.

Elle spent the next fifteen minutes ripping open packages, each one bringing tears to her eyes. Teethers, pacifiers, plush toys, onesies (Rebels and Cubs editions —love!), a car seat, a stroller, a white noise machine, more onesies, bibs—you name it, someone had bought it.

She swiped at her eyes. "I can't believe this. It's too much. Really."

Theo examined everything with the curiosity of a little kid, even going so far as to try on the cool baby carrier for a dad. Cade had drawn a face on Theo's unpopped balloon and slipped it into the cradle.

"What do you think?"

That I'm the luckiest girl alive. "That you've never looked hotter."

His eyes darkened with desire and he moved in closer. "Me and my balloon baby are doing it for you?" His strong arms wrapped her up in the best hug she'd ever received. She didn't come from huggers. Neither was the army touchy-feely but apparently hockey players and their crew were.

"You're much too nice to me," she said with a sniff.

"I have my reasons."

"You do?"

"Sure," he murmured. "I love you."

She could feel her eyes widening in shock, shifting to see if anyone had heard or if a hole had opened in the ground. No one was paying attention to them and the world was still turning. "You-you what?"

He kissed her softly and whispered, "You slay me, Ellie Butler. And I love you." When she still didn't say anything, he frowned. "You okay?"

No! She was *not* okay. She was bowled over by Theo's unvarnished honesty. Of course she loved him, too, but she couldn't say it here. It was too private, and an admission like that needed all her focus. "I—uh, thank you?"

His smile could stop wars. "Sure. Any time." As easy as that, but then that was Theo. He had no problem with annoying things like *feelings*. He cast a look around. "Any chance we could slip away?"

Her phone buzzed with an incoming text. "Hold that thought. It's from my mom."

Duty calls. Headed out.

That was cryptic. She stepped outside to the patio and dialed.

Her mother picked up. "Eloise!"

"Hi, Mom. So the baby shower is practically over. Are you going to make it?"

"I'm afraid not. Something's come up."

Elle bit her lip. "Something? You mean a job?"

"There's always a job, my love. But it's probably better if we're not around for a while. You know how it is."

She lifted her gaze to Theo, who had followed her out and was watching her carefully.

"Better for who? What's happened? Will you be back when the baby's born?"

"If that's what you want," her mother said vaguely, though it was clear that Elle's wants would never be paramount here. "But who knows where we'll be? I wouldn't want to make a promise I can't keep."

No, promises weren't the Butlers' currency. A chill crept through her veins. Always a job, always a score. But there was something else. Something she both knew and didn't.

Before Elle could question that further, the line went dead.

29

"EVERYTHING OKAY?"

Theo had seen the look on Elle's face when she got that text. He had his suspicions and now he had to deal with the fallout.

"My parents have left town."

"Okay."

Her lips tightened. "You don't have something to say about that?"

Oh, he had plenty to say. "Did they say why?"

"No, but they've never been ones for pesky details. I just thought—"

"That this time it was different?"

She cut him a sharp look. "I know I haven't painted them as perfect but you don't seem surprised."

"Because I'm not." He stepped in close, his hands on her upper arms. "I offered money and they took it."

Her eyes flashed. "Of course they did! It's like giving drugs to a junkie. They're addicted to the score and they think they've scored huge with you."

"You can't trust them, Ellie. They're only here because of what you can give them."

"I know that! But you didn't have to do it. They would have been fine if you hadn't ... tested them!"

"Tested them? Come on, it didn't take much. Your dad came to me with some cock and bull story about your mother needing an operation. I thought these people were pros. It was an insult to my intelligence."

She opened her mouth to respond, but he wasn't finished.

"Their presence isn't good for you. I've seen how you change around them, how much they stress you out. You didn't want to fix it so I did. They think they've scored, and now they're on their way to the next scheme. Tell me what I did wrong, Elle."

Nothing. He'd protected what was his. He'd seen a threat and eliminated it.

"You did nothing wrong except waste your money. Because they'll be back."

She sounded so jaded. So sad. He hated seeing her hurt but he had zero regrets about his decision.

"Maybe. Maybe not."

"Oh, because you told them to stay away? I could've handled them, Theo. They might not be the best people but you said it was my call."

He didn't want to have to explain but it was better she knew now. A short, sharp blow instead of long-enduring pain. "They took the money, Elle. They couldn't wait to leave."

"Because you told them to go. You made that a condition." Immediately she realized her error. "You didn't make that a condition, did you? They hit you up, got the cash, and left anyway."

"Ellie," Theo said softly. "I'm sorry they let you down. I'm sorry it came to this."

Her face turned blank, taking on an inexpressiveness he'd thought he would never see again. He wanted New Ellie back, the woman who lit up in shock when he told her he loved her five minutes ago.

"You did what you had to for … for the baby."

"And for you."

"Because we're a package deal. I get it."

Her tone made him uneasy. "You're upset, and this is exactly why it's best they're not here."

"Well, you made sure of that."

"Elle. Your father spun some story about your mother being sick. Your sister almost conned someone into marrying her. And don't tell me that financial services firm isn't a front for worse stuff. I asked Tommy to look into them some more as soon as they showed up."

Her face tightened with pain. "Why didn't you say anything?"

"I was waiting for you to tell me more. To tell the truth."

"I never lied."

"But you didn't come completely clean, either. Not entirely. What about that Preston guy? You were engaged to him and it fell through."

Tommy had dug a little deeper, made a few more calls. Preston Carter claimed he had a lucky escape and had avoided a shakedown when he broke his engagement with Elle. He'd stopped short of blaming Elle but the doubts were there.

"That was … that was a long time ago." She rubbed her forehead. "Wait, do you think I tried to scam him? That's not what happened."

Theo didn't care about this Preston dude. Elle had been

young, still under her family's malign influence. He knew she'd grown, become her own person. But with her family hovering, looking for any way to latch onto a steady source of income, he couldn't be sure, if it came down to the wire, that she'd choose him.

He needed her to choose him.

"I don't care what happened with that guy, Elle. All I care about is the future. Our future. So you didn't tell me everything. It doesn't matter. I know everything now."

She looked at him like he was a fool. "Like that makes it okay. Like that fixes everything."

He crossed his arms. "Sunlight is the best disinfectant. Secrets tear people apart and I don't want that dynamic with anyone in my life."

"I kept it from you to protect you, Theo. So you wouldn't have to wallow in the dirt with them, and now look at you— you're commissioning background checks and buying off scammers. All you had to do was say no to them. People say no to them all the time."

"You don't. You say yes because you can't stand up to them. Or hat least not tall enough to protect yourself, even now when you have someone else to think of. All this time you've thought nothing had to change. That you can manage everything—the baby, a job, your parents, me. Well, things had to change. You can't use the same strategies as before. It's a new game."

"This isn't hockey, Theo. This is our lives."

"Exactly. And I'm going to do what you can't. Eliminate the toxic."

"For the baby?"

"Of course for the baby!" How could she be angry with him for putting the wellbeing of their child first?

She turned away, her voice as small as he'd ever heard it. "I understand. Could you take me home?"

He sighed. "Sure."

~

THIS WAS what it had come to. Her parents performing per their billing. Theo playing his part to perfection, the ideal gull who parts with a fortune and still thinks he's getting the better end of the deal. He'd showed her how ugly her life was. How grasping her parents were. And he'd had to descend to her level to play their game. She hated what she'd turned him into.

She was already tainting him.

Her parents couldn't even stick around for the baby shower, and they would have so enjoyed the extravagance on display, too. She'd hoped they'd be the family she needed instead of the family she was dropped into. She was no longer of use to them.

The ride back to Riverbrook was silent. Theo looked for parking outside the Empty Net but didn't find anything and turned on the hazards.

"I'll let you out and look for a spot."

"I'm kind of tired and could do with some alone time." She looked in the back, piled high with gifts. "Would you mind if we dealt with these later?"

He turned to her. "Elle, I know you're upset. Maybe I didn't handle it right but all I could think of is how negatively this might impact you. You've already had that turn and ended up in the ER."

"You're right," she said.

"I am?"

"You did what you needed to do for the baby. I get it, Theo. I do. I'm just sorry that I put you in that position."

"You're sorry? How is any of this your fault?"

She reined in her irritation. "You shouldn't have to deal with scammers and gold diggers. I brought this toxicity into your life. And while they'll be gone for a while, they'll eventually come back with their hands out. You're a money tree to them."

He shrugged like it was no big deal. "We'll worry about it when it happens."

We. Didn't he get it? She was the enemy. She was the toxic element. He might think he loved her but how strong would that love be after the third handout or the fourth?

"We don't need them, Elle. We have Aurora and our friends and the team."

He had them. They were all his people and she was just a hanger-on.

"It's been a long day, Theo. Could we talk later?"

His brow crinkled. "Sure. I'll check in tonight."

Once inside, she made some chamomile tea and tried not to think about her parents. They'd let her down one last time. Shown their true colors. This was a blessing, really.

But that left her brain space to think about Theo paying them off—Theo *forced* to pay them off so he could keep Elle's stress levels at a minimum and maintain their baby's health. She had placed him in this awkward position. Here he was, getting in the gutter with her awful family. Love needed careful nurturing, even a love as easily given as Theo's. Any feelings he thought he had for her would fray and wither if he was forced to deal with her parents on a regular basis.

Her phone rang with a call from Amy. She let it go to voice mail because she was sick of the whole lot of them.

Two minutes later, she listened to the message with an increasing sense of dread. She called Amy back.

"Elle! Thank God you're there."

"What's going on? Are you still in trouble?" She'd barely understood a word her sister said on the message. Something about Jackson and money and shit-covered fans.

"I thought I had enough to pay them back for the engagement ring, but they want more. I have something in the works, something that might pay off big, but I don't know if it'll come through in time."

Panic made Elle's skin itch. "I have almost ten grand. Maybe we can use it as a down payment on the debt. But Amy, no more scams."

"And where am I going to get the rest? Ten grand won't be enough. Can you ask your guy?"

Elle's blood turned to ice. "No. That well is dry. George and Dee already tapped it."

"That explains why they're not answering my texts. They've gone to ground. I could be at the bottom of the East River for all they care."

Elle's heart sank to the bar below. *Predator or prey.* Her parents had their pound of flesh and wouldn't even throw a bone to bail out their daughter.

"Are you sure Theo can't help?" Amy's pleading broke Elle's heart. Her parents might be beyond redemption but her sister wasn't. Elle should have brought her in from the cold sooner.

"I'll sort this out," Elle said, her tone more even than her pulse rate. "Leave it to me."

30

Game 1 of the Western Conference finals tonight, @ChiRebels v @EdmontonChucks. Who's gonna bring home that trophy?

"Oh, hey, Theo, come in." Jordan held open the door to the hotel room in Edmonton, where she was staying with Hunt. "Everything okay?"

"Have you heard from Elle?"

Jordan blinked in surprise. "Elle? No, not in a day or two. Is something wrong?"

"I haven't heard from her today so I called Tina. She asked for a couple of days off, then left with an overnight bag. We had a fight and she's not answering my texts."

A shirtless Hunt came out of the bathroom, towel-drying his hair. "What's up?"

Jordan's face tightened. "Elle's incommunicado. Have you heard from her?"

"Not for a while." Hunt scowled at Theo. "What did you do, Kershaw?"

"Sure, assume it was my fault. I was trying to protect her

from her crazy family. And now she's skipped town because she doesn't want anything to do with me."

Jordan led him to a sofa. "I'm sure that's not true. She has a job. Friends. Connections."

Did she, though? She could get a job anywhere. And she'd seemed so hurt by her family's departure. When the going got tough before, she ran to Chicago. What if this was her MO and she was bailing again?

He told her he loved her—and she said thanks.

"I'll text her," Jordan said at the same time Hunt took out his phone and thumbed the screen.

Just as with Theo, their phones remained frustratingly silent. He'd be okay with her ignoring him as long as she contacted someone they knew.

"I'm sure there's a good explanation," Jordan said. "She wouldn't leave without saying goodbye." She eyed Hunt. "Would she?"

"She's a headstrong, independent woman, and if a set of circumstances are not to her liking, I think she'd change them."

"Levi," Jordan said softly, with an admonishing glance that told the hardheaded former Green Beret to be more sensitive to Theo and his misery.

"No, he's right," Theo said. He'd driven her away by being so high-handed about her parents. "She has no roots here, a job she could do anywhere. She's pissed as all hell at me and now she's off somewhere with my kid and I can't reach her." He held up a hand to halt Hunt's superior response. "Yeah, I know. Good job, Kershaw!"

Jordan patted his arm. "So what did you fight about?"

Elle likely hadn't shared with anyone about her family and he didn't want to embarrass her. "Her family left town and she blames me for it because I don't think they're the best influence. I can't really get into it, but it amounts to me looking out for her and Elle being her usual ornery self and not appreciating it."

Hunt snorted. "Well, if you can't get into it, I guess we just have to take your word for it."

"Yep, Hunt, I guess you do."

Jordan frowned at her fiancé. Theo had always liked Jordan. "She probably just needs some space."

"Which is your way of saying I'm too much. You think I don't know that? I just want to take care of her." Unable to remain still, he jumped to his feet to work off his nervous energy. "So we have different ways of looking at the world. She expects everything to go wrong when really the second my bad boy sperm met her very receptive egg, we had a bona fide winner on our hands. It's like, how could we possibly fail? It's not an option! And if anything threatens all this winning, of course I'm going to step in and fix it."

Jordan showed a palm to Hunt, who took the hint and closed his mouth. "I think she's worried about letting you down, Theo," Jordan said. "You've got a lot going for you"—His teammate made some indecipherable noise—"And she's worried about living up to your expectations for this winning life you're always so sure of. I don't know her that well but I don't think she's been as lucky as you or me with our families."

Theo knew that for a fact. But why wouldn't she accept the good things coming her way when Theo was so ready to provide it?

"She doesn't trust me. Or trust that I'm in this for the long haul."

"Are you?" Hunt asked. "In it for the long haul?"

"Of course I am."

"Not just as a parent," Hunt said, "but the rest? Do you love her, Theo?"

"Yes, I love her! I told her, but she didn't say it back."

Jordan looked stricken. *That's just great.*

"She's afraid of emotional intimacy," Theo said. "Shit, I shouldn't have told her, should I? That's why she ran."

Hunt folded his arms. "Maybe she felt smothered. You're not the most low-key person I know."

Jordan glared at her fiancé. "That's not it. I suspect Elle's not used to this kind of care. She's overwhelmed by it and doesn't know if she can trust it. She might be worried you're being so amazing because of the baby and while it probably started out that way, she doesn't see the moment when you started seeing her separately from the life you created together."

"The moment ..." How could he explain that Elle had been uppermost on his mind from the second he met her? "There's never been a moment when I haven't seen her. I've had a crush on her from Day One and now it's more. It's deeper. And yes, it's wrapped up in her carrying my child. I can't separate that out but I'm crazy about Ellie, the woman."

Jordan's phone buzzed, then Hunt's. She held up her screen to display a message from Elle. Thank. Fuck.

I'm fine. Out of town for a couple of days.

Still nothing for Theo. A moment ago, he'd have been okay with that, but now not so much.

"That's just fan-fucking-tastic!" Before he could get too mad about it, Theo's phone rang with a pic of a velociraptor, his phone profile pic for Elle, Mother of Hatchlings. Didn't seem so funny anymore.

"Where the hell are you?"

Pause, followed by a quiet, "Hi to you, too."

He stood and headed to bathroom because he had already embarrassed himself enough in front of regular humans. "Tina said you skipped town. You weren't answering my texts or anyone else's. I'm worried."

"I didn't *skip* town. I needed to take care of something. It's no big deal."

No ... big ... Jesus, he was going to smash something. Serenity fucking now. "You can't just up and quit instead of facing your problems."

"Don't worry, my problems travel with me."

Their child, *the* problem. "Are you coming back to Chicago?"

"Theo, did you really think I would leave without talking to you? I just landed and saw all the texts." She sounded a little choked up.

"People were worried about you." *People*, meaning Theo. "And when I heard you were last seen rolling a suitcase down the street, I didn't know what to think. I thought maybe you were ..."

"What?"

Following her parents. That's what he'd thought. That the scam had been successful and she was off to rendezvous with them or something like in a Jason Bourne novel. His first instinct was to not trust her and assume the worst.

It's not like it hasn't happened to me before.

"Nothing. I was just worried. Are you okay?"

"The baby's fine, Theo."

He inhaled deep, thinking about what Jordan had said about seeing Elle as separate from the baby. "But are *you* okay? Where are you?"

"I'm fine. I flew to New York to meet with my sister. She ... she needs me."

But I need you. "Is there anything I can do?"

Tell her you love her again.

Or, you know, stop smothering her, idiot.

"You've already done so much. This—this is something I have to do. Alone."

He didn't like the sound of that. "Elle, what's going on?"

"I'll be back soon, Theo. We'll talk then. Good luck at the game tonight. We'll be watching."

IF ELLE HAD any doubts that Amy's former mark was "connected," they were quickly dispelled by the first choice of meeting location. When she finally reached him—after several phone calls and what sounded like a reroute to a messaging service in the Czech Republic—Jackson's associate had suggested they meet at a dive bar on the Lower East Side.

Elle might be the least talented of the Butler crew but she wasn't born yesterday. Instead she'd suggested a Starbucks in Midtown Manhattan. Nothing bad ever happened to anyone in Starbucks, except empty calorie ingestion. *Zing!*

Sometimes she amused herself greatly, and hell, she needed cheering right now.

Armed with a non-fat decaf mocha with whip (and she was aware of the dissonance), she took a seat at the window. Her backpack sat on her lap, inside it a Chase Bank envelope containing $9,453 in one hundred dollar bills, her entire savings. Like Elle, her sister needed a clean slate to start over, an empty ledger. Elle could give this to her and at the same time, unhook her from the grasp of their parents.

It was a risk. Jackson's family might not be satisfied—she was over two grand short of the cost of the engagement ring and they'd said they wanted more. Amy might not see it for the fresh start it was. Most terrifying of all, Elle would be penniless, needing to rely on Theo to tide her over for the few months after the hatchling was born.

But he was a good guy. He'd do this because Elle and the baby were family to him. She hoped it wasn't too late for them. She loved him so much and wanted to trust that he meant what he said at the baby shower. With her responsibility to Amy fulfilled, balance could be restored. This fantasy life she was living as Theo Kershaw's baby mama might become real.

When she returned to Chicago, they would talk about their future—as a family, but also as a couple.

She checked her phone. Five minutes past the meet time. Some sort of power play, she assumed, but right then, a text came in from Amy.

It's all good. Call me.

What did that mean? About to dial her up, she pulled short when someone took the seat beside her. Someone who sent her hormones into a loop-the-loop because she recognized that scent.

Theo.

She turned.

Scowling Theo.

"What are you doing here?"

The scowl deepened. "I'm here to stop you from being your own worst enemy."

She looked over his shoulder. He was alone.

"Wait, you should be in Edmonton for Game 2 tomorrow night."

He shook his head, not disagreeing with her, but acknowledging her statement and signaling exactly how annoyed he was.

Oh, crud. Leaving in the middle of a two-game away trip during the playoffs was probably not the best preparation.

"Theo, why are you here?"

Anger rolled off him in waves. The words emerged from his mouth like the rat-a-tat of gunfire. "Tommy helped me track down your sister. I talked to her and then I talked to Jackson. I've taken care of it, so we can leave now."

"But—what do you mean you took care of it? You mean you dropped more money on the situation?"

"I didn't have to. Amy and her guy needed their heads knocked together and now that's done—yep, I played Cupid for your sister—so this debt you're here to pay is taken care of. Now, let's go."

Her head spun. "Amy and Jackson are together? You came here to fix this?"

"I shouldn't have had to come here at all. Because you should have come *to me* for help. Instead you kept it to yourself, jumped in to do your lone wolf bit, set up a meeting with some sketchy criminal type to do some sketchy money drop—"

"Theo, keep your voice down." People were giving them strange looks. At least one person was filming.

A muscle she had never noticed before jumped in his jaw. His voice turned low and menacing. "What the hell do you think you're doing flying to another city and putting you and the baby in danger? I thought we were a team."

Pot, the kettle would love to make your acquaintance. "Are you kidding? You went behind my back and paid off my parents. And you think I should have come to you again to beg for *more* money for my sister?"

"If necessary, yes. At the very least, you should have run it by me instead of high-tailing it off on your secret 007 mission and putting yourself and my child at risk. You have no idea how pissed I am at you right now, Elle. I can't leave you alone for a second. I can't trust that you'll include me in the most important decisions."

She opened her mouth and he cut in.

"Yes, I fucked up when I paid off your parents without talking to you first—I get that and I'm sorry—but they're not good people. And they've taught you that it's okay to keep secrets. It's not. It's not okay."

She knew her parents were terrible role models. Given his past and how secrets had burned his heart, she understood he would never be on board with their brand of deception. No decent person would. She would eventually make peace with the lifelong betrayal by her parents but she still had a mission to complete. Amy could still be saved.

"I'm here for my sister. I'm trying to get her back on the straight and narrow. This wasn't about you, Theo."

His expression turned stony. "Yeah, dumb ol' Theo is finally starting to get that. It never is. You're always going to put your bad-news family before us. Before *our* family."

"You don't know a thing about my sister."

He threw up his hands. "Why do you think that is? Because everything with you is army rules, on a need-to-know basis. Your sister seems nice, by the way, despite being a criminal mastermind and all."

"She's not a criminal mastermind. She's just misguided. I wanted to help her sort her life out before I introduced her to proper society. To you."

"And in the meantime, she's fine with her pregnant twin meeting up with mob thugs to drop off money. Oh, she sounds like a peach."

Sarcasm noted. "I insisted. She's too close to the situation and frankly, she's scared of them I'm not and I took precautions."

He shook his head vehemently. "Not good enough. You put your health and the health my child in danger. And you don't sound even the teensiest bit regretful."

My child. "Your golden spawn is safe, Theo. Your precious bundle was never in any danger, so stop being such a drama queen."

"Right, I'm the dramatic one." He stood. Dramatically. "Let's go."

"So you can shout at me in a less public location?"

"So I can put you on a flight back to Chicago and think about what we need to do to fix this."

"What's to fix?"

"The breakdown in trust between us."

Her heart contracted at the pain she heard in those words.

"You don't trust me, Theo. That doesn't sound fixable. That sounds pretty damn unfixable."

High emotion marred his handsome features. "That's it? You're not even going to try?"

An embryonic love might exist between them, but without trust it would never blossom. "For what? You need someone who follows all your directives, plays the subservient WAG, has no agency, and makes none of her own decisions. I'm not that person. Never will be."

"I've done nothing but figure out ways to protect you and our child. You're the one who decided to keep everything inside, lying since the beginning."

She understood that, but he was asking her to change her personality overnight. She had work to do but she refused to apologize for trying to help her sister.

"I should have told you about my family sooner, I get that. I had reasons for keeping those secrets. But I'm not some paragon of human communication, Theo. You want everyone to be an open book, to spill their guts, to keep nothing inside. Not everyone works that way. It takes time to peel back the layers and risk exposure."

His expression turned stormy. "Which is your way of saying you don't want to change. You'd rather be like them, your parents. Keeping secrets, never confiding in anyone, only relying on yourself. I thought we were a team, Elle. Rather than build a life with me and the hatchling, you'd rather pretend solo is better."

"Not pretending. I've done just fine on my own up until now."

His jaw was as tight as a drum, his eyes darker than midnight. They'd reached an impasse—she could never meet his standards for honesty, he would never let make her own decisions.

"Got it," he grated. "I need to catch a flight to Edmonton for the next game. Text me if you need anything."

Still her protector, even as she pushed him away.

Unable to speak, she could only watch as he stormed out and joined the busy throng on a New York street.

31

THEO SAT HEAVILY in a backrow seat on the team bus to the airport and kept his head down. Better that than seeing the disappointment etched on the faces of his team. He'd played like crap tonight and was largely responsible for the Rebels Game 2 loss against Edmonton.

His emotions had ruled his game. Usually he could tune out the noise and let his great game instincts take over. He was known for his excellent ice IQ, his ability to see the plays from all angles and be where he was needed. But tonight, all that had taken a nosedive over the Plexi. He'd missed blocks, whiffed pucks, cleared poorly.

Focus had deserted him, his brain running in perpetual motion, just not on the game. Only Elle. He couldn't recall being so angry about anything or anyone—at least not since his mom. His recovery from Candy's lies and betrayal had required building a callus over his heart. Letting the arrows slide right off him, so that by the time he'd approached Bio-Dad Nick, he was prepared and not even surprised that the man who would reject his mom would reject the product of their teenaged mistake. Being spurned by Nick—twice—

had stung, but Theo had a will and disposition sunny enough to get him through.

But over the last few months, that callus had been sanded off as he got closer to Elle. In its place was his exposed underbelly, at which anyone could take a shot. Elle's go-it-alone attitude and her unwillingness to include him had hurt. Why should he even be surprised that this woman wouldn't want to be a player on Team Theo? He wasn't the kind of guy who attracted forever.

Someone sat beside him. A thousand spots on this bus and he had to pick this one.

Theo pulled out his earbuds because he wasn't rude.

"You played well tonight, double-oh," he said to Gunnar. Tonight the crowd had gone wild when Bond was introduced, a mark of respect for the man who was picking up the pieces of his rubbled life and clawing his way back to the top of his sport.

"And you played like shit, Kershaw."

Good old G-Man, telling it like it was. Gunnar continued with the ego boost. "What's got you performing like a constipated, part-time league rookie who looks like he hasn't seen ice in a millennium?"

Theo held out for the fist bump. "Nice, G. Working on your people skills, I see."

Bond acknowledge the gesture. "How's Elle?"

"I'd be the last person she'd tell."

"Well, that explains tonight's performance."

Theo gusted out a sigh. "She's been keeping stuff about her family from me, putting them before the health of our kid." Putting them before *him*. "We had a big blow-up about it."

"Any of this stuff a deal breaker?"

"It wouldn't have been if she'd come clean about it. It's

not the stuff, it's the hiding of the stuff. It's how she has to do it her way and not consult me when I thought we were a team."

Gunnar waited a long beat. "I've told you before that you're a brave kid, Kershaw. A fighter. Now you're at the top of your game—well, obviously not tonight, but usually— and part of your success is down to how good a communicator you are and how you've always known when to ask for help."

"I'm not afraid of looking like I don't understand something. There's no shame in relying on other people."

"Right. Your mom and dad let you down, but you figured out how to form a circle you could rely on. You're a social animal, an extrovert, a guy who needs other people as a foil." Gunnar's lips twitched. "I'm guessing your girl has a different approach."

Completely. Elle didn't need anyone—but that wasn't completely true. With parents like hers, she'd be better off alone. Is that the lesson she'd learned? But she was starting to come around. She'd been so happy at the baby shower, every smile she sent his way as she opened a gift another brick smashed in the wall between them.

And when he'd told her he loved her, she'd been shocked. Like she couldn't believe it. Like she didn't deserve it.

"She's not had a lot of people she could rely on. Her family's kind of a mess." Including her sister, but Elle was trying to help her twin. So the strategy wasn't fully thought out, but her heart was in the right place.

He just wasn't sure she'd ever want to open up that heart completely to him.

Elle opened her eyes slowly, letting them adjust incrementally to the early morning sunlight streaming across the bright white sheets. Super-soft, they had to be at least 1000 thread count.

Quality linens for the guest room of Jackson's condo. Being part of a "sort of connected" shipping magnate family appeared to pay well.

A light rap on the door snapped her fully awake before her sister's voice called out, "You decent?"

"Debatable."

Amy pushed open the door and entered tray-first. Even at the ass crack of dawn, she looked perfect. Sharp Coco Chanel bob, a wicked slash of red across her mouth, those coal dark lashes that framed eyes bluer than the ocean.

"Breakfast in bed!" On the edge of the bed, she settled a pretty tray laden with OJ, croissants, scrambled eggs and spinach, fresh fruit, coffee, and a cheerful yellow daisy.

"Ames, you didn't have to do that."

"Why not? You came all the way to New York and all you got was dumped."

Elle squeezed her eyes shut.

"Sorry, too soon?"

Her eyes snapped open. "Yes, too soon! It's been less than forty-eight hours."

Blithely, Amy popped a blueberry into her mouth. "I made decaf. And I know you said you were trying to eat more healthily for your super-baby but I figure you can indulge with a croissant while you're on vacation."

"I'm not on vacation." At Amy's fallen expression, she amended. "It's lovely. I just—I need to get back to Chicago."

"But ..." Amy left it hanging. *He doesn't want you. He doesn't trust you. When are you ever going to learn?* "We haven't spent any time together."

"I know. But even if Theo and I aren't friends anymore, or—or anything else—we've still got the baby to consider. I said I'd be at every home game during the playoffs and I need to keep that promise."

Last night's game in Edmonton had not gone the Rebels way. Even a hockey dud like Elle could tell Theo was off his game, and she knew it was because of their fight. So much for Jordan's ludicrous claim that the players were good at shutting out their personal lives. Elle hoped that being in the arena with his child would give him a boost for the next game.

She sat up and grabbed a fork, not really feeling it but knowing she needed to make an effort for her sister. The scrambled eggs were fluffy and surprisingly hit the spot. "Any word from George and Dee?"

Amy rolled her eyes. "We won't hear from them for a while. I can't believe Dad tried the 'mom needs an operation' gimmick on Theo."

"I can't believe he paid up."

"Can't you? He did it for you. He wanted them out of your life because he loves you."

"He loves the baby." He might have said he loved her, but she knew it was all tangled up in his love for their child. "He's determined that nothing harms the kid, so he made a preemptive strike. Remove the poison."

Amy poured out the coffee. "But he didn't have to pay anything at all. That says something. And then he hopped a plane here in the middle of the playoffs to fix *my* problem. Kind of like Darcy bailing out Wickham." Her face registered shock. "Aw, hell, am I Lydia?"

"Didn't you know? I thought the flighty smugness would've clued you in." Theo showing up in New York would have been a lovely gesture if he hadn't been so pissed at her. "Grand gestures or not, we're incompatible anyway. He's all sun and open arms, and I'm clearly not. We'll be co-parents, nothing else." Her heart ached at the thought of getting exactly what she'd wished for from the beginning. Stealing a glimpse of the possibilities of forever with Theo made the idea of going back to before unbearably painful. This was why mortals shouldn't mix with gods.

"Why aren't you compatible? I mean, the sex is good, isn't it?"

"Yes. But sexual compatibility isn't enough. I want to contribute and not have Theo do all the heavy lifting. And I thought I was doing that by taking care of this problem for you without getting him involved. So he wouldn't think I'm this bloodsucking leech." It's what she'd been trying to do since entering the army, but the moment she got pregnant, the scales became heavier on one side. She was taking out more than she was putting in—and Theo was paying the price.

Amy smothered butter and jam on one of the croissants. "He was so mad when he tracked me down and found out you'd gone to that meet. I thought he was going to rupture another aneurysm." She chewed on the buttery pastry, leaving little flakes at the corner of her mouth. "Seems the leech version of you is preferable to the—what did he call you?"

"Lone wolf on a secret 007 mission. He's kind of dramatic."

"He's kind of in love with you. He'd rather you came to him for help, that you'd trust him with these problems. He'd rather you tackled things together and he has a point."

Easier said than done.

"I know. I don't deserve him."

"That's not what I'm saying. But that's obviously what

you've been thinking all along. That this guy who wants to be your partner in all things is too good for you, that he wouldn't like the real you if you showed your heart to him. It's why Jackson and I got into this mess."

Amy's marriage scam of Jackson was a *little* different, but there were obvious parallels. The huckster and the soft-hearted hottie one, in particular.

"I don't understand. How can Jackson possibly forgive you?" An odd pang that she could only label as envy pinched behind her breastbone.

"I marvel at it myself but I've had some time to think about it. None of us is perfect. Jackson knows I have trust issues, that how I—*we* were raised has skewed our views on relationships. I'd always thought falling in love would make me weak. Would expose me to all sorts of hurts."

"It does."

Amy smiled ruefully. "True. I'm not good at it. Not yet. But I want to learn and Jackson wants to teach me. And while I needed his forgiveness, I also needed to forgive myself for some of the things I've done. Which brings me to you and Theo."

"It's not the same," Elle insisted. "I was doing everything in my power not to hurt him. I made sure he didn't give me a penny, that it was all in trust for the hatchling. I resisted all his efforts to ..." *Be kind. Care. Love her. Shit.* "And then when George and Dee showed up, I came clean. Told him what they were like. What *I* was like. And he still made that dumb call to give them money."

Her sister's eyes warmed with sympathy. "So let me get this straight. From the minute you found out you were pregnant you went out of your way to prove to Theo that you were a bad bet and not worth the trouble. You hid—or tried to hide—all the attributes that make you my amazing sister so he couldn't see the kind-hearted dummy underneath. You got mad at him for paying off our toxic parents and told him he had no right to be angry when you went on *your* lone wolf 007 mission."

Put like that ...

"He has this fixer mentality which means I feel helpless around him. He calls it teamwork, I call it patriarchy."

"Ooh, patriarchy! Wish he would throw some of that patriarchy my way." She whipped out her phone. "Let me take a look at this epitome of virtue. I have to say I've been enjoying these little snippets into the life of a baller dad-to-be." She pulled up Theo's Instagram feed. He hadn't posted anything since before their fight, which meant he was ... upset? Busy? Retooling his brand? She had no idea.

"Amy, don't ..." It was too painful.

"Don't what? Show how excited he is to be a daddy? I mean, look at this one." Amy opened up one of Theo's videos from a couple of weeks ago. Fans had sent him hockey-themed gifts for the baby: A pair of mini skates in Rebels blue and white, rompers with "My Favorite Hockey Player is my Daddy," and hockey rubber duckies.

So adorable, but even more adorable was Theo's joy while showing them. She missed him and his exuberance so much. "He's excited to be a father and no one will be better at it. But that doesn't mean we're meant to be a couple."

"So that charm bracelet you're wearing means nothing?"

She couldn't remove it from her wrist, which had swollen because, pregnant. "He likes to buy stuff."

"And put it all over his Insta Stories."

"What?" She grabbed Amy's phone and hit Theo's avatar. He never posted anything in Stories.

Amy was right. Theo had clips in his Stories from the last twenty-four hours, a series of five-second shots of—oh,

God—each charm on her bracelet: the dog tags, the hockey sticks fashioned into a heart, the baby feet. But there was one more, one she didn't recognize.

She played it again. No, it couldn't be.

"What's going on here?" Amy asked fiercely. "Is it a message? A secret code? I love secret codes!"

"Sort of. It's a charm he hasn't given me yet."

Amy played the Stories again, holding the phone between them. "Is that a lizard?"

"It's a baby T-rex. A hatchling." At Amy's blank look, she added, "Theo has a thing for dinosaurs. He's got these briefs that ..." Her cheeks heated remembering his dino-briefs and that first time they'd connected—and conceived a life. "It's an inside joke."

"Do other people know about this dinosaur fetish?"

"It's not a fetish. It's cute and adorable."

"A cute and adorable inside joke that he put on Instagram and only one person would get ... hmm. Listen, Elle-Belle. From the beginning, it's clear that you were desperately trying to not get Theo involved in the family's shenanigans—I understand that, I do. But I think you were also holding him at arm's length because you were worried about falling for him. Worried you weren't good enough when really you're the purest, sweetest person I know."

"You're surrounded by lowlifes and scam artists. Not hard for me to rise above."

"Agh! Why are you making this so hard? Mom and Dad trained us to see every interaction as transactional. What's in it for each party involved. Love isn't like that."

"Let me guess. It's patient. It's kind."

"Yes, my cynical uterus-roomie. And neither of us have had a lot of patience or kindness in our lives. What about

Theo? I'm guessing you gave him hell and he still came back for more."

Elle sniffed. "I was awful, Ames! And he was so sweet, all the time. When he paid off George and Dee I was so angry that he'd had to do that, that I'd brought him down to the gutter level we've always lived in. And then he shows up doing his white knight act again. In Starbucks!"

Amy offered a napkin.

"Sorry, I'm so hormonal these days."

Awkward hand pat. Her sister had never been good at the tea and sympathy thing. "So Theo had to get in the dirt to protect what was his. Big deal. In fact, you're right, it is a big deal. Because it means he's willing to eliminate any threat to your sanity and the health of you and the baby. Don't get too mad at him for taking off the gloves. He's a man in love."

"With his child."

"Right. That dino-charm shit is for the kid. This hot hockey dude—and man, he is hot—is crazy about you. All he's asking is that the two of you work together as a team. Let him help you when you need it because that's how he expresses his love. And you need to stop thinking all this is your fault for inflicting Mom and Dad on him. He's a big boy ..." Her eyes twinkled. "He is, right?"

"Big enough, you dirty bird."

Amy smiled. "He made a call to send the 'rents packing and now he's pulling a Ralphie in *A Christmas Story* and sending secret Insta messages that you have to decode with your heart."

"Sure. Instead of 'Don't forget to drink your Ovaltine,' the message is 'there's a blueberry-kale smoothie with your name on it, Butler.'"

Was she reading too much into this? Theo couldn't really expect that she'd see this feed unless it was a test.

She *had* confessed to being a stalker, though.

She handed back Amy's phone. "You're really in love with Jackson, aren't you?"

"Yes, I am. Do you like him? Say you like him!"

Elle had met the man himself last night at dinner and instantly warmed to him. He had a soothing, Gunnar Bond-like quality she could appreciate. "I like him. And he's clearly nuts about you."

Amy smiled. "Thank you for coming to New York to bail me out. I'm so grateful, especially as Mom and Dad had a big payday courtesy of your man and decided I'm not worth the trouble."

"They're the worst."

"They are. But you're the best. And Theo thinks so, too—when he's not pissed at you. It's time you forgave yourself for bringing all this drama to his life and accept that maybe he kind of enjoys it. He's a bit of a drama queen himself judging by those Insta videos."

He was. She rubbed a hand over her stomach, contemplating her next move.

The baby kicked hard. "Oh!" She grasped Amy's hand and placed it over her belly just as Hatch did another karate move.

"He's going to be a soccer player," Amy said with a smile. "Or a street thug."

"If he plays any sports professionally, it'll be hockey like his dad." Sadness that Theo wasn't here to feel this checked her heart. He might not be present, but maybe the baby was his proxy. Letting her know he was still important. But their kid wasn't the only consideration, was he? Elle had to also think about what was best for her.

Everyone deserves to be happy. Elle had always assumed those well-worn platitudes didn't apply to a girl like her, not when she had so much work to do saving the world and restoring balance to the universe. Like a Jedi.

Maybe it was time for a break from all that.

If she wanted to make this work with Theo, she needed to accept a few home truths about herself and that universal ledger she'd been working so hard on. She needed to make the decision to be happy.

32

The conference finals are heating up with tonight's Game 3 in the even series between @ChiRebels and @EdmontonChucks. @HockeyGrrl's got ya covered!

MORNING SKATE HAD JUST FINISHED when Theo's phone rang with an unrecognizable number. Given that the woman he loved was out of state and not in a hurry to speak with him, he answered immediately. "Hello."

"Theo?"

His blood froze, his heart not far behind. "Yeah?"

"This is Nick. Nick Isner."

"Uh huh."

"So I know you probably don't want to talk to me, but I wondered if you're free for, uh, coffee?"

It was a request, so Theo didn't have to respond. He could hang up right now and go on with his life. For too long, he'd been a doormat, letting his emotions walk all over him. Maybe it would be better to turn off that spigot and become a statue like Hunt.

Which didn't really explain why an hour later he was sitting in Riverbrook Cafe, playing Candy Crush on his phone (sue him, he was old school), and waiting on his bio-dad to put in an appearance.

The door opened and in walked Nick. He held out his hand. "Theo."

"Nick." Theo's voice had taken on a grown-up, deeper timbre. He shook the offered hand because he might be pissed off and heartbroken, but he wasn't a dick.

"Can I get you something?" Nick waved in the direction of the counter, and Theo shook his head. "Do you mind if I ...?"

"Go caffeinate. You're gonna need it."

Nick's eyebrows rose, but he didn't comment. A few minutes later, he was back with his doctored coffee, again asking if it was okay for him to sit. All this deference was doing Theo's head in. Was this where he got his politeness gene from?

"Surprised to hear from me, I bet." Nick looked sheepish.

"Not really. Figured you'd see the light eventually if I made a finals run."

Nick shook his head, like it was too soon to joke about it. Not that Theo was joking.

"I screwed up, Theo. You know I did. All I could see was what I might lose instead of what I would gain. You've done so well and I haven't had a single thing to do with it."

"Got that right." The words sounded tired even though true.

"Could we start over? I'm not asking for cookouts and fishing trips. I'd just like to get to know you and maybe, if you're open to the idea, introduce you to your brothers."

Theo's heart leaped. *Now we're talking.* "Do they know about me?"

"Not yet. I didn't want to get their hopes up in case this doesn't work out. I don't want to put them in the middle of a negative situation if I can help it." He shook his head. "Yeah, I know this situation is of my own making, but I'm trying to do something to rectify it. Even if we can't move to the next level, maybe you could get to know Sean and Jason."

Theo scrunched up his mouth. "I feel like this is really a scam to get playoff tickets."

Nick's eyes blew wide. "It's not, honestly!" At Theo's tilted head, he realized that his oldest son was trying to make light of the moment. "Oh, humor."

"I'm a funny guy. Clearly didn't get it from you."

"No. Candy was the funny one." His mouth twisted in remembered pain, and a moment of recognition passed between them. Sometimes, Theo really missed his mom. "We were dumb kids. Not that it's an excuse for how I behaved then or later."

Theo wasn't sure what to say to that. Kids made stupid decisions all the time. Adults, too.

"I've no doubt you'll do a better job," Nick said, "especially with a woman like Elle supporting you. She's something else."

"She is." Theo wasn't going to get into his problems with Nick just yet.

Just yet? Was he seriously considering letting the guy off the hook? Surely he should punish him for a little longer because he wasn't even sure he wanted a relationship with his father. He'd done just fine without him—Elle was right about that. But he did want to get to know his brothers and that gnawing ache decided it for him.

"Okay, Nick. Here's what's going to happen. I'm not going

to make it easy on you. But I want to get to know my brothers and as I have to go through you to get to them, I guess that makes you and the little dudes a package deal. I'll be monitoring the situation to see if you come up to my lofty standards. In the meantime, you can break the joyful tidings to your other sons and ask them if they'd like to hang with me. And don't even think of forcing them!"

Nick's smile was wry, just like his own. "They'll want to meet you."

"Why? Because I'm a famous hockey player? Maybe they'll hate the idea. Maybe they'll be pissed at you for keeping this a secret for so long. Don't assume you know how people will react." He'd thought he was doing the best thing, removing Elle's parents from her life and fixing her sister's problem. Showed what he knew. "But whenever they're ready—if ever they're ready—I'd love to get to know them. Is the lady Isner in the loop?"

"The lady—oh, right." He nodded. "She's not too pleased."

"Well, I don't want to do anything to piss her off."

"She's not pleased with *me* because of how I handled this. You're blameless in all of this, Theo. She wants to meet you. Again."

Theo let that sink in. He wished Elle was here so he could run it by her. "What made you decide to reach out today? I haven't exactly been responsive."

Nick lowered his gaze, focused on his coffee cup. "I've been thinking of you a lot, though I know you don't believe me. What your girlfriend said when we met and then again, when she called—"

"Called? Elle called you?"

Nick looked up. "Yes. She called me yesterday. Told me that meeting your brothers was important to you, and I thought that even if you and I can't repair what's broken, then I could make that much right. Give them a chance to know the fine man you've become."

Holy shit, Elle had fixed this? She knew how important family was to him and she'd made this happen. His heart ached. He wanted to send her a text of thanks but mostly, he wanted to know she was okay.

"Theo." Casey, Harper's assistant, put her head around the locker room door. "You have visitors."

"Be right there." He put his hockey stick and tape down on the bench, then headed out to the corridor.

Nick Isner was here with Jason and Sean.

"Hey, guys!" Ignoring Nick, Theo addressed himself to the boys. "You made it!"

Two nights ago, Theo had spent dinner with the Isners at their house in Andersonville in Chicago. Awkward at first, but no one knew better than Theo how to navigate awkward. Lady Isner was all brittle smiles, but Theo gave her top marks for making the effort (and her stellar eggplant lasagna). Thirty minutes in, he was speaking the universal language of teenage boys—video games—and inviting them to a playoffs game. Easy-peasy-lemon-squeezy.

"Are you ready?" Sean asked. At fourteen, he was more serious than his younger brother and the one Theo had worried about the most. A Mathlete and a fan of statistics, he'd wowed Theo with game analysis that blew everyone's minds.

"As I'll ever be. Assuming Coach even puts me in."

Sean nodded gravely. "Your plus-minus for the last four games has not been great."

"Sean," Nick warned.

Theo laughed at his brother's honesty and put out his fist for the bump. "No, he's right. I need to do better. Seats are good, right?" he asked Jason.

"Amazing. Right behind the bench. You could turn and see us." Jason shrugged. "If you're not too busy."

"Definitely! Might need some encouragement if we're not doing well." He looked over their heads at Nick. "Thanks for coming tonight."

Nick nodded and said with fake cheer, "Thanks for inviting us!"

Okay, then. It was going to take a while to iron that out. Maybe he'd have a relationship with Nick one day. For now, Jason and Sean were his primary focus, at least until the baby put in an appearance.

Elle had texted him today, letting him know she was back in town. He appreciated the heads-up and prayed that they could be, at minimum, friends. Wasn't that what he'd wanted from her in the first place? So he'd ended up with more than he bargained for—a hatchling *and* a hurting heart—but he had zero regrets about making a move on her one chilly Christmas Eve.

The final call was made. "Gotta go! If you scream my name, I might hear it, so don't be shy." A couple of closing fist bumps sent them on their way.

In the line before heading into the tunnel, Gunnar nudged him. "You okay?"

"My dad's here. With my brothers."

"Thought you were an only child."

"It's a long story."

Gunnar side-eyed him. "Just one long soap opera, Kershaw. You're not really a half-measures kind of guy."

Theo supposed not. He tended to go overboard, letting

his emotions rule and not really thinking things through. Maybe he should have been more patient with Elle, who was a thinker with a different way of processing things. But he couldn't apologize for loving her and his kid too much. All he could do was make every call from his heart.

33

THE PUCK WAS MOVING fast tonight, or maybe Theo was moving slow. Coach called him off the line for the shift change after he flubbed his third pass of the evening.

"Sorry, Coach," Theo said as he took what he expected would be an extended break on the bench.

"Kershaw," Coach said tiredly. Just one word, a shitload of censure.

Burnett was still on. Usually they worked the line together, but he was having a great game, having covered up for a multitude of Theo's sins. Teamwork.

He never wanted to hear that word again.

"Come on, Theo!" That sounded like Jason who was sitting with his brother and Nick about five rows up—close enough to the bench but not obstructed every time the players stood to scream at some ridiculous decision by the stripes.

He knew he was letting them down, but shit, he couldn't get it together. He needed Elle. A text wasn't enough. He needed to see her and know she was safe.

Gunnar came off and sat beside him. "Good work, man."

Coach should really be putting Bond in more. The guy was a beast out there and they did much better with him playing than not.

"Go, Theo!"

Jason again. Theo turned and smiled, giving him a wave.

Gunnar smiled. "Your brother?"

"Yeah. He's loud, like me."

"Just wait until your kid comes along. Loud doesn't describe it."

The Chucks Dimitri Kasparov high-sticked Travis and didn't get called for it. The whole bench stood to protest, but Travis had the advantage, and ... no score.

They all sat again.

"You okay, Kershaw?" Gunnar asked, eyes still on the ice.

"Not having a good night. Or week. Missing Elle."

Theo watched as Burnett smothered the puck and jammed it down the line.

"Aurora's in good form." Gunnar jabbed his stick at the jumbotron.

Theo tended to ignore it because it usually had some embarrassing booty shaking (Aurora) or ridiculous kiss cam stuff (Aurora, again). And yep, there she was in that dumb jacket, along with Dottie and Angelique, the co-founders of Theo's Tarts.

To which they'd added a new member.

If he'd trusted his legs wouldn't turn to jelly, he'd have shot to his feet to salute the newbie to the crew. Elle-oh-Elle, Corporal Cupcake, Mother of Hatchlings. Cheering so loudly he swore he could hear her.

She twirled in one of those pink jackets, that ridiculous "Thirsty for Theo" message on the back now front and center. It was silly but the words sent joy overflowing the brim of his heart.

They're here, the woman and child I love.

His chest grew tight, his throat burned, and his heart made a considerable effort to escape his rib cage and crash the net. Goal! Elle knew how important it was to him to have his child at the game. She might not want anything to do with him specifically, but having his kid in the house meant the world and she understood that.

Coach loomed over him with a clipboard. "Kershaw, if I put you in, could you try to fucking pay attention and actually do what we pay you for?"

"Pretty sure you're not signing the checks, Coach." An uncommon burst of humor from their captain, Petrov, was followed by an even more uncommon wink of solidarity from the big Russian.

"Yeah, I'll do better, Coach. Promise."

Coach shook his head, like putting Theo in was his funeral or something. They called the shift change and Theo bounded over the boards and onto the ice.

He had work to do.

THE LOCKER ROOM was nuts after the game, which they'd won 4-3 in overtime. Reporters, team staff, players, a couple of people he didn't recognize, but no sign of either Elle or Aurora.

Harper stopped by and squeezed his arm. "Good game, Theo. Glad to see you back in the hunt."

"Thanks, Ms. Chase. You haven't seen my grandmother, have you?"

She shook her head and turned to walk away. A second later she spoke over her shoulder. "Could you go to Coach Calhoun's office?"

"Now?"

Her eyes flashed with humor. "Yes, Theo. Now."

Oh, got it. "Thanks, Ms. Chase."

"It's Harp—" But he was already out the door, fighting the tide of people holding him back from his future.

"Excuse me. Need to get through here. Sorry, can't talk." Finally he made it and crashed through the door of Coach's office.

Elle stood there, leaning against the big desk, her hands laced below her stomach. It had only been four days but that bump had to be bigger. His baby was growing like a weed.

"You're here."

She was a vision of womanhood, her dark hair loose over her shoulders, her blue eyes warm and glowing. That pink jacket looked good on her, too, though it barely covered those gorgeous breasts, which also seemed to have swelled in size. (In his professional opinion.)

She rubbed her stomach. "We haven't missed a home game of the playoffs yet."

"Are you okay?" he asked.

"Yes, I'm fine. Well, not fine. I'm a complete dummy but physically I'm fine. The baby's fine." She took his hand and placed it over her swelling belly. It felt like coming home. "Hatch has started moving, usually when I'm asleep. Not now, though, because he knows we're waiting for him."

She was babbling which wasn't like Elle at all. He loved that she was nervous.

"You played so well tonight. I didn't understand everything that was going on but I could tell you were killing it, Kershaw. I could tell ..." She snatched a breath. "I could tell you were doing everything you could to make me and the baby proud."

"Elle, I know you're here to honor my wishes. I'm so grateful, and I—I don't expect anything else from you. I've bossed you around enough. You're your own person and as much as I love you, I can't make you feel the same way."

She curled her small hand into his large one. "No, you can't, Theo. I don't think I could ever do your love for me justice. I'm not good at it. I'm not good at trusting people, which is really the first step to falling in love, isn't it? And if I can't get past that first step, then how can I get to the most important part? Where I open my heart and let someone as amazing as you in?"

It took a lot to make Theo speechless. How could he fix this? Tell her they'd get there in time? That he had love enough for both of them? He suspected that wouldn't fly here. All he could do was stare, willing her to meet him half-way, hoping that she could take this first step. That it wasn't the end.

"You see, people learn how to relate to others from the first important people they meet," she said. "Their role models. We'll do that for Hatch. We'll do our best to get him off to a great start. You had that with Aurora but I didn't have that with my people. My parents created a blueprint I've been following for most of my life—not a great one as you can imagine—and I needed to do a gut rehab of those ingrained behaviors, a complete overhaul of me. Find a better blueprint. That's what I've been working on. Giving back. Surrounding myself with excellent people. And then I met you: a good, kind, patient man."

"I'm not that good or kind. As for patient, definitely not."

She laughed. "You have no idea how wonderful you are, Theo. From the second you found out I was pregnant, you've behaved like an absolute gent. You've treated me with respect and showed me what it means to be in a truly balanced relationship. Balance is so important to me. I thought it would always be uneven between us because you have money and I don't. You're incredibly hot and I'm, well, not. My heart's a closed fist and yours is an open border. I didn't think we could ever meet in the middle, that there would always be one-upmanship and disappointment because one of us holds all the cards.

"I told myself we could never work because I was toxic and would hurt you. But mostly I was terrified of the power you hold over me. I was afraid that loving you would make me feel weak. I couldn't envision the strength that it could give me, because I didn't think I deserved it. I love you so much, Theo, and it's not as much fun as it should be!"

He pulled her close and dipped his forehead to hers. "Fun? We haven't even started yet. But you've got to trust I love you completely. My heart's yours, Elle. Only yours."

"I want to. I want to learn to love with such openness. I want you to show me."

"Isn't that a Foreigner song?"

She clasped a hand to her forehead. "Oh, God, it is! I can't even get my love declaration right without scamming somebody's lyrics."

"There you go being too hard on yourself. I know what you mean. I know what's in here." He touched his fingertips to the top of her breast, knowing her heart was lower but determined not to take advantage by copping a feel.

Not yet, anyway.

"You're new to this love game, Ellie. I'm pretty good at it, like a lot of things, but I could always be better. I've been holding on to some stuff, with my dad, my mom. Not trusting you to make the right decisions when I know you're an adult and you've got this. I know you were only trying to help your sister and I shouldn't have gotten so angry about it. I just want to be the person you turn to when you're in trouble. I want to be your shelter, your rock, your partner, your everything."

"I want that, too. I thought I was burdening you with my problems. My parents were bad enough but here was one more ask from my screwed-up family. Handling it alone seemed like the best but you're right—we work better as a team. I've felt alone for so long and to have someone as wonderful as you open your arms and heart to me? It's kind of overwhelming."

He got that. "I know I can be over the top. But you excite me so much. Our life and all the potential there excites the hell out of me. Doesn't it excite you?"

She wiped away a tear. "It does. Oh, God, Theo, every minute with you is epic."

Perfect. "Let's learn from each other, then. Let's take this epic journey together."

"Are you sure? I know the baby complicates things—"

"No, it doesn't. The baby brought us together but we are more than just co-parents. The baby doesn't define our relationship. We do. I don't love you because you're carrying my kid. I love you because you are Elle Butler, the woman who laughed at my dino-briefs and still wanted to have sex with me. The girl who makes me mad and horny and hungry, often in the same sixty seconds. The person I want to share dumb videos and dad jokes with, who I want to see every morning and night. That's you. All mine. Baby's a bonus. You're the prize."

Her eyes shone with emotion. She clutched his shoulders and kissed him, so sweet and hot. "Thank you for helping Amy and Jackson. I never got a chance to say that."

"You're welcome. I will move mountains and swim

oceans to make things right for you and the people you love."

"I appreciate that. In the future, let's figure out problems like that together. It's too important for unilateral decisions."

She was right. Two heads would always be better than one, but even better were two hearts. "I promise that's how we'll do it in the future. As a team."

"As a team," she whispered, the words a sacred vow.

Their mouths met, sealing that vow, and he allowed himself to get a little handsy and possessive because she was his. All his.

"I can't believe you're wearing this dumb jacket. Aurora has a lot to answer for."

"Of course I'm going to wear it, *baby boy*! I'm Prime Tart!" She laughed. "I have another surprise for you. We're supposed to have an ultrasound at eighteen weeks. Dr. Patel called and asked me to come in—I know, I should have called you but I thought it would be fun to surprise you."

"With what? A secret ultrasound appointment?"

"No. With the gender of the baby." She picked up an envelope on Coach's desk. "I asked her to put it in here so we could open it together. Do you want to know?"

"Hell, yeah, I want to know!"

She gave him the envelope and he ripped it apart. Together they extracted the card so they both found out at the same time, a team effort that boded well for their new future.

"Well, what do you think of that, Ellie?"

"I think I couldn't be happier. I assume you'll be gramming it before the day is out?"

He smiled. "Let's keep this to ourselves for a little while. Some secrets are worth holding on to." Especially when shared by two souls in sync. "And seeing as you came bearing gifts, I should give you something as well."

He extracted a velvet pouch from his jeans pocket and tapped out the dinosaur charm into his palm.

Her lovely eyes brightened. "I saw this on your Insta Stories. It felt like we were connected even when we were apart."

"I hoped you'd still be obsessed enough with me to check my feed."

"I'm not obsessed with you!"

"Sure, sure. Keep on saying it if it makes you feel better."

She plucked it from his hand. "This is so sweet, Kershaw. I don't know what to say."

"That you'll always be my number one fan. Like I am yours."

Her smile sent his heart into the rafters of the Rebels Arena. "It's a promise."

EPILOGUE

THEO MIGHT HAVE THOUGHT he was whispering, but his voice increased in volume as Elle sneaked up behind him, phone in hand.

"So that's your uncle Remy, one of the great centers of our time, but you can never tell him I told you. And that's another legend, Bren St. James, also known as Highlander, Lord of the Puck, though I have it on good authority he goes by Nessie these days because of his resemblance to a certain mysterious loch-based mythical creature from Scotland."

Elle smiled to herself. Her guy must be making introductions to the family.

A happy gurgle lit up the room. "Yeah, it *is* a funny nickname, but he's not. Guy's completely humorless, not like your daddy."

"Who has the greatest sense of humor in the world," Elle said after she stopped the phone recording, "along with the sharpest cheekbones, thickest thighs, greenest eyes, and best tush of anyone we know." She sat beside him on the sofa, patted that famous tush, and murmured, "Nice."

"Not bragging if it's true."

Another gurgle affirmed that the Kershaw men were in agreement.

"I can't believe you let me sleep so long," Elle said. "Want me to take him? You could close your eyes for a few minutes before we roll."

Theo gestured to a Rebels hockey game on TV, which must have been from a few years back because half those players had hung up their skates. "And miss showing our son the moment when the Rebels attained ultimate glory and won the Cup? No way."

Our son. She'd never get tired of that.

Hatch Wayne Butler Kershaw burst onto the scene a week early and had been charming the skates off everyone ever since. Just as Theo had predicted, their son had inherited his good humor and looks, and his mom's brains and stubbornness. (Theo substituted "tenacity" for "stubbornness" because he knew better than to pick a fight with a woman who could castrate him with a look.)

Right now their son was cradled in a Rebels blue and white baby wrap, the promotion of which on Theo's Instagram feed would pay for Hatch's first year of college. Being on the road so much, Theo savored every moment he could to bond with him. Watching their baby's little fist against Theo's chest was one of those indescribable joys she couldn't have imagined a year ago.

"Hey, you know what day it is, Elle-oh-Elle?"

"It's Christmas Eve, and we still need to pack for our trip to Saugatuck."

He grinned, hot and wicked. "Not just any Christmas Eve, it's our anniversary."

"Right. A year to the day when you broke into my apartment under the guise of stocking my fridge."

"And made you breakfast, lunch, and a baby."

"That last part might have been in the early hours of Christmas Day."

Theo shook his head. "I'm 99.9 percent positive it happened that first time. That's when my swimmers were at their most powerful and your eggs were crying out to be knocked up by a hockey god."

She chuckled. "Sure, Superglutes, that's how it happened."

"You hear that, H?" Theo touched his perfect lips to Hatch's perfect head. "Your momma's trying to downplay how she pretty much climbed me like a tree. You are here because she couldn't keep her hands off me and my dino-briefs."

"Yes. Please tell our son about all the sex his parents had before he was born."

He wiggled his eyebrows. (Theo, not Hatch who barely had eyebrows.)

"And after," she rasped, then leaned in to meet Theo's kiss. They'd only recently resumed full-scale Theo-Elle fun times, and it was like discovering each other all over again.

"I've got something for you," he murmured against her lips.

"Is it your D-I-C-K? Because I've seen it already today."

"Yeah, you were all over it, lady. Also Hatch doesn't know what a dick is yet, but he's probably smart enough to understand letters."

"He's only three and a half months old."

"And the smartest baby I know. Much smarter than Cade and Dante's kid, and she's a week older!"

Little Rosie Violet Burnett-Moretti was already a heartbreaker and probably smart enough, but Theo insisted Hatch was a genius.

The last seven months had been a whirlwind. The

Rebels lost the conference finals against Edmonton but had gotten off to a good start this season. Summer in Saugatuck with Aurora showed Elle just how amazing it was to have family in your corner. Not even three performances of *Cats* could scare Elle off.

On the other side of the family ... Amy and her new husband had come to visit and Theo was a prince of hospitality. Elle's parents had gone to ground, sending a few occasional texts and a fruit basket when the baby was born. (Yes, a fruit basket.) With Theo's help, Elle was learning to accept that her parents would never meet her expectations—and she would eventually be okay with that. As for Theo's dad and brothers, progress had been made there, too. The father-son relationship between Theo and Nick was slowly simmering while his bond with Sean and Jason wound tighter and tighter with each passing month.

But Elle was most proud of how far she and Theo had come. They talked all the time—and Theo sometimes even let her get a word in! Keeping those channels open were crucial to making them stronger. Next year, she would start an online business degree with her man's complete support.

She stroked Hatch's cheek, marveling at its softness and watercolor pink bloom.

"I have an early Christmas gift for you," Theo whispered.

"You already bought him that drum set."

Theo chuckled. "No, for you. Look under the cushion."

She checked and found a small blue velvet pouch. "Kershaw, what have you done?"

"It's not much," he said in an uncharacteristic burst of modesty.

She loosened the drawstring and tapped out the

contents into her palm. A silver compass charm, its arrow pointing north. "It's beautiful."

"That's what you are for me, Ellie. True north. My heart and home. The place I'll always return to."

She swiped at her eyes. "How do you turn me to goop every time?"

"Just a talent I have."

"Very annoying, like so many of your talents." She turned the charm over in her hand, admiring its twinkle. "I love it. I love you."

He kissed her over their son's head. "And I love you. Ready to head out?"

"Almost, but first ..." She uploaded the brief video clip to her Instagram and tagged Theo while she was at it. Who was she to deny the world the sight of *The* Theo Kershaw killing it as the best dad ever?

She'd happily spare a few seconds. After all, he'd promised every other one to her.

THANK YOU FOR READING! I hope you enjoyed Theo, Elle, and their hatchling. Please leave an honest review on your favorite book platform. I would so appreciate it.

Ready for more Rebels? Next up is Gunnar Bond's story of heartache, love, and redemption in *Man Down*.

Want to know how Dante and Cade started their own journey to parenthood? Check-in with two of my favorite Rebels at the holidays in *Wrapped Up in You*, available now (ebook only).

NEW to the Chicago Rebels world? Three estranged sisters inherit their late father's failing hockey franchise and are forced to confront a man's world, their family's demons, and the battle-hardened ice warriors skating into their hearts. Start right now with the free prequel, *In Skates Trouble*.

ARE you a fan of hot and heartfelt romance featuring found families? Check out the Hot in Chicago series about firefighting foster siblings honoring the father who saved them while they follow in his footsteps. The Dempseys' motto: fire is stronger than blood and defend the people you love to the last ember.

FINALLY, to stay in touch about new releases, sales, and what I'm working on, sign up for my newsletter at katemeader.com or join my reader group, Kate's Kittens on Facebook.

ACKNOWLEDGMENTS

Thanks to Kristi Yanta for helping me shape this book into the story this couple deserved. She was Theo's biggest fan and I had so much fun exploring his larger-than-life personality through her eyes and making Theo more, well, *Theo*! Thanks also to Kim Cannon for doing such a great job cleaning up all my mistakes—and especially for catching all my Britishisms.

To my agent, Nicole Resciniti—we had another great year, lady, and I couldn't have done it without you. Thanks for supporting me on every path and detour on this journey and finding new opportunities for me.

And finally, Jimmie, I'm blessed to have you in my life. Thanks for being my support every step of the way of this grand adventure.

ABOUT THE AUTHOR

Originally from Ireland, *USA Today* bestselling author Kate Meader cut her romance reader teeth on Maeve Binchy and Jilly Cooper novels, with some Harlequins thrown in for variety. Give her tales about brooding mill owners, oversexed equestrians, and men who can rock an apron, a fire hose, or a hockey stick, and she's there. Now based in Chicago, she writes sexy contemporary featuring strong heroes and amazing women and men who can match their guys quip for quip.

ALSO BY KATE MEADER

Rookie Rebels

GOOD GUY

Chicago Rebels

IN SKATES TROUBLE

IRRESISTIBLE YOU

SO OVER YOU

UNDONE BY YOU

HOOKED ON YOU

WRAPPED UP IN YOU

Laws of Attraction

DOWN WITH LOVE

ILLEGALLY YOURS

THEN CAME YOU

Hot in Chicago

REKINDLE THE FLAME

FLIRTING WITH FIRE

MELTING POINT

PLAYING WITH FIRE

SPARKING THE FIRE

FOREVER IN FIRE

COMING IN HOT

Tall, Dark, and Texan
EVEN THE SCORE
TAKING THE SCORE
ONE WEEK TO SCORE

Hot in the Kitchen
FEEL THE HEAT
ALL FIRED UP
HOT AND BOTHERED

For updates, giveaways, and new release information,
sign up for Kate's newsletter at katemeader.com.

Made in the USA
Monee, IL
05 February 2020